The Greatest Love Story Ever Told!

Eleanor of Aquitaine was the richest, most beautiful and most cultured woman of her time. Married first to the King of France, then scandalously divorced and wed to Henry II of England, she was a queen in every sense of the word.

Her story, lovingly recreated by award-winning author Anne Powers, has all the sweeping grandeur of the age of chivalry, all the breathtaking ecstasy of the most exciting historical romance.

Also by Anne Powers:

SECRET SPLENDOR
QUEEN'S RANSOM
HEART'S JOURNEY

ELEANOR

ANNE POWERS

LEISURE BOOKS ∞ NEW YORK CITY

A LEISURE BOOK

Published by

Dorchester Publishing Co., Inc.
6 East 39th Street
New York, NY 10016

Printed in the United States of America

Chapter One

I knew what I was doing. Why did my ladies always lecture me? I was fifteen and I understood men. They were gay, respectful, charming to me even before I became Duchess of Aquitaine when Papa died. So why shouldn't I go out and meet Armand this afternoon? I still mourned dear Papa, but Papa was too cheerful, loved life too much himself to want anyone to be sad over him. He admitted carelessly he'd committed many sins, but he died repentant on his way to a holy shrine so now he was with the saints.

I smiled thinking of him, scarcely listening to my two women's stern voices going on about men's lust and a girl's frailty. Papa had loved Aquitaine as I did. My home, I'd never leave it. Well, if I married, I'd have to be with my husband sometimes. That is if I'd actually agree to wed—who? oh yes, Louis, the future king of France, or as much of France as the powerful lords let him rule. If I did marry Louis—I hadn't decided yet—I'd come home often to the sunny warmth of the south, quite unlike the bleak climate of Paris.

I've been told of the cold there and how men are more interested in their businesses than in the love our troubadours sang about. Love. The word brought Armand to mind again, and my smile widened. There was no touch of the troubadour's love between us. We'd grown up together, and I thought of him as a kinsman, sometimes quarreling as children do over a game of backgammon or a horse race or nothing at all, sometimes giggling, but never a touch or even a glance of intimacy. From my stone-framed window I could see across the courtyard and castle walls to the cluster of trees where he was waiting for me.

I broke impatiently into the torrent of words pounding against my ears, said demurely, "Yes, yes, I'm sure you're both right. A young maid should be discreet. So now you should see to—" what was there to see to?—"my gown for tomorrow's banquet. I think the sleeve is ripped." I tossed that at the elderly gaunt woman, Adela, turned to Jeanne, a heavy middle-aged lady. "And you see if the altar cloth we promised the cathedral is being properly embroidered."

I ignored their grumbling though their protests were justified. My bliaud for tomorrow wasn't torn, and my silk women embroidered beautifully without supervision. The two left finally, muttering if they hadn't persuaded me not to walk in the courtyard to meet Armand—I hadn't told

8

them I planned to go beyond the walls—I must call them immediately to accompany me for who knew what other men might be lurking nearby?

I said something that was neither yes nor no, waited until the latch clicked behind them and the faint shuffling of their sandals faded into silence. Then I slipped through a smaller door to a circular staircase. It was seldom used. No one would see me leave the place. Briefly I was angry. Why be a duchess if you couldn't do what you wanted to? All anyone could talk about was my being wedded —and I must save myself for that—either to Louis or one of the powerful lords. They watched me if I so much as glanced at a harmless man like Armand who had only a small property.

Laughter bubbled up at the thought of his being my suitor. I wanted to see him only because, when he sent the message to meet him, I was bored with the subdued atmosphere of a court in mourning for a man who wouldn't want to be mourned. Armand was amusing and very much alive.

The staircase ended in a narrow hall that led to the outer yard and the kitchen garden. In my plain dark tunic any casual observer would think I was one of the scullery maids out here to see if the carrots and beets had grown enough since yesterday for today's dinner. I edged my way around the garden wall to reach the gate to the outside world. Here there were guards, alert to any passerby. Their mouths gaped at seeing me walking alone, but there was no one to order them to detain me so they saluted smartly as they tried to hide their astonishment.

My ladies had fussed so much that I was late. I sped across a grassy field where sheep grazed and past a few outlying huts to the grove of birches shimmering white against the dark green of the forest just beyond. I stopped short, catching my breath as much from dismay as from my running. Armand wasn't here. Could he have waited a little for me and then shrugged and left? No. He was too easygoing to be put out by a short delay. But then where was he? Unlike me, he was always early for any meeting, any event.

Suddenly I was—not afraid of course, this was my own land—but, well, wary. I wasn't used to being alone outdoors, and the deeper woods close by could conceal robbers, bandits. I could even imagine moving figures though I knew very well the shadows were from trees bending under the capricious late spring breeze. My uneasiness that made me see strange shapes, hear faint sounds, turned to annoyance. How dared Armand keep his duchess waiting?

Then I swung around gladly, hearing a man-made noise. Armand was galloping toward me, then he pulled up and swung from his saddle and looped the reins on a birch branch and was beside me. But he didn't have his usual casual smile. His dark eyes were alight with an expression I'd never seen there before. As if he were looking at me for the first time and liked what he saw. That irritated me, but I made myself say with our old bantering tone, "Have you been out courting? And stayed too long with your new love?" I pouted. "Do old friends mean nothing to you now?"

A faint color rose in his face. "N-no, no! I mean yes." He gulped. "I—I don't know what I mean." Then abruptly, "Yes, I do." The words were almost lost as his mouth came down hard on mine. I was so surprised, it was a minute before I could struggle free.

Half of me wanted to slap him, the other half to laugh. How dare he spoil our old comradeship. Yet I was amused at the way he looked like an embarrassed small boy. Still, my annoyance helped me say arrogantly, "You forget who you are. And who I am."

"Never!" He caught me again, kissed my mouth, my throat. I was outraged. And yet his male passion aroused a stirring of emotion I didn't understand but which seemed something precious, desirable. But I wouldn't admit the emotion, especially to him. I gasped, "Insolence! L-let me go."

Unexpectedly his hold loosened. That pleased me of course. Or did it? Naturally it did. What could a small landowner mean to me? Even though he was handsome, had an excitement I'd admired in our playtimes together. He was a little like a young uncle of mine who'd shared much of my childhood until he went to the Holy Land. The memory of my uncle, how superior he was to Armand, made me more indignant at this boy's impudence. Did he think we were still children? We were too old for play. I was about to say so sharply when he glanced beyond me, and I could see from his suddenly serious expression that he must realize that too. No, he didn't. His eyes came back to mine, slid down my throat to the low neckline of my gown. Then he caught me to him again as if he couldn't control himself.

His urgency made the blood beat in my temples. This is living, I thought, and knew now why my father, my grandfather, all our family delighted in amorous adventures. And waited until old age before they repented their sensual appetites. How could they be sorry for this joy? I forgot Armand's low birth as his arms tightened, and one hand touched my breast caressingly. I might be only fifteen, but I was a woman.

Abruptly a cold thread of caution wove through the rosy warmth. This time my anger was directed against myself. Why couldn't I be like my relatives and revel in this pleasure? Almost instantly I knew why. His embrace seemed loving, but there was something calculating in it. I realized that when I became aware that gently, nearly imperceptibly, he was edging me around so that my back was to the woods behind us. I might be young, but I knew a man gripped with passion was too enamored to think of anyone, anything, except the love in his arms.

So what was in the woods he didn't want me to—oh! The moving figures I'd persuaded myself were shadows must be men he'd sent ahead of him. The slowest-witted person would have recognized his purpose. So. Thinking me defenseless, he thought to abduct the heiress of Aquitaine and Poitou, force me to marry him. Was that why he'd arrived late, to see if I'd come alone? I'd have to use my wits against this Armand, a nobody. I was too incensed at his effrontery to be afraid. I looked up at him, said furiously, "You can stop your play-acting of love, I—"

"B-but I—I do love—always have—I—"

The faint sounds I'd heard earlier and dismissed were louder now, a creak of leather, a quickly muted clang of steel. My voice was icily contemptuous. "Do you need an escort to prove your devotion? Dismiss them." I still hadn't seen his men, but if I'd had any doubts they were his, they'd have vanished at his shamefaced look, at his hunched shoulders as he backed away from me.

He swallowed convulsively, said just above a whisper, "But it's t-true. I always have cared for—and I knew if I courted you, you'd—you'd only laugh at me."

I did laugh then, mockingly. A mistake perhaps. It pricked his manhood. If he had any. Perhaps I should say his vanity. His mouth hardened. "You won't be so merry, Lady Eleanor, when you're my prisoner." He added as my brows went up, "As you are now since it's the only way I can court you."

Shock held me speechless for a moment. I'd guessed immediately he'd brought his men to abduct me, yet until he said prisoner I hadn't really believed that Armand could seriously plan such violence. And against me. The numbness wore off as I realized the only way to maneuver myself out of this situation was to treat it as though it weren't a serious threat. At least until I could think of a more adequate defense. I said gaily, "I've always been your prisoner, Armand. In friendship. Is that why you're trying to relive those days when we were forever playing pranks on each other?" I smiled. "But it used to be just between the two of us. We never thought it fair to ask anyone else's h-help."

I held onto my smile tightly as one of his men moved up on my left, a shabby serf, his mouth hanging half open. From his dulled expression I could see he'd use his cudgel as his master ordered. Obedience was the only thing he'd ever learned, whether to plow a furrow or take a duchess captive. Impossible to believe. Or was it?

Armand looked uncertain, but he didn't wave his man back. He wasn't strong enough to carry out his action easily, but he knew if he retreated now this chance would never come his way again. That must have given him courage to answer me. "Ah, but we're no longer playing, Elly—Lady Eleanor." He grinned. "Later we will again. When we're man and wife." At the last words he drew himself up and nodded at his serf. Another, armed with a dagger, also came forward and my arms were seized.

The tip of Armand's tongue ran around his lips as if he were already tasting the delight of ravaging me. For a moment all I could think of was the warm safety of my room which I'd left such a little while ago. But it wasn't my nature to want to live in an overly protected cocoon. I glanced scornfully at the smudged hands dirtying my white linen sleeves that encased my arms tightly, said, "I've had enough of this. If you leave at once, I will forget your shocking lack of manners for old friendship's sake. But if you don't—" I looked beyond him as though seeing someone approaching through the field of sheep—"I'm afraid even I cannot persuade my captain of the guard to let you go free after this outrage."

He hesitated, then his eyes followed my gaze. He laughed raggedly. "No one, dear Elly. You—"

"Naturally you see no one. Would I have an undisciplined raggle-taggle like your escort? My guards know how to creep up on an enemy unseen and unheard—" I broke off with a gasp because as I said the words, I saw they were true. One of my waiting women must have found I wasn't in my room and scuttling around looking for me had been told by the sentries at the gate which way I'd gone alone. And no doubt the woman's terrified screams for my safety had sent some of my guards —I couldn't guess how many—to follow me. Discreetly so that if I were in no danger, I wouldn't know of their presence and berate them.

Unfortunately my gasp and staring eyes made Armand start to look behind him again. He mustn't see before my men were closer. I flung myself at him. He was unprepared for the jolt and stumbled backward. I pushed at him again, my hands hard against his chest. He struck the ground, rolled over and came swiftly to his feet. But not swiftly enough. At the sight of me striking Armand and the serfs behind me, my guards charged. Before Armand could rip out his sword, they were on him. I panted, "Don't—don't kill him!" for he had once been a friend. But my words were lost in the angry shouts of the guards, and

Armand fell lifeless under their savage swords. Weapons were turned then toward the serfs, but they'd fled at the first glimpse of my men.

The captain swung toward me, said briskly he'd escort me to the palace. I stammered, "Th-thank you, all of you. I—" I was too shaken to say more. Abruptly I wanted to cry. Partly for Armand and partly for myself. I shrank from admitting it, but perhaps I wasn't as brave as I'd acted. Shut away in his castle with no one knowing where I was, I might have submitted to him. I tried to convince myself that I never would have agreed to marry him, but I wasn't sure. The thought of being his captive forced me to look at his bloodied body, but now I was glad my men hadn't heard my plea for mercy for him. He was an animal who'd tried to rob me of my freedom and my duchy.

For my security I must marry. I was bitter that the decision was made for me and by this scum. Then my natural cheerfulness bubbled up. No matter what I pretended, I'd always known I'd have to wed. So why not Louis? Father had written the French king about an alliance between our families, and I'd heard the king had sent a message to the Pope asking for a dispensation—Louis and I were in the forbidden degree of cousinship—and the Pope had sent the dispensation at once.

My mind was in such a whirl that I was startled to find we'd reached the wall gate where my women were waiting for me. I smiled repentantly at them as they stepped forward to stand close beside me while I crossed the yard and went quickly up the stairs to my room to change from my bedraggled dress which had been caught in brambles I hadn't even noticed. I held on to my smile as they lectured me stridently on my disastrously careless behavior, or I suppose that was what they were preaching about. I didn't really listen.

My thoughts were on Louis. At least he wasn't an ancient dodderer. He was young, only a year older than I. But what if—for the first time the idea occurred to me—Louis wasn't willing to marry? I'd been engrossed only in my own reluctance to wed anyone. I stood patiently as my women, still talking, slipped on a fresh bliaud, fastened a brooch on my shoulder and knotted a silver-edged belt about my waist. But of course Louis would be willing. His father must be avidly pleased to link the provinces of Aquitaine and Poitou with his realm. And from what I'd been told of Louis, he'd obediently follow his father's will.

I caught my upper lip in my teeth. I ached for more than that in a husband. I wanted a man who desired me for myself, not for my lands. I shook my head. I mustn't judge Louis before we'd even met. We had our youth in common, and who knew how much more? I dreamed of him that evening as my ladies and I embroidered silk bands for our gowns in the flaring oil lights while we listened to the troubadours at the hearth singing their love songs.

At the lilting airs, one by one we gave up the pretense of working and indulged in romantic fantasies. I imagined young Louis charging up to the palace at the head of his escort, eager to meet his bride. We'd gaze at each other, try to look away and then look back in our delight that out of the whole world, he'd been chosen for me and I for him.

The next day a messenger came to the palace. My lips tightened. My father's consent had been enough. No one had waited to ask me. Louis had left Paris and was on his way to Bordeaux. He hoped he wasn't being too precipitate for my liking, but the king, who was ill, wished the marriage to take place as soon as possible. As Prince Louis did too, the messenger added hastily. I nodded to my chamberlain to take care of the messenger's comfort and pay him while my first annoyance faded, and I glowed with the thought that my dreams might be true and Louis would come charging up, impatient for his bride.

He arrived two days before we expected him. But our meeting was—well, not quite like my fantasy. As his escort rode into the courtyard, I walked sedately down to welcome him, my scarlet gown bright in the hot noon sunlight. For a minute my seeking eyes couldn't find him, then I saw a young man dismount slowly. His light cape and tunic glittered regally, but there was nothing royal in his bearing. He was fair and tall, but his every movement was awkward, and he didn't charge up to the steps where I waited. In fact he hung back, averting his eyes when our gaze met, and moved forward only when an older man at his elbow prodded him. He bowed gravely, then brushed my hand with his lips hesitantly as if he weren't used to kissing a lady's hand.

I smiled determinedly. "Welcome to the Ombrière Palace, my lord, and to Aquitaine. You must be tired and hungry. Come in and refresh yourself."

He said, "Thank you, Lady Eleanor," in a low voice, and waved to his escort to follow. I gulped at the number of men who stepped forward at his gesture. Our scouts had brought word of his approach only a few hours ago, and our dinner had been cooked hurriedly. Food was garnered from our storehouses and gardens and from our peasants, but was there enough?

I pushed the uncomfortable thought aside as I led the way to the great hall where extra tables were being put up and covered with sparkling white linen. At least everyone would have a place to sit and, I thought with relief, my cooks were inclined to be lavish in their preparations. Chamberlains came up then to bring us to the two tall chairs at the table on the dais, and Louis turned to smile at me timidly. I smiled back at him radiantly and waited for him to speak.

He said nothing, and I had to prod him as earlier one of his men had prodded him forward. Pages filled our wine cups and around us the talk grew noisier and the troubadours sang more noisily, but my polite questions about his journey from Paris brought only monosyllabic answers. Really one would think I was the older the way I had to persuade him to say anything. Then luckily I thought of asking about his boyhood. His thin face brightened as he explained he'd never expected to be heir since he had an older brother. But the brother had been killed when out riding one day because a pig had run into his horse, and when the prince had fallen from the saddle, his head struck a stone. I murmured a sympathetic answer.

Louis nodded, said sadly, "A calamity, my lady. He was trained to inherit while I—I was dedicated to the church and hoped to be a monk. With his death, everything changed. Father summoned me home and said now I was the dauphin and must marry to carry on our dynasty."

I said lightly, "That must have pleased you, to be freed of the monastic life. And one day to be king of France." But I wasn't too pleased at his words that practically said he preferred being a monk to being my husband. Nor when he went on.

"Freed? To leave the peaceful life in a cloister for worldly affairs? Who could wish for a better life than—" He stopped at my cold glance. "I—I—I mean that's what I thought then." He swallowed nervously as he groped for more redeeming phrases.

Maliciously I didn't help him end the silence. Let him suffer for his unbelievable tactlessness. Great roasts had been brought to the tables. He cut off a piece of veal from an enormous chunk on his gold plate, fumbled as he dipped it in a wine sauce, tried to bite into it, put it back as though unable to chew the delicately flavored slice. I said at last tartly, "I suppose meat is seldom permitted in a monastery. You will have to become used to regal manners in more than ways of eating." He appeared so dejected I took pity on him. "Since you were bred to be a monk, these changes must be upsetting. But with all you learned from your churchmen, have you thought perhaps you can improve the world which you shrink from now?"

He smiled at that, a singularly sweet smile that cut through the last of my irritation. "Yes, yes, I can, can't I? And with you beside me, I can do anything." Just as I was thinking I wasn't enthralled at the prospect of improving France and making the people holier, he added shyly, "What I was, you know, trying to say was that at first I thought monkhood was a better way of life. But now—now I've seen you perhaps—perhaps I was wrong about that."

Not exactly a passionate declaration of love but better than his dwelling on the peaceful life in a cloister. And in his quick glance at me I could read that he thought me beautiful. Surely my jongleurs and troubadours could soon teach him how to speak to his lady more gallantly. They were singing a rondel now that was like our usual nightly love songs, warming and subtle with their hidden meanings beneath the intricate words.

Louis's hand touched mine, drew back before I could respond. He appeared to be trying to hide his embarrassment though I didn't know if he were embarrassed at the contact with me or the realization that the troubadour was singing of very human love, not a psalm. I sighed. Then reminded myself he was young, he'd quickly learn our lighthearted ways. It wasn't natural for a sixteen-year-old to be so grave all the time.

As roast pheasant and salt meadow mutton and sweetmeats were brought in, I remembered my earlier concern and looked hurriedly from table to table, let out my breath as I saw there was far more food than would be eaten. I turned back to Louis, trying to think what to say to lighten his seriousness. I seldom had trouble chattering about this or that, but Louis was different. I said laughingly, "I hope you will find married life suits you better than the cloister. There are pleasures—" That was the wrong word. I added appealingly, "Satisfactions in making your wife happy. I need your strength, and our future children will need you too."

He looked pleased, but instead of smiling his face had graver lines and his brows came together as if he were contemplating new and heavy duties. I was exasperated. I wanted to snap at him to enjoy himself as his own escort did, except for one grizzle-haired veteran, after the first quarter hour of restraint before my ladies and guests cut through the men's reserve. What would cut through Louis's gravity?

Before I could find an answer to that, the veteran approached, said austerely, "My lord, it is time to leave for your headquarters across the Garonne River." His expression said he didn't approve of the singing and perhaps of the way wine glasses were refilled the moment a sip was taken. I was glad to see Louis hesitated as if reluctant to go. The veteran went on, "I believe Abbot Suger expects to consult with you early this evening."

At that Louis immediately pushed back his chair. I was indignant. Shouldn't a soon-to-be bridegroom insist on staying with his bride? No one could possibly say he was remaining indecently late when the sun was still in the western sky. I said coldly, "Who is Abbot Suger?"

Louis's eyes widened in surprise. "He's the abbot of St. Denis and the most important man in France next to my father for he's our adviser in all matters."

I wanted to say sarcastically, Does he even advise you on how long you can stay out as if you were a child? I swallowed the words, but I'd remember Suger's name. No husband of mine should be that subservient to an underling. Still, I could wait. No point in antagonizing the abbot yet. So I smiled sweetly as Louis made stilted but proper adieus and left meekly. I glanced at my women who appeared disappointed as the escort rose with Louis and clattered out of the hall.

The days slid by after that in the same pattern except that now we were definitely committed, there was a feeling of urgency in the air. The French king, Louis the Fat they called him because he was too heavy to move without assistance, was ill with dysentery. We should marry soon so Louis could return to Paris though our wedding mustn't appear too hasty for royalty, Abbot Suger told me.

I'd met him the third day and was astonished that this small dark man in a splendid robe that didn't conceal the scrawniness of his body was a power behind the French throne. But I agreed pleasantly with his dictum, saying only that many of my guests had come great distances and must be entertained properly while waiting for the wedding.

Feast followed feast. Swans, ducks, geese,

cranes, peacocks, roasts of pork hot from the turn-spit, mullet, sole, lobsters, oysters, spiced sauces and later figs, candied fruits, rice and powdered cinnamon tarts were served. The washing basins the squires handed around became gray and oily from the many greasy hands. And all the time one heard the rhythms of tambourine, flute, rebec and the troubadour songs.

Louis showed little interest in the food though he kept his eyes fastened on his plate as my countrymen grew more boisterous as each course was washed down with our wine of Bordeaux, and their ladies' bosoms seemed ready to expose themselves as the women drank with the same enthusiasm as the men. But he couldn't close his ears to songs of love and sex and spring that made my Aquitanians laugh and clap, and his escort too when the men were far enough away from the abbot.

I wondered how to make Louis part of the festivities. Then I saw his eyes flickered toward me occasionally, and his softened expression was that of a boy bewildered but loving. So. He didn't know how to say it, but he cared for me. That meant he'd want to please me, follow my wishes. It needed time, but I'd make him into a man. Perhaps not a warrior like the men of my family, but a man who could learn to appreciate lighthearted entertainment, one who could stand up to his enemies and to his adviser. At that moment I was pleased the abbot pleaded for—or rather demanded—an early marriage.

The morning of the wedding, the sky was a cloudless blue, and the sun glittered on our procession to the Cathedral of Saint André. Bells of all the churches rang as we rode through the cobbled streets of Bordeaux, and the cheers of my people mingled with the call of trumpets. My ladies' sheer veils and bright flowing gowns swayed like fans of delicate tints, and the guards' pennants and plumes were scarlet and white and black against the July sky.

I hoped Louis revelled in the pageantry as I did, but I couldn't know if he even lifted his eyes from the ground since men and women were kept sternly apart. A French, not an Aquitanian custom. But that would change, I thought happily, after we were married and Louis learned the pleasures of music and feasting and dancing in a merry court.

The ceremony in the church with its vaulted roof lighted by hundreds of candles was solemn, but the banquet afterwards was gay. Louis's knights took part like children on a holiday, and even Louis smiled though he said little at the jests and swift repartee about us. I spoke only of trivialities too, but I could have sung in my delight that already he was behaving a little more like a young man of the world instead of someone just coming out of a monk's silent cell.

Until some of the men hinted broadly and ladies tittered at the joys awaiting him tonight. Louis paled, fumbled with the crusty bread he was pulling apart. My spirits went down a little for I'd been wondering about the consummation of our marriage, and I'd expected him to share our guests' amusement, not seem withdrawn. The act of course was no mystery to me. I'd heard too much idle gossip, seen animals in heat. Did Louis's pallor mean he wasn't looking forward to his marital rights? Oh no, he'd lost color because he was shy and thought so private an affair shouldn't be talked of in public, especially when the bride could overhear the remarks he considered vulgar.

But I'd no time to think further. The abbot leaned across me to whisper to Louis that he'd just been informed that there were hostile barons who didn't want me married to a Frenchman and they were planning trouble. Because of that he'd send word in Louis's name to the soldiers at headquarters to dismantle their camp. We rose at once, and within the hour I and some of my household staff were rowed across the Garonne. Tents were being struck and pack animals loaded when Louis arrived with his escort, and we were two leagues beyond Bordeaux on our way to Poitiers before we drew up for the night.

But not the wedding night. With the tension that danger brings and the constant coming and going of the abbot and guard, Louis and I slept apart in our gaily striped pavilions. I wondered if the abbot had deliberately planned our separation. But since he hadn't spoken against our marrying, why should he? Four nights later I found my half-suspicions were wrong. We'd reached the fortress of a loyal vassal. Now we could rest within its great stone walls. And Louis came to me.

I rose from my chair near the hearth and smiled at him in welcome. He tried to answer my smile as he walked toward me hesitantly. I put out my hands, and he took them slowly. But instead of easing his shyness, the touch of flesh communicated his embarrassment to me. I gulped, said, "It—it is good to see you, Louis, when—that is, when we needn't fear rebels charging the camp."

Unexpectedly my stumbling words helped give him composure. His fingers slid to the shoulder of my white gold-embroidered robe as he muttered something about the abbot's saying he mustn't forget his husbandly duties. I pressed down my resentment that it was the abbot's wish more than Louis's that he was here. Besides, Louis didn't appear displeased as a fold of my robe slipped back and hinted at the nudity beneath. Faint color rose to his cheeks, but he looked at me steadily, said earnestly, "I'm pleased with you, Eleanor."

His sober words made me want to laugh, but to cry a little too. I had my father's sensuous nature and had hoped, hoped that now we were alone together at last Louis would be demanding, insistent on his husbandly rights. Instead he made me feel self-conscious and stiff. I was sure there were scores of provocative answers to his remark that I'd think of later, but now I could only look down at the stone floor and murmur, "Thank you, my lord—Louis."

Incredibly the words were right. My unusual meekness gave him courage where a livelier response might have turned him away, so little used to sprightly repartee was this young man raised to be a monk. I must remember his cloistered training until I'd taught him the gallantry expected of a prince. He bent his head to kiss my cheek and then my lips tentatively, brushed back my hair. "Pale gold. Our women are dark, but I've always admired fair-haired women."

There was a shade of warmth in his usually coolly precise voice. My breath came more quickly, and my breasts rose, straining for a more intimate touch than his fingers in my hair. I reminded myself again of his cloistered life though I couldn't understand why his own nature didn't break through his rigid unbringing. Perhaps because he—no, I refused to believe his monklike ways were the result of anything except what he'd been so strictly taught. Until now.

I whispered, "We—we must not forget why we are here. You, the heir of your great father, must have an heir to carry on your line." And mine too, I thought, which was far older than the Capetian dynasty that was a mere century and a half old.

"Yes, ah—yes," He appeared uncomfortable but determined. He was ready, reluctant yet ready. I had no fondness for lechers, but I wished he'd had some experience to guide him. Now I must lead him. Gently. I moved toward the great bed, glad now our wedding night hadn't been at the palace in Bordeaux where a horde of courtiers would have followed us, laughing and jesting. Their presence in our nuptial chamber would have frozen Louis.

The silk cover had been drawn back, and I smiled at him as I lay down. He turned away from me as he pulled off tunic and under-tunic and hose. We were in a north chamber and only glimmers of the setting sun lightened the room, and by the time he moved toward me, shadows crept across the floor. The dimness must have given him courage because after I'd unpinned the neck of my robe he scarcely hesitated before pushing the edges back. I knew I was slim, with high breasts, and was sure he'd be pleased. But I couldn't be certain for after one shy glance at my body, he pulled the coverlet over us as if there were something wrong about our being nude. I choked back a laugh. We were married!

My half-laugh faded. His fingers fumbled at my waist. Had I thought to lead him? How? I edged closer to him. Perhaps the warmth of my flesh would urge him on. His hands slid down my hips, pressed on my thighs. And then nature catapulted him across the years of young repression. He flung himself on me. I wasn't quite ready for his urgency, but I welcomed his embrace.

As he entered my body, there was pain at first, and I could feel blood flowing down my legs. I ignored both in my relief that he'd become my husband and held him tightly until he sighed and rolled down beside me, murmuring softly sweet words of love and satisfaction. I whispered drowsily he'd made me happy. I shouldn't have said that. Evidently it reminded him of tales he'd unwillingly overheard that men should take pleasure in intimacy, but only low-born women, whores, enjoyed it. Wives accepted the act as a duty to bear children. I was so accustomed to the Aquitanians' sensual pleasure for both men and women that I'd forgotten the cold practicality of the northern provinces and Louis's own nature.

He showed me by his stiffness as he rose from the bed and the furtive way he quickly drew on his clothes, said "Good night, madame" coolly and hurried to the door. I wanted to spit at him, lash out that his hasty penetration had been painful, that he'd made me happy only because he'd proved he wasn't a monk entirely. I sighed. To teach him gallantry, the ways of the world would take longer than I'd expected. Still, there'd be other nights, nights when he wouldn't rush from my arms.

But he didn't return until we reached Poitiers where we were given a raucous welcome by the citizens for me as their countess and for Louis who'd soon be crowned count of Poitou. The cheers were exhilarating, but after our hot ride under the blazing sun, our answering smiles and waves to the crowds lining the streets were strained.

But not for long. A day of rest and I was ready to have entertainments and wine fountains and roasted oxen planned for the throng outside, and dancing and singing and tumbling for our guests in the palace. Louis agreed all should be fed, but I could feel his disapproval of our amusements. His father and mother didn't encourage such gay affairs at the French court.

I grimaced, then smiled quickly. Wouldn't anyone feel sympathy for a young man whose home life was so dreary? Fortunately Louis noticed only my smile and there was, almost, a glint of apparent anticipation in his eyes. He didn't even frown at one of the bawdier songs a young jongleur sang. Perhaps he hadn't listened to the words. Abbot Suger's frown said he did, but this was my home. No one would be allowed to shorten the time of our Aquitanian revelry. Except my husband since I wanted him to have fond memories of Poitiers, but Louis was sipping more than his usual half-glass of wine and seemed unaware of his abbot's forbidding expression.

That evening I learned why. His thoughts had all been on me, he declared when he came into my bedroom, and the wine and singing and rose-scented air were a fitting background for his lovely wife. I was startled—though pleased—at the romantic phrasing and hoped the effects of our claret wouldn't wear off too soon and turn him back into the hesitant novice.

It didn't. He was as shy as the first night when he disrobed, but his touch on me was surer, caressing me as he pulled my robe aside. Then his eyes became luminous and his thoughts were only on the act of plunging into my willing body. The day had been hot, and his flesh was damp as he held me tightly, but I was scarcely aware of that in my pleasure at having proof of his manliness again. When he moved a little away, his expression was of awe and delight.

This time I was cleverer and said demurely, "I hope that as your wife I have pleased you.".

"Pleased is a tame word for what I feel for you, my love." Then as my breath went out in a flutter of relief, he frowned and edged further from me, and his voice when he went on was too sober. "But—but is it right to feel this way? Lust is wrong. Our greatest saints say it is sinful, a giving way to impure desires."

I gulped back an angry retort that they must have been the saints who knew nothing of wedded bliss so made themselves holy by condemning all desires. But instead of snapping at him I said softly, "The saints are right when they say lust is unchaste. But surely married love is normal and right in the eyes of Our Lord or why are we made as we are?"

"Do you question the teachings of our doctors of theology? We were created with this weakness for lust to test us, to make us rise above our lesser selves. I cannot let my flesh conquer me." He stood up. "I will spend the rest of this night in prayer and ask forgiveness for my sinful cravings."

I was furious, but I managed to speak calmly. "You have a princely wisdom in most matters, but haven't you forgotten—well, that a prince must have an heir? It is his duty."

He pulled on his tunic, fastened his belt and said gravely, "Yes, but the child must be conceived only for that duty, not when one is indulging in sinful appetites. Say no more, dear wife. I know you're trying to reassure me, but I'm a man and understand my wickedness more than the most learned woman could. I will atone on my knees for my vile emotions."

I stared at the door as he closed it quietly behind him. In Aquitaine love was glorified in or out of marriage. And I was wedded to a man who'd been shaped by life in cloisters and a dull solemn court where the king and queen wouldn't countenance even light, innocent entertainment. I bit my lip hard so I wouldn't cry at the bleak country awaiting me. Then I smiled determinedly. Surely, surely I could change Louis into a manly prince who accepted life as it should be lived. Couldn't I?

Chapter Two

My hope that our way of life, our lightheart-edness would soften Louis's stiffness was ruined by a message from Paris. Louis, who'd been out hunting in the early cool hours of the morning, dis-mounted and tore off the ribbons and seal of the document. I'd run down to the courtyard to greet him, but he didn't even see me. He looked up from the letter, said to his captain of the guards, "My father is dying. Have our men prepared to leave by sundown tonight. I must try to see the king my father while he's still alive."

I stared in surprise. Not at the time he'd go, August was even hotter than July so it was almost impossible to ride through daylight hours. But I was surprised at Louis's urgency. Louis the Fat had been reported dying for months. Most men would have delayed to spend at least one more night with the bride. My husband could do nothing for his father, and how often did one celebrate one's wedding? But I was too proud to try to dissuade him from his plans. I'd known the return to Paris would be early, but not this soon.

In less than a fortnight I was glad I hadn't dissuaded him because he sent word he'd been too late in spite of his haste. And now he'd been catapulted into kingship, he couldn't leave his new duties and the burial of his father at St. Denis to return for me, but he was sending a royal escort. I was touched by his thoughtfulness though a guard was unnecessary surely since I had my Aquitanians. And in any case I was safe with my own people as their duchess and the French as their queen. Queen. A pleasant title but no better than my own that I'd inherited. But somehow I didn't feel ready to be queen of an unknown country. My sewing ladies quickly made a mourning gown, and as I put it on I felt some reflection of Louis's sorrow for his father though I'd never met the late king.

Mourning robes were appropriate whether there was anyone to grieve over or not, I thought when I reached Paris and went up the broad steps of the palace on the Ile de la Cité. Was this a royal residence? Hundreds of years old, it appeared as if no one had taken a thought to brighten the ancient heap since it'd been built. Only fingers of light slanted through the narrow slits of windows, and I had the sensation of everything being gray, the few tapestries on the walls doing little to lighten the gloom.

My chambers were like the rest of the castle, stark and bare except for a bed ringed with curtains to keep out the drafts, drafts that filtered through the whole heap of stone. At least I could gaze with pleasure at my ladies who came trooping in after me. They weren't in mourning white. Gauzy veils and silk gowns were a rainbow of gay color in the bleakness. And later the great hall below would come alive when my equally gaily clad troubadours would make the walls ring with their singing. I smiled.

I smiled too soon. When I went down to meet the Queen Mother Adelaide, a large plump figure standing at the hearth, her face showed instant disapproval of my attendants, deepened into horror when she saw my minstrels with their lutes. "Madame! Our good king—" she could as well have said gluttonous—"died less than a month ago. Your people are dressed for a revelry. Music too! It is indecent, quite indecent."

She'd probably lived contentedly in this primitive dull place, but I thought it unwise to argue with my mother-in-law the first day. I said graciously, "We will follow your wishes, Your Highness. I'd thought to please you, but if you believe songs are unfitting today, I will dismiss my troubadours." I added pleasantly, "As to dress, I am the one bereaved and wear mourning as you see." Her expression had been cold, now it was icy as her eyes fastened on my low-cut bliaud saying without words it was immodest and no doubt indecent, quite indecent.

While I struggled for an answer to her unspoken criticism, Louis hurried into the hall. I breathed with relief when he took my hand and turned proudly to his mother. "Isn't my wife beautiful? Beautiful and kind." He went on to me, "I heard of your arrival only a few minutes ago, or I'd have been outside to welcome you." He rubbed his eyes with the back of his hand, and I could see how tired he was.

"Poor Louis! You've been working too hard. Couldn't your ministers—no, I suppose you must meet with them until you know their ways and whether you have to read every document they hand you before you sign them. I understand because my father often took me to his council meetings, and since I've been duchess I've attended many of my own. At least I hope we can lighten your leisure hours with some entertainment."

The queen mother cleared her throat, and I put in quickly, "That is, when it's the proper time." Inwardly I resolved the proper time would be tomorrow. A young man, a boy really at sixteen, shouldn't be so burdened with all the tasks of a new king without an occasional hour of gaiety. Perhaps hawking? We'd be away from Adelaide's censorious gaze and in the open air and sun, and my troubadours would sing a few, just a few, solemn tunes. If they knew any that were serious.

Louis repeated, "Entertainment?" and glanced at his mother. "I'm afraid—so soon after Father's death and—and there are so many duties I scarcely have time to eat." I swallowed the retort that I hoped he remembered another duty. To sleep with me. He added, "But after you rest from your journey, quite exhausting I know, I shall see you have some pleasant diversions."

I hadn't realized until he mentioned it that I was worn out from the long hot miles we'd ridden over rough roads that were sometimes scarcely more than lanes. I'd been upheld with the resolve I'd learn to love Paris and France as much as my beloved Aquitaine, and that was still my resolve. I said, "By tomorrow I'll be quite refreshed. And oh, Louis, if you can't leave your work, I will help you. As I said, I'm used to administrative details, and that way we won't be separated so much."

He glanced at his mother again. I didn't need to see her face to know she was readying an acid remark that kings of France didn't share their authority with a wife who should be attending to household management. But before she could speak, Louis put in eagerly, "I'd like that! That is if—if my ministers will allow a woman in their consultations."

I was annoyed. He was king, such decisions should be his. But this wasn't the moment to be insistent. I said lightly, "But why do I talk of such dull matters now? Let us just enjoy the sight of each other. And enjoy our dinner. I'm hungry." I'd been reminded of eating by the scraping noise across the stone floor behind us from servingmen setting up trestle tables. I'd thought eating would strike an ordinary note that'd please Adelaide, but in spite of her ample proportions her expression said appetite was unseemly in a mourning period. Or perhaps it was because I was the one who'd mentioned food. Was it impossible for me to please her?

At first I didn't care, especially that night when Louis came almost surreptitiously into my bedroom. I stifled a giggle at the way he slipped in as if he were an illicit lover, not my husband, then realized his mother would certainly frown at lovemaking now. I put out my hand to him, remembered his shyness and dropped it quickly. I said primly, "I'm happy to see my dear husband. You look tired. I hope you will sleep well tonight."

He said eagerly, "I will if I can be with you. My bed has been lonely." He stopped abruptly and his face flamed at the unexpected boldness of his words. "I—I mean—the abbot—an heir."

I nodded soberly. "You are a good man, always ready to do your duty." I must not, must not smile. Or think regretfully what a joyous hour this could be if he were an ardent Aquitanian lord. I moved over in the bed and touched the pillow invitingly.

He hesitated, walked slowly forward as if willing himself not to be too precipitate. As if he ever would be! I lay quietly while my senses screamed for a loving kiss, his hands on my breast. He pulled off his clothes, slid in beside me. Our bodies touched. He started to edge away, then surprisingly he turned toward me and shyly drew me closer to him. I realized he was as hungry for love as I, but his early training or his own nature refused to let him understand his need was human and right.

Slowly his hands searched my body more intimately, sliding from my back to my thighs. I wanted to snap that I wasn't fragile, but I only made murmuring sounds like a mother to a child. The soft words eased him. I was elated as he held me with more confidence. I felt him harden against me. Then with a swift movement he plunged into me, moaning words of love, of delight.

I felt a brief flare of resentment that he hadn't tried to give me pleasure, forgot it in my relief that he'd acted the husband. Almost at once both resentment and relief were swept away, and I could only stare at him numbly as he said, "I—I must tame my gross appetites, pray for forgiveness." He rose. I should have expected this reaction, I suppose, but I'd fondly hoped that our separation after he'd tasted marital gratification would have crushed any repentance for tonight. "And my—my mother would be distressed if she knew I'd indulged myself so soon after Father's death."

I said tartly, "Only because you were with me, not with some meek and humble woman. She doesn't dislike the lands I brought with me, but—" I said aloud what I'd thought earlier today—"it's impossible for me to please her."

He tried half-heartedly to defend his mother, realized abruptly he was naked, rushed to dress and left with the same furtive air as when he'd come. I shrugged, tried to laugh. After all, I knew Louis cared for me no matter how uneasy he was over the passionate side of marriage. And if the queen mother disapproved of me, so? Still her attitude was oppressive in the days and weeks that followed.

She said tight-lipped, "My dear, I don't want to criticize, but your ladies—perhaps you will speak to them. At table I have them seated as far from the young men as possible, but they are forever giggling at the men and giving them unseemly glances. And their gowns aren't what should be worn in a royal court." Her eyes, scraping over my bliaud which was laced at the sides to fit closely at the hips, said not only my attendants should dress more properly.

I said sweetly, "I'm sorry you find the gowns displeasing, but they are the fashion in the south as are my women's manners. It's regrettable but it's as hard to change one's way of life as it is to learn the Paris dialect."

She snorted. "If they spent more hours in prayer and improving their pronunciation of our *langue d'oil*, they'd have little time to think of singing and flirting and painting their faces."

I bowed my head and turned away, refusing to give her the dignity of an answer. That heightened her antagonism, and next time she directed her grievances at me, perhaps because she could hardly place the blame for this on my ladies. She said with an air of sadness for having to speak,

"My dear, I wonder if you realize how many Aquitanians you have with you and how lavishly you entertain them? I fear the royal treasury will soon be depleted."

I saw with relief that Louis had come up and overheard her. "Mother! What harm in giving the court a few pleasures? It'd be inhospitable to send the southern lords away. Besides, it's been too long since the hall was filled with song and laughter."

It was a moment before she could get her breath, then gasp, "You—you always side with that—with your wife. Well, it seems I'm useless here. I shall retire to my dower estate."

He shook his head, but not too decisively, said as if forcing himself to be filial, "No, Mother, your home is here. We would miss your presence in Paris."

She too was aware how weakly he protested and within a week flounced off to Compiègne. And the next we heard from her was that she'd remarried, a nobleman of Montmorency. I tried not to laugh, but even Louis smiled at the report after all her talk of a decent mourning period for the late king.

I didn't smile long for she wasn't the only one to leave. By late Autumn my Aquitanians were becoming restless. The days were dark too often and night came early with the advancing year. And there were few fireplaces to gather around, all of us being expected to stay warm by huddling over braziers. And the chief nobles, except for the ministers and their ladies, went to their country estates which I'm sure were more cheerful than our drafty mildewed palace. So my "lavish entertaining" was curtailed from lack of guests. As for outdoor activities, my Aquitanians who'd have gone through blizzards for a war were too chilled indoors to indulge in sports under the gloomy, usually dripping, skies.

The few who were left soon came to me with one excuse or another—they must consult with their stewards, husband or wife had been left alone too long, a thousand business details they'd never bothered about needed their immediate attention. In short, they were pining to go home. How could I fault them? So was I! I gave my consent as I reminded myself Louis was a gentle and considerate husband, and I'd find other matters to while away the time.

My first thought was the council. The ministers hadn't invited me to join them though they knew less than I of affairs in my own provinces. When I suggested to Louis that this lord had a better right to a strip of land than the man suing him, or that a vassal was demanding more of his peasants than our laws permitted, he was ready to listen. But not his ministers, especially Abbot Suger, when they heard the advice came from a woman.

I soon learned they were reinforced in their hostility to me. A confidant of both Louis and the abbot who had been north on some business of the king's returned to court. Thierry Galeran, a eunuch. Louis was delighted with his presence. I was not. We had little chance to speak to each other as Louis was pressing questions on him about one northern lord after another. Thierry answered them readily, but he kept turning toward me, and his bleak expression said what he dared not say aloud, that this was not the woman he'd have chosen for his king. Though he hinted at his thoughts by making uncomplimentary remarks about how superior the northern lords— and their ladies—were to southerners. In the north they were easily governed, had respect for old-fashioned virtues and women knew their place. Evidently he'd been told I wished to share Louis's work. Perhaps by the queen mother who wouldn't have described me kindly.

I was annoyed. With time the ministers might accept me, but I doubted if Thierry ever would. Now with the winter stretching ahead, I must look for another interest. I hadn't far to look. I would make our palace less gloomy. There were days I'd rather have sat warming myself at a brazier, but when I set myself a task I carried it through. I had my needlewomen work on new bed curtains to replace the present faded ones. And I called in masons to change the slits that let in only dreary fingers of light into larger windows like ours in the south, though I prudently had them add close-fitting shutters for nights and cold days when the sun didn't shine. And most important, work was begun on fireplaces and chimneys for other rooms besides the great hall. I'd had enough of a brazier futilely trying to heat a room.

I'm sure many thought me mad to be busy at construction when I could have sat with my ladies playing chess or backgammon, guessing riddles or laughing through blindman's buff. Idle pursuits to fill the dull, dull days. But there was more than construction to see to though my next plan would do more than make people think me mad. They'd be highly irritated.

After a particularly tasteless dinner had been served—Louis of course didn't notice the fish was half raw and the mutton unseasoned—I visited the kitchens where supposedly the cooks were beginning to prepare for the evening meal. I looked at the hearths unbelievingly, then turned to the cooks and their helpers who rose shufflngly to their feet. I jerked my head at the chef in charge. "There is wood stacked beside the hearths, but only one has a fire in it, and the flames are scarcely alive. Light them all. No wonder our food is undercooked."

The chef, a heavy man with a ruddy face and sullen mouth, shrugged. "We do our best, Your Highness, can't do no more. The king has never complained." But he nodded at three apprentices who scurried to pile on wood and light the logs from the single hearth that held a flame.

I peered into a great pot hung above the cold hearth. My eyes snapped. "I should think everyone has a right to complain. Look at this. Pork, isn't it? The pan isn't even warm, but it's so old that grease is dripping from the bottom. And why isn't the meat on a spit?" I answered before he could give some grumbling retort. "Too much trouble to turn, I suppose, though you have enough boys here to do twice the work needed. From now on roasts will be baked on spits." I glanced at a long table where a man had risen lackadaisically to shape bread into round loaves. I said sharply as he started toward the hearth with them, "Wait until the fires have heated the ovens so the loaves will rise properly."

I examined buckets of vegetables which no one had bothered to sort or clean though they were being poured into shallow pans for cooking, said they must be washed and went on into the store room where great jars of honey stood uncovered, a lure to insects. The chef who'd followed me said hastily, "We always scrape off any bugs, Your Highness, before we stir up the sweetmeats."

I told him incisively what I thought of his careless methods. His ruddy face paled as he assured me, his sullenness gone, that the kitchen staff would change these old ways. In spite of his humble expression, his anger at my interfering showed in his shaking hands and tight mouth. I thanked him coldly and left to summon the chief palace chamberlain.

A tall gangling man, he too had trouble masking his indignation at my demands. I said, "Has no one here ever heard of tablecloths and napkins for dinner?" He started to stammer the custom was too extravagant. I cut him off. "Buy bolts of linen tomorrow and have the seamstresses cut and hem the cloth. And the pages! Call the boys together.

Tell them they must wash their hands before serving even the lowliest guests, and between each course they are to hand around finger bowls.'' He stared at me open-mouthed, then an angry red crept into his cheeks as he fought down his wish to protest.

They obeyed, but all the servingmen and women showed as openly as they dared that they thought my notions of cleanliness and well-done food were effete nonsense. I ignored their dark looks. Christmas would soon be here, and our guests at the palace must be properly served. And impressed. I looked forward to the gay times we'd have in that season from Noel until Twelfth Night. Once again the palace would ring with singing and laughter that would entice Louis out of his shell. I was particularly hopeful because when I mentioned the entertainments I planned, tumblers and mimes as well as troubadours and dancers, he objected to none and said not a word about the costs of my merrymaking.

I was hopeful too soon. Christmas day he was shyly affable to visitors and appeared to enjoy the minstrels and acrobats and lavish banquet, though as usual he ate little of the chicken and eel and cheese turnovers and great roasts of beef and pork and marchpanes and comfits. Still he drank more than his customary half-glass of golden wine. And that night he entered my bedroom with a light and confident air.

But after we'd come together, he was completely sober and left, as always, bemoaning his sinful nature. And the following days he joined us in the great hall for only brief periods and scarcely touched the red Bordeaux as if the amusement were a painful duty, and he was anxious to escape our frivolities. His awkwardness and stretches of silence wouldn't have been noticed if he'd just been one of the invited throng. But as the king and the host, his attitude dulled the spirits of our guests.

I wouldn't let myself become angry, only thought resignedly that it would take more than a few months of marriage to change Louis from a shy, repressed young man into an amiable, outgoing prince who'd be eager to be part of his wife's revelry. Would he ever change? I crushed the unbidden thought quickly. Besides, the fault of dullness wasn't his alone. In Aquitaine his bashfulness hadn't quieted my people. The Parisian nobles didn't have the southerners' enjoyment of life and their wives—whose taste in dress was priggish—didn't have the quick wit of the women I'd grown up with. But I couldn't deny our guests were more uninhibited when the king wasn't with us.

I was almost relieved when the holiday season was over, and Louis didn't disguise the fact he preferred our dull routine to a horde of noisy guests. I stifled a sigh as we rose from dinner and Louis started to leave for another council meeting, stopped as a messenger arrived and held out his hand for a document. But the dispatch was for me. I tore it open, said delightedly, "Raoul is coming to Paris. He's my deputy—did I tell you I'd appointed him?—in Aquitaine." I added at Louis's questioning expression. "He's my cousin, Raoul de Faye."

Louis looked grave, apparently seeing no reason for my pleasure. "He can meet with my ministers and give them any administration details they should know. But will you have time to see him? Your duties—"

So that was the reason for his gravity. I hadn't expected him to be jealous, especially of a young man he'd never met, but I said, "I'm sure I can manage an hour or so between embroidering and giving the cooks their instructions so Raoul will realize what a fine court you have." I couldn't keep a note of excitement out of my voice. Raoul would be a breath of air from my own province. I didn't realize how homesick I was until I'd read his letter which hinted, since the south was quiet, that he was visiting more to discover how I was than for a discussion with the ministers.

He arrived two days later. When I saw him striding into the hall, gay and darkly handsome, I stretched out my hands to him. He caught them, pulled me to him and kissed my lips heartily. We both smiled. Louis didn't, though he welcomed Raoul courteously. Still it was obvious he didn't share our pleasure and immediately suggested my cousin join him and Abbot Suger in the council chamber. I made a moue. But neither Raoul nor I could find a reason to refuse.

Fortunately in less than a week the abbot

thought there was no more to talk over—Louis told me soberly at the evening meal—and implied there was no reason for Raoul to stay on. I ignored the last part of the sentence, thinking only that now Raoul and I would have more time together. My eyes probably gleamed as Raoul's did as I said to Louis that then we should entertain my kinsman properly. Perhaps a hawking party tomorrow? Impatiently I brushed aside Louis's objections. That the weather was too cold, he himself was too busy, my cousin wouldn't wish to remain away from his post too long.

The horses were saddled and in the courtyard next morning as Raoul and I waited for Louis. I bit my lip irritably when a quarter of an hour, a half hour, passed. Then at last a page brought word Louis couldn't join us, his duties—I was tired, tired, tired of that word, and I didn't listen to the rest of the message. I frowned, debating what to do. We'd have an escort, but was it proper for me to ride out with Raoul? Then I caught sight of his grin, and I laughed with him and shrugged away my hesitation which must have come from living too long in Paris.

The clouds that had obscured the sun earlier were swept away and the light was brilliant as we clattered across the Petit Pont to the south bank of the Seine. The trees were still bare, and through them we could see a few birds circling high in the air. We spurred our horses forward, their hoofs almost silent on the leaf-strewn path, to a clearing beyond. Two grooms hurried to us with falcons they strapped to our wrists. We waited until a blackbird and several woodcocks flew closer, then we unhooded our hawks and slipped them from their leashes.

They sped upward like arrows, swerved as their prey scattered in a desperate attempt to escape from beak and talons. They were almost out of sight when our falcons closed in and plunged downward each with a victim in his claws. Raoul and I galloped toward where we thought they'd hit the earth. Or at least I thought so. There was no sight of the birds where I drew up. I turned to Raoul, started to say, "I was sure they were—" and broke off.

His dark eyes were glowing, and his mouth widened into a grin that had a hint of deviltry. I could faintly hear our grooms beating the bush well ahead of us. So Raoul had known I'd draw up too soon. Before I could do more than shake my head at him, he slid from his horse, took two steps to me and lifted me out of the saddle. I stumbled against him. He caught and held me closely. Instinctively I tried to step back. He chuckled but his grip didn't loosen. He said airily, "I prayed Louis wouldn't be with us today." His voice deepened. "I wanted to be alone with you, I had to."

"No, no! Raoul, I'm married."

"To a monk, as anyone can see. You deserve a better husband, my sweet, someone gay and loving." His fingers slid under the low neckline of my gown to fondle my breast. At his touch my lips parted. I wanted to put my arms around his neck, to hold him tightly as he held me, but I didn't move. My body felt pliant against him, wishing, demanding he ease my suddenly roused desire. He sensed my mood, laughed triumphantly and swung me off my feet to lay me on a knoll under a leafless aspen. Then he was beside me, one hand crushing my gown as he pulled it up.

For a moment I yielded against him as I smiled joyously. Then I heard the grooms' voices calling for us. That brought me to my senses and I rose swiftly, horrified at how easily he might have seduced me. He stood up too, grimacing wryly. I gasped, "We—we mustn't. It—it isn't right."

He shrugged good-naturedly. "I was afraid the queen would say that. But at least as a woman," he grinned wickedly, "you didn't say my attentions were displeasing."

I wished I could look indignant, but his words made me smile unwillingly. He helped me mount and we rode to where the grooms were searching for us. But after that morning's incident I was careful to meet Raoul only when others were around, at dinner or wandering—well escorted— through the narrow twisting streets of the city where the crowded overhanging houses prevented the sun from seeping through. Even then there was a sparkle between us that I hoped no one noticed. If my ladies and the guards did, they said nothing, only grumbling over the stench of the streets with the mud and refuse underfoot.

I didn't listen to their complaints, too pleased to

have Raoul's companionship though it was under watching eyes. And it was cheering to talk with him in our own dialect, the *langue d'oc*, which I'd missed since my Aquitanians had gone home. That is when we could hear each other outdoors. Bells pealed almost continuously, and the street vendors shouted their wares of wine and waffles, cakes and pastries. Bread and fish carts rattled past milch goats and swine, making an unbelievable din.

But we enjoyed being together until he could find no more excuses for not returning to Bordeaux. I knew it was as well. For though we spoke only of everyday matters, his eyes were forever wooing me, and on the last day his expression said we wouldn't be separated too long. Yes, it was time he left.

Chapter Three

At first the court seemed empty, but soon I almost forgot Raoul because a week after he'd gone I woke one morning feeling slightly sick but delighted. Wasn't this how a pregnant woman felt the first months? I'd almost given up expecting a child, but that Christmas night with Louis must have made me pregnant. My hope of motherhood gave me new life, melted my restlessness. I was told by everyone, a boy, the baby should be a boy. I wasn't concerned. Since I'd become pregnant this time, I could again. What if the child were a girl? Our next one would be a boy.

Our delighted anticipations were brief. In the third month when I was rising from my lonely bed —Louis said that since I was in a delicate condition, we'd sleep apart so his hours at prayer wouldn't disturb me—I felt dampness along my thighs, saw with horror it was blood flowing. My cry brought my ladies instantly, then the surgeon. He stood a respectful ten feet from my bed and ordered an opiate while he shook his head wisely and said he feared I was miscarrying. The soporific would do little but make the pain easier for me.

But he couldn't ease the pain in my heart that I'd failed. And there were few distractions to help me forget. Abbot Suger, who'd been born a peasant, had met Louis the Fat at Saint-Denis, and my late father-in-law had raised him to be a royal counselor. My husband had inherited the minister. I admit the abbot really loved Louis, but his devotion to his king and country worked against me. And Thierry Galeran showed only contempt for my loss. It'd been irritating to be allowed no voice in government when I'd first come to Paris, but now they made me feel that a woman who couldn't provide an heir was of even less consequence than a girl bride.

So I'd little to do as I recovered slowly except walk in the royal garden at the tip of the Ile de la Cité. It was lovely. Not with the luxuriance of Aquitaine which I missed more every day—I wouldn't think of my cousin here—but the walks were bordered with flowers pushing up through the soil, acanthuses, roses, lilies, trellised vines. From here I could gaze at the Seine where river craft were frantically plying from bank to bank or larger ships sailing west toward the Channel.

I enjoyed the everchanging scenes at first, but as

my health improved my old restlessness took over. Crews of ships and pilots of river boats were part of the great world and could go where they willed. But I the queen was held here as if I were a criminal. My prison might be handsome, but what if it were? I too needed to be part of the world.

Well. Louis wanted to please me. He might be afraid to look at me if a glint of moonlight shone through my new windows, later pray the night away for his sin in his unwilling joy when he touched my nude body, yet in his own way he loved me. Not all the abbot's training about women being Eves, necessary to carry on the human race but never to be listened to on important affairs, had made Louis into a monk. Or would.

So the abbot must go back to his own duties. It'd take time for me to persuade my husband that a young woman who had ruled Aquitaine and been trained by her father could give him more sensible advice on her own provinces than an aging, ascetic abbot was able to, even though all the elderly ministers nodded sagely at his advice. Louis was being treated like a schoolboy. So naturally, I excused him, he was weak as he wasn't given the chance to grow. I must plan carefully or I'd forever be the schoolgirl wife of my schoolboy husband.

Occasionally I was allowed to go off the Ile de la Cité as summer approached and the budding trees now had leaves of tender green. My ladies and I, with the usual guards but also with troubadours which I insisted on, went riding in the fields and woods south of the Seine. I delighted in the warm breeze ruffling my gown and blowing across my face, and in the sunlight away from the dreary palace and in the songs the troubadours sang of Arthur and Roland while we ate in a sheltered nook. Though the singing of those long-ago heroes' exploits depressed me too. Why couldn't Louis have some of their daring?

He hadn't even the mettle to be with me and listening to our jongleurs. The abbot and Thierry said he must sit home every day and attend to his administration. The thought angered me on a June evening when I dismounted in the palace court-yard, an hour, two hours later than usual. In the swarms of riders and servants and grooms, I didn't see Louis until I heard his voice raised sharply. "Eleanor! Do you take no notice of the time? You should have been home hours ago!"

Had his tone been pleasant, I'd have said I was sorry if he'd been worried. But the rasping question, as if I were a child who must answer to a governess, honed my resentment of him. I snapped, "My days are so filled with excitement the time slips by. This morning I spent making tremendous decisions. Should I embroider bands for my new gown with silver or gold? And this afternoon deciding what lays I wished sung to me." I admitted to myself I'd enjoyed the after-noon. The outing had passed the time. Then I choked in horror. Could one call that living, searching for ways to pass the time? And this pale-faced young man—boy—dared to reproach me for not returning early to his gloomy home and half-frightened embrace.

Louis said firmly, "Women who value their reputations should be home at a decent hour. Thierry and Abbot Suger say—"

At those names I forgot I'd intended to try sweet persuasion and stormed, "Since you feel I should be under my husband's eyes, I will be. At the council table beside you. Your abbot is restoring his church of St. Denis. Instead of preaching to you, let him be about his own work. And leave you to yours. You are the king." I didn't wait for an answer but strode past him, wishing I could think of an equally good reason to send Thierry away.

Louis didn't speak to me when we sat down to a delayed supper. Yet I sensed the reason wasn't annoyance but a search for the right words. Finally he blurted out, "You—you said—yes, I am the king." His shoulders straightened. "I—I no longer need Abbot Suger's constant advice." His voice was uncertain, and I knew he'd waver if he waited until tomorrow.

I gave him a radiant smile. "You recognize your own abilities. Send the abbot word now, tonight, that he needn't appear again until you send for him."

That easily it was done. And to prove his manhood further, Louis turned savagely on cities which rebelled against his authority. The first was soon defeated, and I let him see how I admired him though it was hardly a great victory. He flushed with pleasure and begged I accompany him when he confronted the next hostile town. I agreed, smiling at his wish to show off his new authority. He was just too and sent for the mayor to negotiate. But the mayor refused to talk with us and Louis gave the signal for our army to attack. Our charges were driven back, and the troops pitched their camp around the walls so that no townsman could leave to ask help from a neighboring city and no supply wagons could be driven in.

Louis said complacently, "Let them starve a little, and they'll be on their knees pleading for my forgiveness."

I nodded. "But they should be punished. How can they revolt against the king that God placed above them?"

After a fortnight there was still no sign from the citizens that they hoped to placate their ruler. Louis looked disgruntled, then frowned. "They'll be weak from hunger. Tomorrow at dawn we attack."

I rose while it was still dark to be ready to watch the swift charge and victory from our pavilion on a hilltop. But it was midmorning before the signal was finally given, and the army rushed raggedly at the walls with battering rams and ladders. But the ladders came only within inches of the parapets before they were flung back. And the shields protecting the men with the rams were broken by the great rocks hurled from the walls so the rammers had to retreat.

I was astonished at the ease with which towns-men repelled our onslaught, but I said nothing when Louis rode up to me, his hauberk with its flat iron rings sewed onto leather gleaming dully in the noon light. He dragged off his helmet, ran his hand through his damp hair. Surprisingly he appeared cheerful. "It may take a few hours longer than I expected, my dear, but we'll soon conquer."

I said sharply though I hadn't intended to speak, "If your French start acting like soldiers. My Aquitanians—" I broke off at his startled expression which changed to one of annoyance.

He said with dignity, "Our first charges were to test their strength. Now we know the state of their readiness we have only to change our tactics." He swung away and galloped down the hill toward a dozen officers who were talking earnestly.

In spite of their consultation and an increase in protecting rammers and men bearing ladders, it was almost sundown before a breach was made in the wall. Immediately our men poured through. I could hear a clash of steel and anguished shouts, then saw flames shooting upward from some building near the walls. Soon the gates were flung open. Men streamed out, our own soldiers, some burdened with gold and bronze vessels with lengths of velvet and silk swirled around their shoulders, others empty-handed in pursuit of ter-rified girls who tried desperately to escape them. Within minutes the girls were caught and thrown to the ground. I knew this was an accepted part of war, but I looked away. Though not before I saw lustful hands tear at their gowns, leaving the girls naked, and the men ripping off their own clothes to plunge savagely into the young women while their comrades stood around laughing and yelling encouragement, waiting their turn to violate the girls.

When I'd said the town should be punished, I meant fined, not that the innocent should be raped. I rode toward the city searching for Louis as more flames and smoke swirled above the captured town. It was an hour before I found him. He was more horrified than I at my story and sent his captains to restore order, an impossible task with the night coming quickly. So it was morning before creeping fires were put out and slack-mouthed men drawn into lines about Louis and the town officials. Louis summarily ordered the mayor hanged for the rebellion and fined the city heavily before we rode back to Paris.

He didn't ask me to be with him when another town, Vitry, revolted, demanding a city charter, probably not liking my comparison of my soldiers' efficiency and his. I was happy I stayed behind when I heard how Vitry was defeated. It was a victory to his soldiers but not to him. A thousand women and children and elderly men fled to the village church for sanctuary when the town was overrun. Some of Louis's troops set fire to the church, and for months afterwards Louis could still hear their screams of agony whether he was waking or sleeping.

He must atone for his terrible sin. Useless to point out he hadn't ordered the church set afire, that no blame was his. He could only repeat in anguish, "The fault is mine in the eyes of God. I must atone." Then with a flicker of hope he added, "I will go on a pilgrimage to the Holy Land. Only then will I be forgiven the desecration of the Lord's house."

I'd been invited occasionally to a council meeting since the abbot's departure, but Thierry saw to it that I'd no authority to sign documents. So I wouldn't be needed in Paris. My first thought was that I'd return to Aquitaine while Louis was away on his pious mission. I swept the plan away almost immediately. Not yet. France must have an heir. I frowned considering. Louis hadn't come to my bed since the flames at Vitry. No use to try to lure him at our midday dinner today for afterwards he was seeing another abbot, Bernard of Clairvaux, whom many called Saint Bernard. He was ascetic enough, God knows, to be thought of as a holy man with his hair shirt, constant fastings and rare bathing. He thought bathing was self-indulgent.

Still, the challenge of enticing Louis to bed after hours of talk with—or being talked to by—Bernard about the pilgrimage and how Louis must prepare himself by good works and penance made my eyes sparkle with determination. I sent for my troubadours. They must spend the afternoon learning songs they'd seldom heard and which were not to their taste. Godly hymns of praise, the Gregorian chant. I laughed at their expressions, said encouragingly it'd be only for a short time while we supped, then they could sing their own love songs, but not too bawdy. Airs that wouldn't shock the proper Parisians.

Louis returned from his meeting with Bernard thin-lipped and pale. Briefly I was depressed, then reminded myself his expression was little different than any other day since Vitry. As usual he scarcely ate, just tasting the broiled lamb with its spicy sauce. Fortunately he was thirsty after the long hours of discourse and sipped more wine than was his custom. I signalled the troubadours and smiled at him. "I've some entertainment for you, music that will comfort you."

He started to protest he was in no mood for gaiety, stopped as the gentle notes of the Our Father rose and fell pleasantly in the sudden, surprised silence. And when praises to the Virgin were chanted, he said, "Surely there's no evil in enjoying such music."

I slipped my hand over his. "It's like praying, isn't it?" I swallowed abruptly. The troubadours had evidently used up their recently learned repertoire and were now singing one of their love songs, less lusty than most but still not exactly decorous. I went on hastily to distract him, "Praying is a duty for all Christians. But you, the king, have other duties." Before he could interpret that as a reason for hurrying off to his endless documents, I added, "Your first duty to France." I held out his goblet, waited until he gulped down the red wine, then whispered, "You are a great ruler, but can you go on a pilgrimage and leave no heir for your country to take to its heart?"

Color rose to his face, whether from the thought of intimacy or the wine I didn't know. I lowered my eyes demurely. After a moment his fingers tightened on mine. "You—you are right, my love. We must put aside our own inclinations to live chastely and give my people what they need."

I hoped he wouldn't forget his resolution and before I went to bed later that evening, I was massaged and perfumed, had my hair brushed until it was a cloud about my head. My ladies had scarcely left when the door opened again. Louis crossed to me, his face half uncertain but with a struggling ardor in his eyes. He sat on the bed, touched my hair softly, saying it was pale gold in the firelight.

I said, "I wish my whole body was of gold so that you'd plunder—" He drew back slightly. "So that I could spend it on you. What woman would not wish to spend what beauty she has on a king and for his loyal subjects? If that would give my lord pleasure." Again I used the wrong word. "I mean the pleasure a strong man takes in doing his royal duty."

He looked gravely pleased, or tried to be grave, but the ardor in his eyes deepened as he stepped modestly away to take off his tunic and hose before sliding in beside me. His hands were less fumbling than usual as he stroked my shoulders and went tentatively to my waist and hips. I pretended to be hesitant to allow him the freedom while my body screamed to have his embrace more forceful, not to be denied. My hesitancy aroused him and I thought hopefully, perhaps tonight a child will be implanted, and surrendered to him.

My hope became reality, but this time I told no one until I was past what I'd heard called the dangerous third month. Then I could laugh gaily, spontaneously, over nothing, trifles. And the court smiled with me. Until the child was born, healthy, a lovely little creature, bright-eyed. But a girl, Marie. Now there was no reason for Louis to delay his pilgrimage longer. In fact he wanted to hasten it, certain God wouldn't grant him a son until he'd atoned for Vitry. He'd leave soon, in the spring. He'd recall Abbot Suger to take charge while he was away.

I shrugged, hardly caring as I recovered from the birth. Besides, now I'd have a child to watch over. But I didn't. Half-a-dozen nurses hovered over Princess Marie, and they allowed me into her rooms grudgingly and hovered about us every moment I held the soft and dimpled baby in my arms. So through the long bleak winter I was mother and wife in name only. Louis in his depression frowned on my jongleurs' merry songs, and finally they drifted away to other courts where they'd be welcomed wholeheartedly. I had nothing to brighten the gray days and thought, I'm scarcely over twenty but my life has ended. What have I to look forward to?

More dull days and duller nights. I needed

gaiety, companions I could talk and laugh with. I needed a husband, one who'd be a real lover like—like Raoul who could answer the restless stirrings of emotions within me, make me feel a woman. Then as I was wearily embroidering the sleeve of a robe for our bishop, Louis came to tell me of a bull from Pope Eugenius.

In the east the great city of Edessa which, like Antioch, guarded the Latin kingdom of Jerusalem, had fallen to the Moslems who would now try to sweep all the Christians into the sea. The Pope urged Louis to gather up his lords and vassals and lead a crusade to prevent the infidels from overrunning the Holy City which the Christians had held for half a century. Louis's face shone. This would still be a pilgrimage for him, but now it was more, much more.

The robe fell from my lap as I rose excitedly. His pilgrimage had been planned as a small group of men, mostly monks, praying their way to the east. But a crusade! That meant that the nobles, many with their wives, would ride triumphantly across Europe, lightheartedly adventurous. I was excited, but I tried to make my voice solemn. "Louis, you can see God is smiling on your wish to repent. He calls on you to lead our people to His own land in a holy war. You must send out a proclamation to all the provinces."

He nodded with more life than he'd shown for months and hurried away. But my thoughts weren't on him now. Antioch was in danger, and the city's ruler was my young uncle, Prince

Raymond. I remembered how much we'd liked each other when we'd played together—was it ten years ago? twelve?—in Bordeaux, and how I'd looked up to him, trying to follow him in everything he did, hunting or fishing or falconing, before he'd left us for a more brilliant future than he'd have in Aquitaine where he was only the second son.

Would he remember me? Yes, yes, he would. We'd cared too much for each other for either of us to forget. He might even be dazzled at the young woman I'd become. Was that vanity? Perhaps, but my own polished silver mirror as well as the courtiers told me I was beautiful.

But in the days that followed, I realized with dismay that Louis's appeal for followers aroused little enthusiasm. Instead of blazing forth the glory of a crusade, he talked of his need for penance and went on and on about how he was taking the cross to atone for Vitry. The barons yawned. I sent for some of my Aquitanian lords, the best fighters in Christendom, but they too only shrugged.

What did they care for Louis's soul? A second Crusade would but repeat the disasters of the first one which some still remembered; and others had heard from their fathers or grandfathers how they'd mortgaged their fields to rescue the Holy Land only to be wounded or killed before they reached Jerusalem. Life at home was too pleasant to exchange it for dusty roads and parched deserts and the savage onslaught of marauding Moslems.

I understood their feelings but my desire for adventure didn't lessen, though Abbot Suger also disapproved of the crusade. He thought Louis should stay home and administer his kingdom's affairs. But then the other abbot, Bernard of Clairvaux, was commanded by the Pope to preach a Holy War. Bernard agreed to go to Vezelay. Louis, eager to hear him, prepared to leave Paris immediately with a following of reluctant lords and vassals.

I was so used to the grumblings of our suite that I was astonished when we rode north. Highways were filled with noisy crowds swarming out of cities and towns and farms, shouting enthusiastically they must see the famous abbot. Though seeing him was all they wanted they said to any inquirers. I wished, if that were all they looked for, that some of them had stayed home. I enjoyed masses of people usually, but the road was narrow, and they pressed in on us from all sides, gaping at Louis and me and our courtiers in bright cloaks and caps and tunics.

The last month had been dry, and dust from the shuffling feet settled on our clothes and filled our nostrils so that it was hard to breathe. Still that had some advantage. The fragrance of budding trees and hedges was overlaid with the odor of unwashed bodies and soiled clothing. Some of my ladies held their veils against their noses, but I shrugged off the unpleasantness and enjoyed the crisp breeze that played over my face and ruffled the flaring skirt of my bliaud.

The last day of our journey we had an occasional shower so we were glad when we reached a convent outside Vezelay to dry our clothes and sleep before we rode into the cathedral to hear Abbot Bernard. We didn't go to the church. A guard ran up to tell us as we were mounting that no cathedral could hold the overflow of people so the abbot was being taken to a field to speak.

There was no need to ask directions. When we left the convent yard, we saw streams of lords and peasants hurrying down the lane on our left. And our guard had a difficult time breaking a way through to a place near a small rise on which a dais had been raised. I waited expectantly for the abbot to arrive, wondering if he really thought he could touch this throng. The people were merry as if at a vast fair, laughing and singing and elbowing their way around us, shouting witticisms to each other and scrambling up to vendors who came out with carts of bread and honey and fish.

The noise was deafening when I saw Abbot Bernard and a monk walk slowly up the hill and climb on the wooden platform. He was so thin from fasting he seemed too weak for speech. Yet when he stood facing the crowd, the voice from that emaciated figure rang out powerfully. At his first words, the impossible happened. Everyone fell silent, staring at him. He unrolled the papal bull and read Eugenius's call to arms for every man here to march against the wicked infidels.

There were some snickers at his demand for

men to leave home and family to fight and perhaps die in some far foreign land. But the snickers faded as he went on. "Fellow Christians, fellow sinners, we must hasten to rescue Christ's tomb from the proud followers of Mohammed. You will be rewarded gloriously. Raise your sword for Christ, and our sins, great and small, will be absolved. Every transgression will be forgotten by the merciful God who reaches down from heaven to save you. Do you not marvel at his everlasting mercy? He wants all of you in His service in this holy crusade. The meanest sinner will be forgiven, murderers, adulterers, the perjured, brigands, all, all will be welcomed in this army for Christ who needs you and you and you to wrest His tomb from idolaters."

He said more, but I could hear only an occasional word above the shouts of rage from the crowd against the blaspheming infidels. And when he finished, cheers rang out and cries of "On to Jerusalem!" Louis wiped his hand across his damp eyes and pushed forward to kneel before the abbot, begging to be the first to be accepted in Christ's army. The abbot's gaunt face was transformed by a smile as he turned to a monk behind him who held a supply of crosses and took the top one to give to Louis.

About us lords and peasants forgot their indifference to Louis's appeal to join a crusade and yelled, "Crosses, give us crosses!" Soon the monk's crosses were gone, and Bernard had to take off his outer tunic and was tearing it into crude crosses for the crowd as I made my way through the throng and went down on my knees. He started to hand me one, stopped, his dark eyes fierce. "Women! The holy crusade has no need of women to tempt men from their prayers and work."

My ladies and the wives of lords who'd taken the cross sputtered with anger, but I pushed aside my wrath and said humbly, "We too wish to be pilgrims to Christ's sepulcher, to have the joy of absolution from our sins. Weak though we are, we will encourage our husbands to greater effort to aid Jerusalem. Surely you cannot deny us the way to heaven."

Bernard's bloodless lips drew back as he thundered, "No! I do not deny you heaven. Husbands and sons on this crusade will secure redemption for their families as well as themselves. We will have no women to distract them from their holy purpose."

My mouth tightened to hold back a furious retort. It was true I did want to do my part for God and His church. What was wrong if I also wished to share in a great adventure that would take me far from a gloomy place? I rose and stepped back, my eyes lowered so he wouldn't read my resolve in them. I'd wait for a quiet moment when Louis and I would be alone.

But when I spoke to Louis that evening in the great pavilion that had been set up for us near the field, he stubbornly repeated Bernard's refusal. I pleaded, "Husband and wife should be together, and who knows how long it will be before you return?'' He only shook his head. Like most weak men, he thought obstinacy was firm strength. I flared, ''Very well if that is your final decision. But if I don't go, not one of my Aquitanians will follow you, and you know what great warriors they are. How will you fight the infidels with only men from your provinces?''

He paused, then shook his head again. ''We must do as Abbot Bernard says.''

''You are the king and the leader of this holy crusade. The abbot is a saint, but no man of the church can tell a commander what knights should follow him.'' This time I paused, readying a more persuasive plea. I let my shoulders droop. ''I must obey my lord and king. But you will not insist I remain in Paris where I'd be so lonely for your company. I shall wait for your return in Bordeaux. Raoul is studying new laws. It is my duty to read them and be sure they are just. We'll be working long hours together, but you have showed me one must never turn one's back on one's duties. Raoul and I—''

There was no need to say more. Louis's mouth opened, closed, opened again. ''You are right now I've had time to think it over. How would Christ judge me if I allowed someone else to give the orders—holy though the abbot is—and lose the support of many fine fighters? And it is true that women will support their men on our great crusade. As for the new code of laws, you can appoint someone to study them with your cousin.''

I said demurely, "Thank you, Louis, for I too want to serve Christ," and hurried out, my mind whirling with plans to persuade my Aquitanians to join me on the crusade.

I'd summon them to Poitiers to talk it over—No. Tournaments and festivities would bring lords and knights together, put them in a pleasant mood and make them more willing to listen to my pleas than any solemn discussion would.

Chapter Four

The day was sunny with wisps of clouds making lazy scrolls in the clear blue sky, and the light wind only ruffled the gauzy veil pinned on my hair. Below my canopied box vassals and their retainers sat on the tiered seats leaning forward eagerly, and further down freedmen and peasants pressed against the railing protecting the sandy lists as they shouted for their favorites. At either end pavilions of scarlet striped with white were set up for the knights who'd engage in today's jousting. It would be bloodless, lances and swords blunted. I wasn't risking having my best fighters wounded or killed before we set off for the Holy Land.

I turned smiling to Raoul who as my deputy sat beside me. He grinned back, his dark eyes sweeping boldly over me. "The duchess has avoided me since she returned to Poitiers, but this morning I can enjoy gazing at the woman behind that ducal facade."

I said primly, "You may forget, but I don't. I have a husband." He pretended to be crestfallen at my words, and I couldn't hold back the laugh bubbling in my throat. Still, when his fingers crept toward mine, I drew my hand away and waved toward the excited throngs around us. I'd told him of my idea that tournaments and festivities might help persuade our warriors to go on the crusade, started to ask what he thought, stopped as a trumpet call rang out and two knights thundered down the lists, lances aimed at each other's chests.

The weapons struck true, horses reared back but were quickly controlled as the crowd cheered wildly. They circled to charge again. One knight was flung from his saddle, his squire ran up to help him from the field and the victor galloped to our box to receive my badge. The crowd cheered, then turned to watch the next fighters spurring down the lists. The jousting ended in a wild melee when a score of knights from each pavilion strode out to mount their horses and strike against their opponents just below me. The people screamed encouragement and laughed immoderately at the difficulty of finding their favorites in the cloud of dust the hoofs stirred up.

The merry mood of lords and peasants continued through the day when the people drank from wine fountains and feasted on oxen in the squares, and my vassals and their wives banqueted in the great hall of the palace. Raoul, good-humored as always, chewed on a chicken thigh while he drifted from table to table to speak of the crusade and say that their own duchess had taken the vow to journey to the Holy Land.

I was applauded by all, and the lords stood to toast me. Most of them, forgetting their earlier indifference, promised to follow me. Those who didn't promise apologized, saying they couldn't because the new taxes I'd had to impose—as Louis had done among the Franks—made their presence on their fields necessary for survival. Otherwise they'd have to sell their holdings. A practical viewpoint I could well understand. And they would donate to our army more than the tax levied.

I thanked them, pleased at their generosity. The abbeys too supported me, and I gave them special privileges in tithes, especially to my favorite abbey, Fontevrault. This was a hospital connected to both a convent and a monastery, but the person in charge was an abbess rather than an abbot. My father and I had often visited there, impressed with the serene quiet and the way anyone was cared for, serf or lord, with tender efficiency.

But now with my provinces behind me, it was time to leave them—and Raoul—for Paris where Louis and his ministers and warlords were planning the tiresome details of food and camp equipment and guides for routes through the foreign countries. We'd go by land as it was thought to be safer and cheaper than the sea. Winter was coming on, and the city was drearier than usual with these conferences where there was only talk and more talk about arrangements that couldn't be made until the sun shone and melted the snow drifts.

Still, there were some bright days when we received letters from Germans and Hungarians giving us permission to cross their countries that seemed to bring the day of departure nearer. The emperor of Byzantium also promised us support and begged us to be his guests when we reached his city. That was exciting, but first we had to take the first step on that long road. Would the time never arrive?

It came at last on a blazing day in June. We stopped at Saint Denis cathedral, which was awash with flags and on fire with the thousands of candles lighting the great interior. Here the Pope, who'd crossed the Alps to bless us, gave the sacred banner of France, the oriflamme, into Louis's hands, and from there we took the road to Metz. There was the clatter of knights, the whipping of pennants overhead, the sound of music that was almost lost in the tramp of thousands of marchers and the crash of hundreds of supply wagons.

That first evening out Louis came hesitantly into my pavilion. I could guess from his awkward movements, his half-lidded eyes, why he was here. I nodded dismissal to my waiting woman who was brushing my hair and smiled at Louis with relief. I'd been afraid he'd use our holy mission as an excuse for us to sleep apart, and I was still eager to be the mother of the heir to France and to

Aquitaine. Then I laughed silently to myself. I also needed the feel of a man's arms around me, the sensation of being one with him.

I said dutifully—he'd be shocked if he knew my passionate nature— "Welcome, Louis. I hope I can give you the wifely support you should have to carry on the journey you've undertaken for God. Why else am I here?"

His face brightened. "You are quite right, my dear. We should use all the help God has provided for His sinful children." He stumbled over the word sinful, frowning doubtfully as if he wondered now if he should have come.

I said quickly, "Do sit down and tell me your plans for tomorrow." He went into incredible detail on the next day's march as if trying to persuade himself he was here only to discuss our daily routine. I nodded, but I heard little of what he said, my mind on how to bring him back to his first mood. I said at last, "Ah, now I know what I should do tomorrow. But since that's settled, you must rest so you'll be fresh for the long ride." I looked down modestly and moved toward the bed.

"I—I thought—but then I—do you believe we—we should—"

I sighed, thinking of Raoul's demanding farewell kiss and his eyes that caressed me, said with gentle firmness, "Whatever will make you ready for your pious work is good," and unpinned the brooch at my shoulder.

He caught his breath audibly at sight of my pale flesh, but turned resolutely away as I slipped off my bliaud and long-sleeved undertunic and jerked off his own tunic and hose. A moment later he was beside me, his fingers just touching my waist. Even that small gesture warmed me, and I had to restrain myself from drawing his hand to fondle me intimately. At least he pulled me closer, and I felt the damp heat of his body against my breast and thighs. He muttered, "My—my dear love," and kissed me, not like Raoul's mouth hard on mine but gently.

My lips parted under his, but I made no other response though I ached for the sweetness of caresses, of insistent exploration of my body. Instead, as if the kiss were wooing enough, he took me quickly. But his glowing, unfocused eyes pleased me. Until he fell back and stared at me with something like horror. "Abbot Bernard was— right. I should have heeded him. Women are —are a temptation like Eve. I vow I will not come to you again until our holy crusade is triumphant."

I whispered, "An heir, France needs an heir."

He shook his head. "Until I have expiated my sin for the burning of Vitry, God will not grant me a son."

There was no answer to that, or none I could think of as he hurried into his clothes and left me alone in the great bed which was transported in our supply wagons. I tried to shrug, but I was too hurt. I was said to be the most beautiful woman in France, yet my own husband could turn from me refusing, probably for months, to possess me.

The next day Louis in his pilgrim tunic surrounded himself with monks, and I chose my own escort, my ladies and knights and troubadours from Aquitaine. Troubadours had been forbidden to accompany the crusade, but I was happy now I'd ignored the prohibition. Their gay songs lifted my spirits and were laugh-provoking as we rode east.

When we reached Metz, the throngs there were unbelievable. A hundred thousand people I was told. Tents were pitched on the banks of the Moselle, and beyond them were horses, sheep, mules and cattle in the strips of greenery which with difficulty were saved for the animals. Wagons loaded with arms, baggage, tools for building siege engines were placed in the rear, and near them field kitchens were set up. And when we left, the highway was filled with new recruits, crossbowmen, cavalry, foot soldiers, shabby pilgrims, washerwomen, criminals and vagabonds.

People lined the road to watch us pass. When I came into view I was cheered wildly and pleas were called out for me to pray for all of them in Jerusalem. Louis was dressed plainly, but my velvet robes were embroidered with fleurs-de-lis and my horse had a saddle trimmed with silver. At the admiration showered on me I was delighted I'd packed chests of clothes and jewelry, cosmetics and furs and veils. When we reached Byzantium, we wouldn't look like beggars but like a queen with her entourage. I thought of Byzantium, and later Antioch where my young uncle would welcome us. If he remembered our childhood days and was pleased to see me, that would lighten the hurt Louis had dealt me.

Through the next weeks we moved briskly, covering ten to twenty miles a day. Our army was like a huge animal padding along highways or narrow roads through forests that seemed greener than our own woods and past castles on a mount and small villages huddled in the hollow below. Everything was different from home, and I found it all exciting. I felt vivacious as I hadn't been in Paris and forgot Louis's neglect of me. How was that different from other times in our married life except that his vow of chastity was for a longer period than ever before?

Surprisingly our marching with separate escorts was frowned at by Louis's monks. I thought at first they disapproved because a husband and wife should be together, but I soon discovered their real reason. They said, tight-lipped, this was a crusade for God, not a tour through strange countries for the light-minded that encouraged a too-easy familiarity between men and women which would lead to vice. It was true I enjoyed my own people and the flirtatious glances from young knights, but what harm in that?

Fortunately Louis, always praying with his eyes downcast, was unaware of the gossip about my escort so when I saw him occasionally he only spoke solemnly about his joy that he'd been chosen to lead this holy army to Christ's tomb. And I did share his dedication. Each morning when I was awakened before dawn by the camp noises of tents being taken down and mules harnessed to the wagons, I'd rise shiveringly to say my early devotions and decide I'd try to match his gravity and remember why we were here. But as the hours wore on, and the hot sun was dazzling on bright gowns and cloaks and fields bursting with life, I couldn't suppress my pleasure in the company of my countrymen and the constantly changing scenery.

Some days riding through the mountains was exhausting, and all our energies went into guiding our horses along overgrown paths and avoiding branches above our heads. But that made us more eager for the evening when we'd gather around a fire and debate about love and chivalry and sing the merry songs of the south while our evening meal was prepared for us.

Tonight, though, I glanced around, frowned in surprise as the supper was being served. The lords and ladies had trays heaped with bread and meat, but page boys and servants were given crusts and small portions of fish. I sent for my steward. He shrugged helplessly. "This is the best our provisioners could do, Your Highness. There was little food to buy in the towns we passed through and, and even if there were an abundance, we could not purchase much. You see—well, the money changers—at home our francs could supply our needs, but the farther we go, the less the money changers give us in guilders, or whatever coin is used in the countries we pass through. Pilgrims and foot soldiers are lucky to have one meal a day, and the king has forbidden looting.''

At that last word there was a burst of laughter, hastily stifled. I looked at my plate on which a page was now adding eels and greens. "Do you mean this was—stolen?"

"Not your meal, madame, no, no, no. We slaughtered some of our cattle, and the fish were caught at the last stream we crossed."

I said firmly, "Now divide the food more equally among my household," and held out my tray. I realized it had never occurred to me before to notice what our servants ate. But at home while they had the second choice of delicacies, there was always enough for everyone. More than enough as we fed beggars at the gate with the leftovers of any meal.

The steward signalled the pages, who looked delighted as they made a fairer distribution of our supper. Before they were finished, there was a commotion behind us from the river bank where we'd made camp. Angry shouts, a loud splashing answered by happily profane screams rose above the usual hubbub of our night quarters. I rose and walked toward the din, stopped in astonishment at the scene before me.

A large fishing boat was being towed ashore by a group of soldiers while in the river five men, evidently the crew, started floundering toward us cursing furiously. However, apparently seeing how many men lined the bank, they turned and swam clumsily toward the opposite shore, which luckily was close since they were dragged down by their drenched clothes. I saw only the first reach safety as the others were cut off from view by the surge of our own people onto the boat to haul out nets of fish which they dragged toward a fire.

I was shaken at the thought of how hungry our crusaders must be. When we'd set out, our provisions seemed as though they'd more than last the army until we reached Byzantium. I'd speak to Louis, who was probably as ignorant as I'd been of the state we were in. But when he heard of this plundering, he'd know how to provide for all our followers.

At first he dismissed the affair saying it was sinful and the looters must pray for forgiveness, but the fish stealing was merely the result of high spirits and no great harm was done. The fishermen had lost a day's catch, but tomorrow they'd return for their boat, and we'd also replenish our supplies. But when we moved on the next day, towns refused to trade with us, and all Louis's orders couldn't prevent our men from dropping out of line and breaking into shops and lonely farmhouses.

He sighed at the looting, said his counselor Thierry Galeran would handle the matter and returned to his prayers. I wondered why I'd expected him to show leadership at my request when he'd scarcely glanced at me for months and when we met acted as if he were afraid I'd seduce him from his high resolve.

As for Galeran, Louis might as well have called

on his equerry as that eunuch who appeared, as always, to blame me for our difficulties. I was too extravagant and with my women, there was a constant drain on supplies. I confess I felt a malicious satisfaction that the only result of his bungling arguments with the stewards was to drive away many crusaders. My Aquitanians remained loyal to me, but many from the Frankish provinces said even if shops further from the disturbance would sell to us, how would they pay for the food? Only the wealthy could meet the money changers' rates.

They said too that if the king had trouble feeding his men in what was supposed to be friendly territory, what would it be like when we marched beyond Byzantium into enemy lands? Soldiers slid away into the night to go back to their homes. There weren't hordes of deserters, and I believed that those who left would be of little help when we faced the Turks so I wasn't overly concerned.

But I was worried over our army. Men who marched all day must be fed. I consulted with my vassals who shrugged tiredly. Then they exchanged glances, a glint of deviltry in their eyes. An hour after I retired that night I heard muted sounds outside my pavilion, mumbling voices and an occasional scraping of a boot against a stone. I turned over unthinkingly, frowned suddenly, realizing these weren't usual camp noises.

I slid swiftly out of bed and ran to the entrance, the ground cold under my bare feet. One of my women grunted drowsily, slept again. I threw back the tent flap. Instantly a sentry stepped toward me. I was about to question the young man, then saw the answer in the cool light of the full moon. On my left a small group of men were moving cautiously down a slope that led to a wide field where buildings and wooden enclosures for animals were smudged shadows in the night.

I whispered, "No, come back!" then saw the sentry was grinning. Because tomorrow our troops would be fed. I couldn't give the order I knew I should but watched fascinated as the men crept across the meadow and climbed over the wooden walls. Abruptly the quiet darkness was torn apart by bellows from watchers inside who were on guard with an army camp so close to their holdings. Swords clanged and wood thudded against wood as dim figures fought savagely. But our men were well prepared, and the struggle was brief.

Soon they were on their way back, staggering under bags of grain on their shoulders or darting back and forth as they drove sheep and cows up the rise near my quarters. I turned hastily to go inside where I could lie in bed and pretend I knew nothing of the night's looting. And I continued to close my eyes against the plundering that went on until we crossed the Danube.

There on the far bank when we disembarked from fishing boats and scows was a sight that made us all gape. Banners and pavilions with gold and silver stripes lined a grassy field between river and forest, and issuing from them was a vast entourage surrounding two men in silk robes and turbans, each with a staff of office in his hand. But our attention strayed from them to scores of wagons drawn up to our right, their slatted sides bulging with food supplies.

I forced myself to look back at the two ambassadors who came forward, stopping every few feet to bow to Louis and me. The first one said through an interpreter, "Greetings from our glorious master, Byzantium's emperor, Manuel Comnenus, to his glorious brother king from the West. His humble wish is that you accept this small token of his good will." He waved toward the wagons. "A trifling gift for so majestic a prince as you who are known throughout the world as the very epitome of wisdom and piety." He bowed again, the gesture repeated by all his followers, and went on extolling Louis's virtues.

One of our bishops finally said shortly, "We are grateful for the supplies you bring, but I beg you, do not repeat majesty, wisdom, piety again. We all know our king so we wish to learn if your emperor has some slight favor in mind that we could do for him to show our appreciation."

They couldn't quite forego a few more ornate phrases, but said at last that their great emperor asked first if we came in peace and would not attempt to take any of his cities. They smiled fawningly as Louis assured them his only purpose was to go to the Holy Land to pray at Christ's tomb and was happy to have Byzantium at his back since he'd have to cut through Turkish territory.

They permitted themselves smiles at that and said the majestic Louis was sure to be successful. So the emperor's second request was that any city or castle we captured which had once belonged to his empire should be returned to Manuel. Louis bit his lip indecisively, but his counselors surged forward saying the request was completely unreasonable. Louis said, "Well—perhaps—" I edged toward him and whispered, "No need to agree yet. Why not wait until you meet the emperor?"

Galeran scowled at my advising Louis, but the other ministers appeared pleased since the king accepted my suggestion. Now they'd have time to stiffen him against handing over any victories to the Byzantines who, everyone knew, were never trustworthy. As if to bolster that opinion, word came that Manuel had already signed a peace treaty with the Turks, and anger spread through the camp. So instead of being our ally, the emperor would give us no help yet expect our crusaders to fight the Turks for him. Many shouted we shouldn't visit Byzantium, we should besiege and take the city.

Louis was horrified. Fight a Christian prince when our enemies were the infidels? Never. These people were our friends. It seemed he was right when we reached the city gates for we were welcomed by a parade of satraps and merchants and clerics who begged him to go at once to the palace where the emperor waited, his one desire to meet the glorious leader of the crusade.

I was not invited, but I was too interested in the

city to care as I stared about me. Byzantium was said to be the wealthiest city in the world, and its harbor the largest. There were hundreds of ships in the Marmara Sea and in the Golden Horn which edged the triangle of land the city was built on. I gaped at the double curtain walls as I passed through the gate and at the shining domes of the great churches that reflected the noon sun. In every square it seemed was a splashing fountain which, I was told by the obsequious lord who accompanied my women and me, was fed by aqueducts cut through the walls, with water stored in underground reservoirs. Obelisks towered against the sky, and the tall homes were decorated with paintings on either side of clean-swept streets which were so unlike the muddy and stench-filled streets of Paris.

We were led through shady passages to arcaded bazaars. I blinked my eyes against the gold and jewelry from the Orient, looked delightedly at brocades from Tripoli and Baghdad, carved ivories, perfumes, linens from Egypt and beautiful illuminated books. But there was no time to do more than glimpse the dazzling displays before we were escorted to a palace outside the walls where dozens of servitors seated us at long tables and brought course after course of highly spiced meats and fish and curious-looking vegetables and sweetmeats shaped in intricate designs.

My attention strayed from the food to the enormous chamber where we ate. Above us were chandeliers set with jewels, the walls were decorated with gold and mosaic and columns were striped with gold. Other rooms we'd passed through were hung with brilliant wall tapestries that made our French hangings appear dull. I wondered why we weren't lodged within the city—though I had no complaints about this elegant palace—but soon discovered the reason.

Our huge army was camped outside among orchards and vegetables gardens. It was well to be with our own soldiers who, I suspected, weren't allowed through the gates because Manuel had heard rumors many had wanted to capture Byzantium. A wise decision to keep them out, I supposed, since soldiers, already hostile, could easily become unruly, their needs sharpened at the sight of the wealth in the streets and bazaars.

But my ladies and I were invited into the glamorous city by the Empress Irene, who'd been a German princess, and I found the Blachernae Palace even more awe-inspiring than the city. Gold and silver glittered everywhere, and the empress also glittered in robes heavily embroidered with gold and strings of matchless pearls falling across her breast. At first I was content with admiring the lavish Eastern ways where slaves and eunuchs surrounded Irene, and no one spoke to her without kneeling. Our palace was a pale shadow of this magnificence, and I felt a twinge of envy.

Very soon, though, I was irritated. Irene and her ladies made it clear they thought the bliauds I'd packed with such care, tight-laced with flaring skirts, the undertunics with close-fitting sleeves, weren't magnificent enough for an imperial court. Was anyone whose gowns weren't stiff with gold dressed dowdily? But I was angrier when the empress raised her brows as she asked through the interpreter, "Is it true that you, a queen, are traveling to Jerusalem with a horde of rough soldiers?"

I said sharply, "They're skilled warriors, madame. And I ride at my husband's side where surely a wife should be." If I weren't exactly at Louis's side, he knew I was close by and supporting his venture.

Irene's blue eyes widened. She was fair like most people with Germanic blood, young but with a heavy, unwieldy body. She gasped in horror. "You ride? Surely you can't mean you aren't carried in a litter? How can any highly born lady endure such discomfort?"

Her women muttered something which I took from their expressions to be "How primitive!" I was tempted to retort that, considering Irene's heavy bones which were too well-padded, she'd be fortunate if she could ride more than an hour, but I swallowed my annoyance and said sweetly, "We ride for the glory of Christ. If we were in litters, the army would be slowed."

She shrugged and yawned. "We have enjoyed meeting you. We will meet again later today to dine. The morning has been fatiguing. Perhaps you'd like to rest now?"

I couldn't suppress a laugh at that, and my ladies smiled at the suggestion that an hour of conversation was so tiring I'd have to lie down. "If the guides who brought us here will be so kind, I'd prefer to see more of the city before we return for the banquet."

She nodded wearily. Fortunately our escort was more enthusiastic, showing us with a flourish into Santa Sophia. The church was dazzling with its brilliant paintings and gold and mosaic, but we had too little time there as the satrap in charge insisted we must also view the tower above the Golden Gate. From there we could see caravans of camels which brought, I was told, brass and sandalwood and spices and silks from the Far East. And across the Bosphorus was the hazy tongue of land that was Asia where we would soon be marching.

I'd have been completely fascinated by it all if the empress and her suite hadn't made it so evident they thought us inferior. An opinion, I had to admit, that was reinforced when I saw Manuel and Louis together at the feast that afternoon. Both were in their twenties, but like his wife Manuel glittered in his gold and purple robes while Louis wore his colorless pilgrim tunic. And the dark Manuel gave the sense of enormous power which contrasted with Louis's humble attitude. Though in spite of his diffident expression, Louis was firm in not promising to turn over any castles or cities his army captured.

Still, he was a sorry figure for a king. Or was that my frustration over my lonely nights when I spent too many hours sleepless in my need for a man? My anger at his too rigid self-discipline intensified as I saw that while he could control his own natural urges, he couldn't control his soldiers who were bored at their inactivity and forever brawling in the streets outside the walls, sometimes going as far as to set fire to homes or attack peaceful citizens. Louis paid for their vandalism, sighed at how low the treasury was—even Galeran couldn't complain I was the source of the rowdiness—and wrote Abbot Suger he must have more money at once. So between the empress's disdain and the army's being out of hand, I wasn't sad when Louis decided to leave this splendid city.

I was eager too to reach Antioch and see my uncle Raymond. He, I was sure, wouldn't be a disappointment. I smiled at the thought of him as we were rowed to Asia Minor and marched across the plains toward the hills in the distance. The days were sunny, and the soldiers in a good mood now, ready to meet and destroy the Turkish troops. We were all elated at the hope of soon reaching the Holy Land, certain our men would slice through any infidels who might try to delay us. But Louis was prudent and instead of taking the shorter route inland, he decided on the longer way near the seacoast where we'd have a better chance to buy supplies or meet any ships coming from France.

The villages the Greeks had colonized were well supplied, but prices were unbelievable. When coins ran out, our hungry men had to trade helmets and shields and cloaks for food. And Louis no longer gave orders. He said God was providing since we were on a holy mission, but God would have had to come in person to prevent the army from becoming a mob as each division camped and ate and marched as it pleased.

Or perhaps God was providing. We were near Ephesus on Christmas Eve. As the tents were being put up and fires lighted, I swung around at a sound across the narrow river. A band of shouting, screaming Turks seemed to have come out of the ground, scimitars gleaming in the late afternoon sun. Our captains yelled to their troops, and astonishingly our men became an army again. Steel clattered as they caught up their weapons from where they'd laid them on the ground for easier working on setting up camp.

Horses neighed and reared as grooms rounded them up. Leather jingled as the cavalry snatched at the reins and mounted. Then with the infantry at their heels, the force forded the bitterly cold water and fell savagely on the enemy, our war cries drowing out the menacing shouts of the infidels. Our lines held steady when the Turks charged again and again, trying to break the solid resistance. It was a pandemonium of clanging swords against scimitars, bellows of rage, screams of the wounded, the pounding of hoofs. The setting sun glittered on helmets and shields and touched the dark faces of the Turks, their open mouths screaming, "Allah! Allah! Allah!"

Our troops moved relentlessly forward,

pressing the enemy back. The Turks broke into small knots of fighters, then swung their horses about and fled to the hills, our mounted men thundering after them. We were wildly gay when our crusaders returned, bringing with them horses and gold from the camp the Turks had abandoned. We laughed as we sat around eating our evening meal of bread and fish at how easily the enemy had been defeated. And our bright confidence wasn't dimmed even though the next morning we woke to sleet pounding our pavilions and a rising wind that brought the first taste of winter.

Louis was also buoyed up by the confidence and said our march was taking too long. We should turn inland for the more direct route to Antioch from the coast. The Turks struck again and again, but each time we drove them off. Our successes helped us endure the winter storms that otherwise would have made our march a nightmare. Without native guides, we had to take our bearings from the sun and stars, but sometimes neither were visible, and we halted so we wouldn't be lost in the mountainous hills. But after three days the sun shone brightly, and Louis said he'd march with the rear division.

One of my vassals, Geoffrey de Rancon, offered to be in the van, and I rode forward with him, eager to reach the summit where I hoped we'd see some city or landmark to help guide us.

The officers had agreed we'd all camp there, but since we had no baggage wagons to slow us we were at the top by noon. Geoffrey shook his head when the soldiers drew up. Impossible to put up tents here, the winds would tear through them. Besides, we should make a longer march today if we were ever to reach Antioch. And his scouts, sent ahead earlier, brought word there was a pleasanter place to camp a few miles ahead. So we rode on.

This lower plateau was shielded from the wind's fury, and the sun was warm. At first Geoffrey was pleased at the site, but as the day wore on he appeared nervous when none of the rear had joined us. He paced restlessly up and down, then at twilight he called for knights to ride with him to discover what had delayed the rear. I wasn't anxious yet, knowing how straggling the army had become in their belief the Turks were easily defeated. But I couldn't sit still as the hours went past and still no one was seen on the road winding down from the summit.

Geoffrey returned after midnight, the king beside him. I hardly recognized Louis. In the firelight I could see his face was smeared with dirt and his pilgrim's tunic was torn. I gasped in shock, "What—what happened?"

The story came out brokenly from him and the groups who strayed in after him. The rear, thinking they'd only to reach the summit to meet with us, had loitered so the divisions were strung out haphazardly on their way up the mountain. And then, howling, "Allah! Allah!" the infidels struck against the disorganized mass, maiming and butchering. Some of our men escaped by hiding in bushes and near crags, but the blood of hundreds, perhaps thousands of crusaders flowed in the narrow rocky path. Louis's bodyguard was massacred, but he reached the safety of a tree. He wasn't pursued because his pilgrim tunic made him appear of no consequence.

I laughed hysterically, shakily relieved he was safe but in such a way only Louis would have managed. My laughter was misinterpreted as were other matters I discovered the next day after a sleepless night filled with the sounds of weeping, and men and women calling out names as they searched for absent loved ones.

I didn't hear the comments at first. I was too horrified over the loss of so many of our men in yesterday's disaster. But as I went through the camp, trying to help where I could, I heard whispers that grew louder against Geoffrey—he was the reason for our defeat, he should be hanged—and lowered voices blaming me for letting him camp on the plateau instead of the mountaintop. There was more. I'd laughed on hearing of Louis's escape, and if the rear hadn't been so loaded down with chests holding gowns for me and my ladies, they'd have reached the mount earlier and seen we'd gone on.

I wanted to scream furiously that my baggage was nothing compared to the wagons of equipment and weapons and provisions. And that if the rear had stayed in close marching lines, they wouldn't have been vulnerable to the Turkish attack. But how can one answer accusations blown in the wind so I didn't know who spoke them? I was silent, tight-lipped, as lords and officers pulled their followers together to descend to the plain below. This time they allowed no stragglers so the remains of our army marched in tight formation and could hold against the infidels who swept down against us.

But the stricter discipline couldn't replace weapons and clothes stolen by the Turks nor the wagons of food. Soon we were killing what horses we could spare and eating the roasted flesh with bread baked in the ashes of our campfires. We had one hope to keep us plodding on. We'd soon be in the Greek city of Adalia on the coast. That hope changed to anguished moans when we reached what we'd thought would be a safe place where we could reprovision our starving army.

The citizens there were little better off than we were. Afraid of Turkish attacks, they couldn't cultivate their fields and relied on ships for all they needed, so had little to share with us. And that little was priced so high we could purchase few supplies. Worse was the news that if we continued across the mountains with their waiting infidels, the journey to Antioch would take at least forty days.

Gloom settled on our camp. Our remaining horses were dying for lack of feed, a day of sunshine would be followed by a week of sleet and snow, and inevitably disease swept through the army. Then we were told that by ship we could reach Antioch in three days. That is, when enough ships arrived and if we could pay four silver marks for each passenger.

I felt I could breathe again and ignore the malicious whispers that still blamed me for our situation. But my revived hope faltered when I came upon a group of lords surrounding Louis. They stormed we must take they sea route. I wondered why they raged until I realized they must have had earlier disagreements on this. For Louis was saying in a monotone, as if he were repeating earlier pronouncements, that since we couldn't bring the whole army by sea, we'd continue on the land route.

They shouted, "Then we'd lose all our men. By sea we could save many of our forces."

Louis shook his head stubbornly. "God will lead us." He added quickly before they could interrupt, "If it's to a martyr's death, what matter? That very day we will attain everlasting glory in heaven."

One minister said furiously, "You promised to lead us to the Holy Land. We are prepared to die fighting for its freedom. We aren't prepared to die of starvation along this impossible land route. We must sail to Antioch."

The argument went on for hours until Louis finally agreed when they pointed out that every day our army was worse off here, men dying for lack of food or from the sickness sweeping through the camp.

But it was an unhappy scene when ships arrived in the harbor. Louis and his councillors and I were helped to embark on the largest of the score of ships. Briefly I was pleased to have the swaying deck under my feet, then I turned to look back at the shore and was stunned to see that the army wasn't following us as they'd been ordered. Instead of those chosen by the officers filing onto the ships, there was a mass of men struggling through the water, thrusting their companions aside savagely, not caring who drowned in their desperate battle to clamber aboard. I cried out in shock at the sight of crusader fighting crusader, wanting to weep at my helplessness to aid these men.

Louis came up to stand beside me, his face sad too as he looked at the thousands in the rear who'd given up the fight to scramble for the ships which were now overloaded. He said, "I should not have agreed to sail. But do not feel too sorrowful, my dear. I've done what I can. I've promised that as soon as we've raised money for more ships, we will send them here to sail all to Antioch."

I found little comfort in his words, doubting if Abbot Suger would be able to raise enough in taxes. And if it were possible, how many of our men would be left? A pall hung over everyone as our ships beat their way out of harbor. We felt a little more cheerful when we were at sea with the hope of reaching our destination soon.

Then a winter storm broke over us, and most of us were too dulled by seasickness to think of anything except that we'd been told we'd be in Antioch in three days. Sailing in summer might take the three days so optimistically predicted, but with the icy winds carrying us far out of our course, it was three weeks before we reached the port of Saint Simeon.

We disembarked shakily and white-faced. And ragged since the Turks had plundered our baggage. But with the earth steady under my feet and the sun shining and a warm breeze blowing on my shivering body, I was able to smile and feel again a zest for life. Only ten miles to Antioch where we would be welcomed. As the words slid through my mind, I heard a distant singing and the high sweet notes of flutes. We all turned to stare at the bank above the harbor. The music grew louder, and over the top of the rise we saw staffs with gaily colored pennants followed by horsemen and people on foot all singing, their voices mingling with flute and tabor and viol.

Leading the procession was Raymond. In spite of the years since I'd seen him, I couldn't mistake that tall lithe figure and dark smiling face. He must have heard of the ships' arrival with the king's banner on the mast, and he wasn't like Manuel who'd waited comfortably in his palace for Louis to go to him. At sight of me he leaped from his horse and strode forward. He hadn't forgotten me. In a moment I was in his arms, half laughing and half crying, not caring that the crusaders and his followers could see me. My heart beat happily. It had been so long since a man had shown pleasure in me.

I felt I'd come home as he held me strongly

while smiling over my head at Louis. And the voices around me made me feel at home for Raymond was surrounded by families from Poitou and Aquitaine who spoke my tongue, the *langue d'oc*. They shouted for us as Raymond placed me tenderly in a litter and nodded at his men to bring up extra mounts for our people. It was a merry procession to Antioch through a valley with hills on either side that were aflame with scarlet and purple anemones. Here it was spring, and gardens and orchards and fields were a misty green as we made our way to the city that was built on terraces.

It was late when we arrived, but the palace was aglow with lights. It was hard to believe in the color and warmth after our months of wandering. And to believe I was actually with Raymond again. In contrast to his vigorous figure, Louis appeared a tired monk with no spark of vitality. Even when we were given fresh clothes that were as fashionable as those we'd lost, Louis's purple robes—which he put on reluctantly, preferring his crusader's tunic—couldn't make him look like a king. In any garb Raymond would have been taken for a prince.

And after a night's rest, his entertainment was princely. Days were spent falconing or hunting gazelles, and evenings were gay with the songs of minstrels and Saracen dancers and witty conversation that bordered on the ribald. Fish from the Orontes was served with a spicy Oriental sauce, mutton and beef and veal were placed before us on gold platters, vegetables and fruit and sweetmeats heaped in silver bowls. Pages circled the tables continually, refilling our trays and goblets. I sat beside Raymond, and under pretense of helping me to meat or bread he touched my fingers and occasionally his hand dropped to my thigh for a brief caress.

But the most exciting moments were when Raymond and I exchanged glances when he escorted us from the hall. Perhaps tonight we would . . . But each time we were disappointed. Louis insisted on seeing me safely, safely! to my room before he went on to his own chamber. Did he think a few private words between Raymond and myself, perhaps a cousinly kiss, were wicked? We hoped only for the stimulation of being a man and a woman together since we were each restrained by the knowledge we were married to another.

I seldom saw his wife, Princess Constance, who he said was too young for the festivities. And who, I could see for myself on the few occasions I met the young, palely pretty wife, was at one with Louis in her disapproval of the court's festivities. But Raymond smoothed away some of Louis's frowns by continual small attentions and by his gratitude for the army we brought.

"Now Antioch will be secure. We can retake Edessa and the towns between that the Moslems captured. Jerusalem, of course, will also be safer once all the sea coast is in Christian hands. That's necessary because now Antioch is the only power between here and the Holy City. If our city fell, nothing could prevent the infidels from sweeping down on Jerusalem."

I nodded and turned to Louis, expecting him to say his army was at Raymond's command to save the Holy Land. But Louis said—I couldn't believe it but he said gravely—"My friend, I took the cross to make a pilgrimage to Jerusalem, not to go to war. I must worship Christ at the Holy Sepulchre before I can think of a campaign."

Raymond's brows came together briefly, then he shook off his irritation and said pleasantly we could discuss military affairs another time, perhaps tomorrow, and swung away to speak to other guests. I said angrily in a low voice, "Louis, have you forgotten the purpose of our crusade is to help the Christians regain captured cities? Why, even Abbot Bernard would advise you that the thousands of crusaders who followed us came to fight for Christianity, not to pray while the Moslems attack."

His lips tightened. "You need not echo your kinsman for I've made my decision. I will fulfill my vow to pray at Christ's tomb before I think of worldly matters."

"But—but Antioch's in danger, and it is the only city that protects Jerusalem."

He drew in his breath sharply. "In danger? How can it be? Look at how the people live in their mosaic-tiled homes and with gardens that are overrun with fountains. And how Christian is Raymond? He wears loose gowns like an Oriental ruler and even invites Moslems to his table so we have to dine with the enemy. Is that how a fearful man conducts himself? No."

My mouth opened in astonishment, and closed as I realized abruptly why Louis was so adamant. He was jealous that the warm friendship between Raymond and me was more than friendship. He added, "My ministers are in complete agreement with me when I spoke today of going on to Jerusalem."

That too, I thought, was out of jealousy. Raymond and his court were from Aquitaine. Why should northern barons fight to give more land into the hands of southerners? I wanted to fling that at him, but I forced myself to swallow the bitter words, aware I'd say too much if I spoke. I told myself he cared for me, even loved me in his own way. But what way was that? He was dull, dull, dull, firm when he should be flexible and too flexible when he should be resolute. As a leader of a bold crusade, he'd conducted himself like a ten-year-old. How could he expect to hold me, me as his wife? Wives, especially queens, were supposed to accept their husbands as God created them. But I was not any woman nor any queen. I would, yes, when I was calmer I'd point out to Louis we were too closely related. Our marriage wasn't lawful. Why else had we but one child and that one a girl? He was right. God was punishing us. There was no way out for us except to have an annulment. But would Louis agree?

Irritably I wiped away tears of anger. I must talk to someone. To Raymond. He'd understand.

He did when I met him in the garden half an hour later. His smile was comforting, and his arms were a haven as he murmured he'd seen this coming. A woman like me should never have been tied to a half-man. As his words flowed over me and I felt his muscular body against mine, my heart seemed to stop and then beat violently as if some vital spark in me flamed high. I'd never felt like this before—I hadn't allowed myself to with cousin Raoul—avid for something unknown. But now I could for I felt I wasn't properly married to Louis.

I looked up into Raymond's face. His dark eyes were luminous, and his hand slid down my back to my thigh. I shivered. He muttered, "You were born to follow your passionate heart. You can't go back to that man, not you."

I whispered, "No, but, Raymond, what shall I do?"

His voice was anguished. "I—don't know. You are what I've always—" He broke off, stepped back. "You are my niece. We can't—we must not—but we need each other." He glanced swiftly at the cypresses that circled the colorful flower beds in this private corner of the garden. Then he stepped back again, but this time he drew me with him toward a garden house that looked like a pagan shrine. A pulse beat in my temple. I'd been deprived of love too long.

Inside the shrine were chairs and a long bench covered with silk. He closed the door and stood gazing at me. "To see you alone, my love, after all these days of eyes watching our every move, every expression, this is heaven." I half-smiled agreement but held myself from moving to him. After years of marriage to Louis, I put a restraint on myself without thinking. Raymond touched my cheek gently, then kissed me bruisingly. Then he drew away. "You say nothing. Have I offended you?" I shook my head. "Or, or despite your beauty, does ice run in your veins instead of warm blood?"

I laughed softly, joyfully. This man desired me and wanted me to return his love openly, sensually. My arms went around him, holding him close to me so that he must have felt the wild beat of my heart. I pushed back his oriental robe and pressed my mouth against the dark curling hair on his naked chest. His delighted laughter joined mine. He swept me from my feet, and in the same movement placed me on the bench and pulled up my gown. Then he tossed aside his clothes and was on me, his eager hands searching my body intimately. A small cry escaped my lips, and he took me forcefully as my back arched to meet him.

Were we clasped together for minutes or hours? Time had no meaning as we clung happily to each other, our aroused bodies finding new pleasures until our passion was satiated. He murmured, "Beloved, you have given me—I don't know how to say you're the most wonderful thing in my life, the most—"

I put my hand over his mouth. "You've said it very well, my love. But now," I sighed, "we must think of the world outside." I edged away and smoothed down my skirt.

He nodded gloomily and reached for his clothes. A moment later he grinned, said triumphantly, "There'll be other times. Your husband insists on abandoning Antioch. A pity, but while he's away to Jerusalem, we'll keep you here. Why should you leave this comfort to ride more dusty highways, perhaps be attacked by Moslems? This is where you belong, beside me."

"Yes, yes, I do. I will stay here. If Louis objects—but why should he?"

Object was too tame a word. Louis was horrified the next morning at my flat statement I'd remain in Antioch while the crusaders went on. Never would he permit that. He added sulkily he knew why I wished to stay here. To be near Raymond. He'd seen the way we looked at each other. I almost giggled at the understatement, sobered when he said he wouldn't allow me to make such a mockery of our marriage.

I snapped, "Mockery! When you refuse to have us live as husband and wife? Yet you say you don't agree with the churchmen who question whether our marriage is legal even with the papal dispensation."

He shook his head, said miserably, "I am punishing myself for the burning of Vitry. But," more firmly, "you are my wife, and we shall not be separated."

I swung about and left, half contemptuous for his lack of aggression, half sorry he missed so much of life. And wholly grateful that in the next few days he said nothing more about my staying in Antioch. I glowed at the thought of being here with Raymond away from prying eyes that prevented us from again being alone together. My heart sang at the memory of his masterful loving and how soon we'd once more delight in secret rendezvous.

There were malicious whispers of course when people heard I was not going to Jerusalem, but in my happiness I scarcely heard them. A happiness that flamed high two nights later when one of my ladies said the crusaders were marching in the morning. I tried to sleep but could only toss in my silk-hung bed waiting for the night to pass. Faint noises drifted in from the streets, unusual at that hour but too far away for me to wonder what the sounds meant. Then a racket was closer.

Scuffling feet were in the anteroom. I sat up frowning. The door was flung wide and unbelievingly I saw half-a-dozen soldiers at the opening. For a moment I couldn't speak, then I screamed at them to leave. At once. But they advanced toward me as if they hadn't heard my command. I gaped at the incredible scene of men-at-arms in my bedroom.

Before I could order them out again a veil was thrown over my head, and a hand clamped over my mouth. I struggled savagely, my breath coming in sobs. One of them shouted to my women who were hurrying in that they should dress me and then pack my clothes and follow. Orders from King Louis and his minister, Thierry Galeran. I would be with the army which even now was marching out through the gates.

I tried to cry out these soldiers were mad but could only gasp through the clenched hand. And not even that when another veil was tied tightly about my face, and I was carried down the stairway into the street and placed in a litter.

Hours later as the sun was just rising I was brought to Louis who was riding in the van. The men saluted triumphantly as if they'd accomplished a great deed by overpowering one woman. I faced Louis raging, almost incoherent in my fury. He tried to soothe me, it was for my own good, to protect my reputation, to have me share in the glories of Jerusalem with a loving husband. But there was a complacent smile on his narrow mouth that, with the night he'd just put me through, killed forever any chance of a reconciliation.

Chapter Five

My anger hardened, and a desolate sense of loss overwhelmed me as we made our way across the stony roads of Palestine and on through olive groves and fields ready for the harvesters. There wasn't even a skirmish to distract me from my despondency. The route was peaceful because the fortress at Antioch protected it from the Moslems. How could Louis leave that city—and Raymond— open to invaders while he marched piously eastward? My vassals were also furious at his ignoring the needs of war, but no persuasion swayed my husband.

Not in military matters. Was there hope he could be persuaded to a divorce? He must know he couldn't hold me forever against my will unless he shut me into a prison. That he wouldn't do, partly, I admitted, because he wasn't cruel by nature, but equally because if I were a prisoner and still his wife, he couldn't remarry in the hope of begetting an heir.

Today I'd been allowed to change from a litter to a horse, and I leaned forward in the saddle as the white-walled city of Jerusalem loomed before us, shining church domes just visible above the stonework. As we drew nearer, a gate was flung open, and it appeared the whole city poured through to greet us, singing and fanning the air with olive branches. I forced myself to forget my private pain as I smiled and waved at the procession.

At the head of the throng was a dark plump woman who must be Melisende, queen regent of Jerusalem, and the quiet boy beside her King Baldwin. Melisende threw out her arms in an extravagant gesture of welcome, she was enchanted to see us, and immediately embarked on the entertainments she'd planned for us. I was pleased at the prospect of any escape from my weary thoughts which whirled dully through my mind, going nowhere for the answers to my questions were in Louis's hands. As were the queen's eager suggestions of falconing, hunting, banquets.

Louis was shocked. "Entertainment in this holy place, Your Highness? Our great joy will be to walk in the steps of Our Lord and pray at His Sepulchre. We will have no leisure for idle pastimes."

I wasn't sure if I wanted to laugh or scream at his narrow attitude—as if all gaiety were sinful. After all, Christ hadn't looked down on pleasure. But I said nothing, only exchanged a speaking glance with Melisende, who bowed her head resignedly and motioned a captain with a large escort to guide us. We rode through streets decorated with olive branches and great banners stirring in the light wind, past streets on either side which were stairs rather than lanes circling up and down. Booths in colorful bazaars jutted out so that we had to straggle around them. As we were delayed, the captain pointed out the platform where slaves were sold, and beyond them camel caravans winding in with spices from India and musk from Tibet, the drivers shouting and waving whips at the disdainful camels.

We moved slowly through the crooked streets, the procession around us as much of an obstacle as the shops with gold and silver ornaments and dazzling lengths of silk. We finally reached the Via Dolorosa leading to the Church of the Holy Sepulchre. Stone had been cut away at the foundation, and from this rocky base the basilica rose, solid and magnificent, its domes shining against the clear sky.

I walked reverently through the atrium and nave and the Chapel of the Angel to the tomb beyond that was encased in marble. All of us who could crowd in after Louis fell on our knees as he led us in prayer. The quiet and peace of the small chamber touched me, and my heart felt light for the first time since I'd been forced to leave Antioch. I shared some of Louis's triumph too when a knight handed him the oriflamme he'd carried from France, and the scarlet banner was laid on the altar.

Still, I was exhausted from the hours of pilgrimage and pleased when we were finally shown to our lodgings in the Tower of David that rose above the city walls. Little else pleased me when Louis and I were left alone in the chamber that separated our bedrooms. His gratitude for being actually at Christ's tomb soon changed to a wary watchfulness as if he expected me to fly out of the tower and back to Antioch.

And wherever I went in the following days, I was aware of being discreetly followed. Louis had to make it discreet as my vassals were already angered at how he'd treated me in Antioch. No southern lord would have abducted his wife from her bed because she had eyes for another man. An Aquitanian would shrug and, in the arms of another woman, wait for her return.

Less personal matters were also upsetting. The Latin Kingdom wasn't as welcoming as it had appeared on our arrival. Knights and their sons from the crusade fifty years ago had forgotten about being soldiers of Christ and greedily strove after gold and land. Now they feared they might have to divide some of their wealth with us. Though they didn't object to using Louis's forces to acquire more territory.

They invited him to an assembly and, unbelievably, instead of striking north against the waiting Moslems, they decided to attack Damascus. That seemed only curious to me at first since we had to show Christendom some victory we'd accomplished. But then I heard Damascus was the one Moslem city which wished to live at peace with the

Christians. I told Louis, Galeran, his ministers, hoping one would listen. No one did.

So our army attacked, besieging the city for four days. And were sent flying ingloriously. Insults were flying too. Our army said the soldiers of the Latin Kingdom were cowardly, and they accused us of having lived too softly and knowing nothing of how to fight the Moslems. I wearied of their constant bickering, but that was nothing compared to the sickness in my heart that what should have been our splendid crusade was finished. Our forces, disillusioned by Louis's lack of leadership and the scanty supplies of food, retreated to the coast to find passage home.

I packed too, expecting to ride to the coast today or tomorrow. Not only was our army a shadow of itself but Louis's mentor, Abbot Suger, wrote letter after letter, begging him to come back to his country which needed him. But Louis, God knows why, refused to move. One month slipped into the next. I saw every sight, every holy landmark, so often I lost count. The only break in the boredom, and it was hardly cheerful, were our arguments over a divorce. Louis promised me anything, anything I wished. Except an annulment, though we still slept apart. Or to pull himself away from his shrines to go home and face the problems of his country.

I said finally as we walked down the Via Dolorosa, "Louis, we've stayed for Lent and the Easter celebration, we can't delay longer." I pushed back my veil that the April breeze blew across my face. My heart lifted at the thought that we'd return to Antioch. And to Raymond.

He hesitated, then agreed reluctantly. "I'll send word ahead to have ships waiting for us—at Acre."

"You mean we—we won't sail from Antioch?"

"No." He turned quickly to one of his escort before I could protest. And he hardly exchanged a word with me as we made for the coast almost two years after we'd set out for the Holy Land, and with less than three hundred followers, all that remained of our forces in the east.

In my sadness at having to leave without seeing Raymond again, I was relieved Louis had me escorted to one vessel with my ladies and baggage, and he sailed on a sister ship. I didn't want him to guess how often my thoughts were on Raymond and the fear we'd met for the last time.

Spring winds buffeted us and sent us off course, and it was July before our ships were washed up on the Sicilian coast. In spite of my sorrow over Raymond, I had too much love of life not to share Louis's joy that we were both safe. Until we had news of my uncle. Raymond had attacked to the north, which the crusaders, or rather Louis, had refused to do, and was slain in battle.

I kept whispering, "No, no, not Raymond, he can't be dead." But I knew the story was true, and that my fears were right, I'd never again see his laughing face or feel the warmth of his body against mine. I wept for days and stayed away from Louis, who'd thrown away not only Raymond's life but hope for the Latin Kingdom. How long before the victors would move from Antioch to Jerusalem?

In my bitterness when finally I spoke to my

husband I said we should go home by way of Rome. Pope Eugenius had been driven from that city, but he was nearby in Tusculum. Louis's eyes shone. "An excellent thought, my dear. I'm eager to tell the pope how we prayed at the Holy Sepulchre." He didn't guess that my purpose was to have the pope declare our marriage unlawful, a decision Louis wouldn't dare argue with him.

I wasn't well after those months at sea, but it would take more than illness to prevent me from making this journey, though we had to stop occasionally for me to rest. But my hope in meeting Eugenius spurred me on. He wouldn't take Louis's side after the shameful way my husband had bungled the crusade.

The aging pope greeted us warmly and listened with pleasant attention to Louis, too pleasant for he said nothing about the failure of our expedition, only asking Louis to repeat his descriptions of the holy places. When they were finished, I moved closer to his throne-like chair. I couldn't tell him my real reasons for asking for an annulment. How could I explain my unwifely feelings of contempt toward Louis, or that it had become unendurable to be married to a half-man whose petty jealousy had driven Raymond to his death? I said, "Your Holiness, I wish I needn't say this, but during our pilgrimage I realized that those people were right when they claimed Louis and I have lived in sin because we are too closely related to be man and wife. God Himself has showed his disapproval for after years of marriage, He sent us only one child, a daughter instead of an heir to the throne."

He heard me out compassionately. But then Louis said tearfully he loved me dearly and would not give me up. The pope smiled at that. "Why, if your fear, dear daughter, is that you and Louis sinned in living together, I'll put that right. I'll write out a dispensation though it isn't necessary since you were dispensed when you wed. And now no one can ever again whisper a word about your union being unlawful."

Automatically I answered his smile, too shocked to feel anything at that moment. And in the evening before I'd recovered from the shock, the Pope —with every sign of happily fulfilling his duties— led us into a bedroom which was decorated, he said, with valuable hangings from his own chamber. I half drew back at sight of the enormous bed with its embroidered cover. He thought I was charmingly modest. After years of marriage? I tried to speak, found there was nothing to say.

Louis, with the papal blessing on our mating, took me in his arms ardently. He whispered, "My love, how I've hungered for you. You cannot guess how long my lonely nights have been, how I lay sleepless until dawn yearning for you."

I was still too stunned by the defeat of my hopes to answer him scornfully. He must have taken my passivity as the proper attitude for a dutiful wife. He stroked my body with a new confidence, even dared look at my nakedness and murmured passionate declarations against my breast.

It was too late. Beyond him I could see Raymond's dead face, the thousands of crusaders lost, the first years of my youth wasted in his dreary palace. I wanted to move away, to run from him. Where could I go? I stayed, submissive as any meek wife, while he entered me and then fell back sleepily content. I wasn't drowsy. What if—? I might find a way around the pope's dispensation, but what if this night had made me pregnant? If that were true I could see nothing ahead but gray inactive years with a husband I could neither love nor respect.

The fear haunted me as we rode to Paris. And there on a cold autumn day within the damp walls of the Cité Palace, my foreboding proved horrifyingly right. I was with child. Louis, the whole court were delighted. An heir at last. The news was the only thing that made Louis smile as he was buried under the problems Abbot Suger and his ministers laid before him. I thought cynically he smiled partly because he had an excuse to stay away from my bed. Except for that one night when he'd made what he probably thought was wild love, he hadn't changed but was a monk again.

Still, I admitted he had other reasons for his satisfaction. Paris, the whole country, hadn't cheered him when he'd returned home. He'd neglected his kingdom for two years and what had he to show for his great crusade? Too many women had lost loved ones, fields had gone untilled, shops were closed. But if he'd returned with an heir—everyone assured me we'd have a son—there was hope, and the citizens forgave his mismanagement in the east and he was their king again.

There was little else to please them that bitterly icy winter. And nothing, nothing to please me as I gazed out at the frozen Seine. When one could see the river through the snow or mist. But it was a better sight than Abbot Suger and Galeran hovering over Louis. I'd thought to escape all this, to be in my beloved Aquitaine, not here huddled near the fire as I shivered with the cold while day by day my body thickened.

Spring came at last, and as it drew to a close I was brought to bed. Bonfires were made ready to be lighted, bells to be rung. But when word went out of my chamber, no flames leaped toward the sky and there was no glad pealing of bells. Another girl, Princess Alix. Louis clumsily tried to comfort me. Next time I'd give him a son. That was kindly of him, and I thanked him. But everyone else let me know that I had failed again.

Dejectedly I thought so too. A son would have given me some standing in the court. A girl child only tied me to this dreary city and made me more ineffective than before. Abruptly my chin went up. I was Eleanor of Aquitaine, and I would not accept this dull existence. So. I must throw off this apathetic sense of failure and act. I bit my lip thoughtfully as I sat embroidering a band of fleurs-de-lis for the loose sleeves of my bliaud. A moment later the silk strip fell into my lap. I glanced around at my ladies, lowered my eyes quickly so they wouldn't see they were shining.

I said hesitantly, "I—I wonder—two daughters. The king—and the court—their disappointment—" I broke off while my ladies leaned forward though they tried to mask their eagerness for what I might say about having a second princess instead of a prince. "I wonder if—if I can have only girls, would it be better—better if the king took another wife? A sorrow for me, but if an annulment of our marriage would be for the good of France—"

They murmured, "No, Your Highness, no, never." They looked shocked but pleased too at such a startling suggestion as neither Louis nor I had mentioned divorce to anyone.

I went on, "We all know some churchmen have said Louis and I are too closely related. We thought the pope's dispensation—but maybe that isn't enough when God refuses to give us an heir." I sighed, dismissed my ladies, saying I wished to be alone. I bit my lip again to hide my smile at their hasty leaving. As I'd expected they couldn't wait to repeat what I'd said to their families, probably adding this was confidential and mustn't be mentioned to anyone. Which meant it would be all over the city and seep into the countryside within days.

The fact that even the queen questioned her marriage brought into focus the people's discontent with me as a mother. My spirits rose. Until Abbot Suger said, "No, madame. Louis and you are still young. You might yet have a son." He didn't add, though I knew he was thinking, that through a divorce not only would France lose Aquitaine, but that if I remarried my husband would be lord of Aquitaine and possibly an enemy.

I was briefly despondent, then decided hopefully the abbot couldn't stand out forever against the people's and the lords' disapproval of me. I thought over the words, if I remarried. I smiled gravely at Louis, who was entering the hall for our midday meal. There was no if. I remembered

Armand, who'd tried to abduct me that summer when Louis came to Bordeaux for our wedding. Other men would attempt that, and one might succeed. I could not rule alone. But this time I'd choose my own husband. He'd be strong and vital and demanding. He'd be like my father who didn't care who knew how he enjoyed women. Like my uncle Raymond. At the memory of their masculine vigor, I felt soft and yielding. If—when I married again, it'd be a real marriage. With a man I could respect as well as love.

My fancies were interrupted by Louis's muttering, "Normandy! I have to lead an army against that province. It's under the Plantagenets, you know, and Duke Geoffrey swore fealty to me. But now his son Henry is named duke by his father so there'd be no question who'd succeed him, but Henry refuses to give me his oath of loyalty though I'm his overlord."

The names meant nothing to me though naturally I knew Normandy was too strong a neighbor to both France and Aquitaine, so the newly proclaimed duke should submit as a vassal to Louis. But I also knew Louis was no leader. I said, "Must you go to war, endanger your life and the lives of your subjects? Why not negotiate?"

He shook his head stubbornly. Normandy must understand what was rightfully owed him. But the war was conducted so much like Louis's usual ventures that Parisians were sardonically amused. Within a week after he'd left with his army, he was back at the palace with a fever and took to his bed. Then not only I but his advisers too could suggest that a crusading king shouldn't shed the blood of

Christians. He agreed finally to discuss terms though he thought young Henry insolent in his neglect of his overlord. The mention of Henry reminded Louis he himself had no son. Would his fretting for an heir give me reason to hope our marriage would be dissolved?

Hope! The word was too tame. Henry came to a sweltering Paris with his father, and within days I was too excited to think of such an everyday emotion as hope. One didn't hope. One performed what must be done. Geoffrey the Fair was handsome, swaggering, not to be intimidated, a man I admired. But it was his son I couldn't look away from. Not handsome like his father, but there was something about Henry that put him aside from other men.

He was broad and stocky and muscular and seemed to have the energy of ten men. His face was only a little less red than his hair when he was angry at some demand of Louis's, probably the surrender of Vexin and Gisors, a city on the border, and his light gray eyes darkened until they were nearly black. Not really attractive, but his vehemence drew me, it was so different from Louis's indecisive mannerisms.

Henry was certainly decisive enough about refusing to return any territory in exchange for being recognized Normandy's duke. I thought the price wasn't too high to put a stop to the endless bickering. Because until this haggling was over, Henry and I had no chance to meet except in public. I wondered again why I should even glance at him. He looked more like a servant than a prince. He wore his clothes of silk and velvet as if he'd been brought up in a peasant's hut, and his hands were rough as if he'd plowed that peasant's land and carted in the hay. Nor did he have any of the gallantry of Raymond. But, he had a masculinity and vigor that were magnetic and helped me forget my uncle. And when Henry's head turned toward me, his eyes sparkled as he gazed at my face and slim body in its tight-fitting bliaud with its wide flowing sleeves over the narrow sleeves of my undertunic.

He wanted me. I was amazed Louis wasn't aware of Henry's ardor. But then what did Louis know of passion? Or perhaps, if Louis thought of it at all, he believed Henry too young for me. Henry was over ten years younger than I, but years had never meant much to me, and I knew I appeared far more youthful than my age while Henry looked much older than his eighteen years. He'd lived hard, helping to fight the battles of his mother, Empress Matilda, to wrest the English throne from King Stephen. And now it was almost certain Stephen would keep the crown for life but pass it on, not to Matilda, but to her son Henry.

Though a crown was of little moment to me. Hadn't I been trying for years to put aside the crown of France? I'd be quite content with being duchess of Aquitaine and of Normandy. I was beside Louis at the next angry conference where neither he nor Henry was willing to concede an inch. Henry finally stalked out of the room. My eyes followed his stocky, energetic figure. This futile arguing must not go on or there'd be war, more deadly than the last fiasco which had brought Henry to Paris.

Well. I could put a stop to it. There's little privacy in a palace so I waited until all but the guards outside would be asleep, then sent a waiting woman to the tower rooms where the Plantagenets lodged. If a sentry woke enough to question her drowsily, no harm done. She'd say I sent her for a physician. And if it were a Plantagenet man, Henry would silence him with a wink and leer that would say plainly he was on a nocturnal adventure with some unknown woman.

He strode into my room so soon I wondered if he'd been waiting for my message. His boots clanked on the floor, and I tried to hush him laughingly. He laughed too, pulled off his boots and threw them across the chamber, but he didn't lower his loud voice as he greeted me brusquely. He knew nothing of discretion. "Time for us to meet, eh? Began to wonder if you were like a slut, your eyes inviting me, then getting all coy and ladylike and backing off. Should have known better. Come here!"

I didn't move. He knew nothing either of the pretty knightly phrases one expected from a lover. Still, I had to smile at his very ineptness. At my amused expression he was beside me, his lips hard on mine. With one arm he crushed me to his powerful body while his free hand slid inside my robe and caressed my breasts and thighs.

He grunted, "Ah! This is better. Knew you'd be all soft curves under those stiff gowns you wear. Now let me see." He jerked off my silver robe and lifted me onto the bed. I trembled, feeling delight in his aggressiveness.

He was shaken too, muttering something about

"too delicate" and "not like the usual jade I've mounted", then tried to gulp back his words. I smothered a smile. Could he think I believed him an inexperienced lover? If I had, I'd never have sent for him. Then all thought was submerged in an uprush of pleasure as we came together, clinging to each other, his mouth on mine, the tongue darting out to savor sweetness between us. Did he take me forcibly or did I give myself to him? I was too dazed with happiness to know or care.

We lay back sleepily yet vibrantly aware of each other. Then we talked desultorily about affairs that should be important but now seemed merely shadows. Would Louis give me a divorce? Would Henry inherit England? To me that last question mattered little, but he was determined he must and would. He came out of his drowsiness to say gaily that with England and with my lands, he'd have an empire. Anjou and Maine as well as Normandy from his father when joined with England and Aquitaine would give him a sweep of country from Scotland to Navarre.

He'd been gazing at the ceiling. Now he turned to look at me, his voice trailed off. He forgot royal ambitions and crushed me to him again. With our first desire quenched, we were less intense, and our love play was lighthearted and brightly pleasant. Laughingly he kissed my breasts while his large hands searched my body until I dug my fingers into his shoulders to let him know I was ready for him to take me again.

We had no chance to repeat that dazzling night, but when our eyes met we both glowed with a pleasure that was hard to conceal. Everyone at court grumbled at the stiflingly hot summer, but I only noticed when I saw bushes and flowers wilting under the blazing sun, and the stench from the streets reached into the palace. But our stolen hour had the result I'd hoped. With Aquitaine in sight, what was Vexin and Gisors to Henry and his father? They gave up fortress and town with a show of loyal obedience, and Henry was confirmed duke of Normandy.

My triumph at the peaceful settlement was brief. With no reason to remain in Paris now, the Plantagenets left for their own provinces to put down sporadic outbreaks among their own vassals. Without them the court was empty and dull, and who knew when we'd meet again? I must hasten that day. I went to Louis in the council chamber when his ministers had left for the day. My heart was thudding, but I forced myself to speak quietly as he drew out a chair for me.

"You are the king, my dear Louis, so perhaps you don't hear what is being whispered in the streets." I went on as he shrugged tiredly. "The people are saying we aren't lawfully married. They want an heir which I haven't been able to give you. So they believe you must wed again." I stopped breathlessly.

His thin mouth set. "I have had enough of the foolish argument of our being within forbidden limits of kinship. What if we are? We were dispensed twice. Our marriage is valid in the eyes of God." He rose abruptly and left before I could open my mouth.

Week after week when we were dining or walking in the garden with its vines and budding flowers, I repeated the city gossip, that he must marry another if France was to have a dauphin. He pretended deafness or changed the subject to desultory talk on how chilly it was for this time of year or how beautiful my bliaud was—though he'd seen it dozens of times—with its exquisitely embroidered bands.

At last I went boldly to a meeting with his ministers. They looked up frowning at the interruption by a wife who couldn't give their king a son. I wanted to lash out at them for their contempt of me, Eleanor, but I said deferentially, "My lords, I am saddened to hear that many citizens believe I'm not the king's true wife, that they demand an annulment of our marriage so that France will be given an heir. This is a sorrow to me, but I must not stand in the way of your country's future. What would you have us do?"

They looked at each other. They'd no need for discussion, having heard the same news and repeated it among themselves. One after another they said grimly that they'd advise the king to seek an annulment. Louis's shoulders hunched forward as he said desperately, "My lords, I will consider what you say, but the matter is too important to be settled in a day." He turned toward me, and from the way he gazed at me he must have been thinking more of how, monk or not, he loved me.

If I hadn't met Henry, I might have felt some sympathy for him. I couldn't now when he stood so obstinately between me and happiness. He'd snatched me from any happiness with Raymond. I would not again be cheated of a man who was a great lover and soldier by a husband who was an awkward boy in the marriage bed, an indecisive leader in the field. I glanced from him to the ministers and said sedately I would abide by whatever decision they made.

They smiled, obviously pleased at my respectful manner. "Madame, as His Highness pointed out, this will take time, but we will call an assembly to weigh whether or not this royal marriage should be annulled." From their determined faces, I was sure they'd invite only those lords and churchmen who agreed Louis must find a new wife.

In spite of their willingness, I had to wait impatiently for months before the assembly convened. But when they met, the lords saw to it that the business was concluded quickly. Louis and I were pronounced too closely related to be married in law. However, my daughters Marie and Alix were proclaimed legitimate. But now I had to pay for my freedom because unhappily they were to be brought up by Louis. They were my only regret. I hadn't been allowed to see them often, their nurses and governesses too eager to hover over us, but at least I'd known they weren't far away. My sorrow at their loss was a gray thread weaving through my excitement at the new life waiting for me.

We had a tearful good-bye. Then they were taken from me, and the next day I started for home, for the city of Poitiers. The road south was a shining mass of greenery, towns were bustling with citizens who cheered me as I rode through, and farmers left their work in the fields and ran toward me waving loyally. My spirits rose and soon I could put the past behind me and joined my escort who laughed and sang as we went along the dusty lanes.

Until one afternoon when we stopped at an abbey to stay for the night. We'd scarcely finished our evening meal of bread and fish and honey when one of the younger monks hurried into the abbot's dining chamber to say he'd been told that the count of Blois planned to abduct me the next morning. I stared at him horrified, then said, "Will you see that my escort meets me at once in the yard? And have the horses saddled. We must be on the march within the hour."

We rode through the dark, the half-moon scarcely outlining our way as we swung west from Bois. After that I sent scouts ahead and learned another lord had set up an ambush for me. Again we had to make our way through the night with only the stars to guide us. I thought wearily I'd known that as a woman without a husband, I'd be prey to any ambitious lordling. But I hadn't expected it would be so soon. We rested in abbey or castle through the day and continued our secret progress at night until at last, with an enormous relief, I saw the walls of Poitiers rising ahead of me.

I was safe, but there was little leisure when I reached the palace. I needed a larger household. One pleasant addition was Alicia, a young woman sent to me by the nuns at Fontevrault. She was a round-faced girl, eager to please and anxious to see the world. I liked her immediately, and she was delighted to be appointed one of my waiting women. But I also needed clerks to write my vassals of my divorce and ask them to swear fealty to me and to draw up special grants to be given abbeys and a study of new laws that had been passed in my absence. That last reminded me of my cousin Raoul. I smiled spontaneously at the thought of him, but I was glad he was in Bordeaux. Since I'd met Henry, I knew I could resist Raoul's charms, but as I was no longer married Raoul might be more demanding, thinking of me as free now and more willing to indulge in the pleasures of love.

My most important task, and this I'd trust to no scribe, was to write Henry that I was in Poitiers and ask his plans. There was need for secrecy. As duchess of Aquitaine, vassal tradition demanded I have Louis's approval for my marriage, and how could I ask for it? He wouldn't want me to wed anyone. He'd be incensed at my request and doubly so if he discovered the bridegroom was his potential enemy. So I entrusted my letter to a captain I had confidence in, and soon he brought the answer, that the day Henry settled an affray between two of his knights, he'd be on his way to me.

I was delighted at the decisiveness, but that meant there was more work to be done in haste. Henry and I were as closely related as Louis and I, and I had to ask our archbishop to write out the dispensation we needed to marry. Fortunately he didn't need any persuasion as he'd a poor opinion of the French king after his mismanagement of the crusade so I was ready when Henry, with only a few companions, rode exuberantly into the palace yard.

I ran out to meet him, the blue skirt of my bliaud swirling above my ankles. He flung himself from his horse, swept me into his powerful arms and crushed his mouth against mine. Then I stepped back to gaze at his tousled red hair, his square face and strong body. His brown curt-mantle was pushed back, showing his usual sloppily worn tunic, but I liked that too, it was so much a part of him. The thought hardly came to mind when I was in his clasp again, my head resting on his broad chest. Around us servants and vassals laughed and cheered, and I turned to smile happily at them.

We were married the next day. Quietly, with only a few friends and house staff as witnesses. But our chamber wasn't quiet when we retired for the night. Henry's great laugh and booming voice echoed from the walls as he swept me into his arms. My fears that Louis would somehow have our wedding proclaimed illegal were washed away. What could make me anxious with this strong protector at my side?

My body tightened against him. I could feel his heavily beating heart as he must have felt mine. His breath came in gasps as he picked me up swaggeringly. Then he was calmer and laid me on the bed gently as if I were fragile. His calm mood lasted only until he'd jerked off his clothes. He was on me at once, urgent and demanding as if he hadn't had a woman for months, and I was laughingly happy.

I soon found these changes of mood were an integral part of Henry. On a sunny afternoon he was reading his handbook on Roman war—he knew a little of many languages but was fluent only in French and Latin—and exchanging an occasional remark with me, his voice light and casual. Then a messenger arrived with a letter from Louis. He read it at a glance and burst into a rage which I'd never seen though I'd heard about his family's "black bile". I watched with astonishment as he rolled on the ground, saliva trickling from his mouth as he gnawed at the parchment, his feet drumming the earth.

He spat out the document and I picked it up. The writing was smudged, but I could make out enough to understand why he stormed. He was angry enough for both of us so I wasn't irritated when I read we were summoned to Paris to answer Louis's charge of treason. We were his vassals, but we'd married without asking his permission which he'd never have given since we were too closely related. I shrugged. It would take more than Louis's written command for us to put ourselves in his power. I waited until Henry was over his fit of fury, then said we should ignore the letter, and he agreed hoarsely.

I thought that the end of the matter, but within days we had word Louis was gathering his barons and marching toward Normandy. I expected another tantrum. Instead Henry laughed, said he'd teach Louis a lesson and was pounding out of the courtyard with his men before I recovered from my surprise at his good humor. I sent scribes with him to write me every day, but when I asked my vassals to go with him they said almost with one voice, "Impossible, my lady. We must be prepared here. King Louis may change his mind and strike against our province. We cannot leave our borders defenseless."

I had to accept that though I knew their real reason for holding back. They were fiercely independent. They hadn't worried about Louis's encroaching on them, but Henry was a different matter. They eyed him warily and let me know I was their duchess, but they owed Henry no loyalty except as my husband and wouldn't take orders from him.

I was concerned about their attitude. What if Henry needed more soldiers? I needn't have been upset. My scribes wrote Henry moved so fast that horses fell dead as he prodded his men onward. And wrote later that he'd bypassed Louis's army and invaded French territory, striking against the lords one by one and sending them home in defeat. And Louis again came down with a fever and returned to Paris. I almost felt sorry for him, but after weeks of not knowing if Henry would be successful and our marriage safe, it was difficult to spare a moment for Louis.

Now I discovered I had another anxiety. Like Louis, Henry longed for an heir. When he'd left, I convinced myself I was pregnant, but soon I admitted the depressing fact that I hadn't conceived. Would I be a barren wife? If I were, could I hope to hold Henry? I was afraid he'd leave Normandy for England to stake his claim, and how then could he breed sons?

But as I mulled over the discouraging thought, Henry clattered into the courtyard, outriding any messengers my scribes may have sent. I hurried down to be at his side as he dismounted. "My love, my love," but I could say no more at my joy when he told me he could stay for months. His Normans were raising money and hiring ships to take him to England so he could come to me while they made preparations.

Briefly he was delighted to be in Poitiers, to spend loving nights together. I was content with having him near me and with my household officials and troubadours and gay banquets, but by the fifth day I could see his growing restlessness. He'd spring up from a chair to pace the room, mutter at how long it was taking to gather a fleet, snap his fingers until the small sound made everyone nearby on edge.

I adjusted a thong of my silk and leather sandals, glanced up. "Since we have the time, I'd like you to see my provinces. Would a tour through them please you?"

He looked so delighted at the prospect of activity there was no need for him to answer. We rode along lanes between fields from town to abbey, stopping when we wished to hunt or hawk. And in the evenings there was singing and laughter under candlelight in the great halls or in our pavilions when we made camp in the open air. Our days weren't made up of only pastimes. Henry insisted on our visiting every harbor town and bargained over hiring extra ships to meet him at

Barfleur where other vessels were gathering.

Too soon he had word his fleet was ready to sail, but I wasn't overly downcast when I waved good-bye to him. I was pregnant. Now the time sped by. Days I spent with my councillors, working on administrative details, and nights I had friends and music about me. Every week I had news of Henry. Always in a hurry he'd embarked for England in the winter Channel, marched inland to face King Stephen's army and won a bloodless victory because a storm raged high. Henry strategically had his back to the icy gusts while the full force of the gale struck Stephen's men. Stephen agreed to negotiate. They rode to London together to complete a treaty, and Henry was again confirmed as Stephen's heir.

Good news, but I too had great news. I was brought to childbed, and this time the midwife held up the baby for me to see I'd borne a son. I had him baptized William, the name of so many dukes of Aquitaine. Henry hurried to me. He was disgruntled that though he was named heir, he was given no voice in the English councils. But he was overjoyed with our son. And two months later I could tell him gaily I was pregnant again so I wasn't the barren wife I'd so feared to be.

Henry wasn't disgruntled long. Four months later a courier arrived from London. Stephen was dead, and Henry was to take possession of the kingdom immediately. There was no need for the English lords to beg the impetuous Henry to come at once. He hastily assembled a retinue of soldiers, lords and clergy so we'd be royally escorted when his new subjects greeted him.

But when we reached Barfleur, crossing was impossible. Winds and sleet slashed the Channel day after day. Henry, wet through, strode around the town, raging at the weather and asking old seamen when the storms would abate. To his fury they only shrugged and said who could predict what November would bring.

I was depressed at leaving Aquitaine for the chilly northern country, yet I was almost as impatient as he because of the child in my womb. If we were delayed much longer, I might miscarry on a rough crossing, and what other kind of crossing would there be with winter again coming on? Finally in early December the wind was less menacing. Fog crept in so one couldn't see beyond the harbor mouth, but Henry swore he'd wait no longer. The choppy waves made me miserable, but after a day and night we landed on the English coast.

Scarcely stopping for food, we rode north toward London. The weather was still wretched and the child heavy within me, but I was heartened by all the people who came out of their homes to line up on the icy lanes to cheer us. Many of the villagers and barons joined our procession, gossiping cheerfully that now after the civil wars in Stephen's long reign there'd be peace. I was pleased at their instant acceptance of Henry and me, but I wished the rugged climate matched their warmth of heart.

Henry decided to ride through the snowy streets of London to show himself to his new subjects.

The city was even more crowded than Paris, or perhaps it only seemed so because throngs of citizens were in the streets and banners and pennants adorned their homes. In Chepeside drapers had silk mantles from the East on display, and goldsmiths' wares glittered on their open counters. We rode up to the great Tower, then turned back to lodge at Westminster Palace. I was exhausted and dreamed of hot fires and bed.

I stared in disbelief when we walked into the palace. The great hall was a shambles, trestles and benches broken, tapestries on the wall torn. Our rooms were little better. Stephen's men must have ransacked the whole place. Henry grimaced. "Well, better than camping in the wet fields."

I eyed him coldy. "If we were at war, we'd sleep where we must. But you are bringing peace to this country and see the welcome we get. Your servants must clear this up before I—" He started to speak, but after the Channel and the ride through the country, my aching bones and the kicking of the unborn baby, my last bit of patience deserted me. I said with shrill firmness, "I will not lodge in a place scarcely fit for animals."

His red face turned purple, and I wondered with icy indifference if he'd have one of his tantrums. Instead he shouted at the household, demanding someone find us comfortable lodgings. A knight stepped forward to say there was a Saxon palace and a new abbey in Bermondsey, a village across the river from the Tower. We were there within the hour, and I saw with fervent gratitude that fires were blazing, fish and veal and bread and wine ready and great beds with soft wool blankets.

I rested for a week while Henry dashed about the city, consulting with ministers about the government and with guildsmen and the chief men of London commanding them to prepare a splendid coronation. And it was splendid. Westminster Abbey was in little better condition than Westminster Palace, but its dreariness was forgotten when our procession moved in, pages, knights, lords, bishops, abbots all gleaming with gold and jewels and silk and velvet in the bright light of myriad candles.

I felt solemn as the choir of monks sang and bells pealed while Henry and I walked to the altar to be anointed and crowned by the Archbishop of Canterbury. Then we rode along the Strand to the cheers of our subjects whose faces grinned with goodwill. I hardly noticed how I shivered though there was reason with the Thames so frozen that children were skating on it with pieces of bone tied to their shoes. Henry ignored the cold too as—between saluting the citizens—he went on and on about how the government was at a standstill, the administration must be started again to bring order to the country, new officials must be appointed.

When we finally returned to the Saxon palace, he sank in front of the fire, booted feet near the flames, and continued to go on about all the problems. "I'll begin in the morning, call back Stephen's clerks and stewards who all seem to have scattered. And then—hmm, think my first appointment will be Thomas à Becket. The Archbishop of Canterbury recommended him as chancellor. Now as to the judiciary—"

I stopped listening. Why not let business wait till tomorrow? We should be celebrating with music and troubadours with their slightly ribald songs and gay conversation now that Henry's ambition to be King of England was at last achieved. But even if we had troubadours with us, I knew it would be useless to suggest any merriment when he could think of nothing but the state of affairs in the country.

I swallowed my yawns and said I must go to bed for the sake of our coming child. He was growling something about who should be chief justiciar, and I doubt he was aware when I stood up and left the chamber. I felt sleepily happy. I missed our Aquitanian evenings, but the loss was offset by thought of the baby. Little William was being well cared for so I could take time to recover from the stresses of the last months. Later I'd be interested in officials and government, but for the moment I was content to think only of the child.

The winter was still with us when I was brought to bed, but what did I care that drafts ruffled the tapestries on the walls and searched out my body when the covers had to be pulled back? The midwife was relieved at how easily I gave birth and laid the infant against my breast. I had another son. I'd name him Henry for his father.

I wondered briefly how Louis would take the news when I'd brought him only two girls, forgot him when Henry strode in, eyes sparkling. "Another boy, my love! We'll have a dynasty of

Plantagenets." He laughed his booming laugh, and I echoed it. Now no one forever could call me a poor breeder, little better than a barren woman. The Duchess of Aquitaine and Queen of England was also the mother of two sons.

Chapter Six

A week later I was playing with little William near the open hearth in Bermondsey's small hall— I saw my children when I wished, not like in Paris where the governesses were between me and my daughters—when Henry came in. He impatiently brushed snow from his curt-mantle, cut short for easier riding, and said he was off to the north.

I sighed resignedly. "I suppose you may as well be out of the city since I seldom see you when you are here." He leered at that, and I added laughing, "And now not even at night for weeks. As to your day, you're forever with your ministers or dashing madly to some outlying town and no doubt forget I'm even alive."

His eyes gleamed. "If it weren't for that month's prohibition after a birth, we could—" He brushed that aside. "Stephen almost ruined this country. I must bring it back to life, not only in London but in every city and village. Then there are the farmers, artisans, sheepherders who have to give away half their produce or animals to pay taxes to corrupt sheriffs. And the brigands have gone unchecked. I must make it safe for people to travel without an armed escort."

He paused for breath and I laughed again. "Do you have to do everything at once?" I answered my own question. "Being you, yes. So you might as well look into another matter." He'd started to turn away, swung back at my words. "I'm tired of our cramped quarters here. When will Westminster Palace be ready for us? It should have been cleaned and refurnished by now."

"No, because I've had some ideas about the palace that I talked over with Becket. We need more space, but we have to wait until the weather warms. We—I—thought we could use the old palace for business offices for state officials and possibly living quarters for courtiers and build a new one joined to it for us to live in. Would that please you?"

"Y-yes, but won't that take years?"

He chuckled. "Not with the man I've chosen to oversee the building. Becket of course." He left then, and I made a moue at his retreating back.

I'd liked Thomas Becket well enough when I first met him, a lean, tall man with dark hair and sharply chiseled features. But as weeks went by I didn't like—and neither did many at court—the intimacy between him and the king so that Henry treated him as an equal and showered revenues on him. As his wealth increased, Thomas dressed and entertained more regally than Henry ever did. Though with me as hostess, we could easily have outshone a chancellor who was taking too much power to himself.

However, I couldn't complain about his restoring Westminster. We all thought it would take at least two years, but Becket managed the impossible. He employed so many men that the work was finished in less than four months. He asked with a humility that didn't quite mask his self-assurance if he could escort me to Westminster where I could give him suggestions on improvements he hadn't thought of. I agreed coolly, but I forgot my chill indifference when he showed me the land to the Thames that was covered with orchards and stretches of sunny lawn.

But when sentries swung open the doors to the new palace, my thanks about how much he'd done and so quickly weren't repeated. I said flatly the rooms were pleasantly large, but the bare floors? I'd expected carpets like those we saw in Byzantium. And what did he think of having mirrors and inlaid furniture instead of the unadorned chairs and tables? I was sure, though I didn't say so, that his own home was far better furnished.

He was enthusiastic. "Carpets. I'll send to the east for them. I knew you'd have ideas that a mere bachelor would never think of. And I'll exchange this furniture for pieces more worthy of you. I'll see to it at once." He bowed and left me with my ladies. Like Henry, he was always in a hurry.

Alicia said, "At least it's better than Bermond-sey." I nodded agreement while I admitted to myself that my critical feelings might have more to do with the man who'd supervised the work than with the palace. So I wrote Henry I was satis-fied and would be even more so when new furni-ture arrived. When it did, and every piece was beautifully inlaid or etched with silver, I ordered my household to prepare to entertain officials from foreign countries. Now we were in a spacious palace, I looked forward to living as I had in Aquitaine.

No announcement of arrivals came. Puzzled, I turned to Alicia. I felt close to her though she hadn't been with me as long as many of my ladies, and she was efficient. "Find out why ambassadors seem to be suddenly avoiding London. Surely a few of them or their staffs must be here." It was early September with breezes still mild and the sun golden on the green fields. I'd have our guests dine above the Thames in the gardens Becket had so cleverly laid out, and there would be boating and archery contests and music and dancing to amuse them. And in between we'd talk of state affairs. I'd been away from government matters too long. I smiled happily at being again part of the greater world.

Alicia returned an hour later, her plump face anxious when she saw my expression of pleasure. She knew me well enough to guess what I was thinking. She cleared her throat, said nervously, "The ambassadors from Austria and Castile and France and Flanders—all the ambassadors, I mean, are in the city, madame, but—but—" I gestured impatiently for her to go on—"instead of presenting themselves at Westminster, they—they wait on Chancellor Becket. I'm—I'm sorry."

I was shocked, but I was too proud to complain to one under me, much as I liked Alicia. I said coolly, "No need to be sorry. The chancellor is simply trying to save me the trouble of officials always being underfoot."

Ironically, when Henry returned briefly, he said almost the same to me. I answered more sharply than I intended. "It is more proper for foreign dignitaries to be at the king's table, not at the chancellor's."

He laughed, "My love, you know how bored I am with keeping a great court—"

"I am not, and I certainly know more about entertaining than any small merchant's son."

He waved a big freckled hand. "Yes, yes, but I refuse to be burdened with all the ceremonies that impress visitors when I've someone who'll do the tedious labors for me." He yawned, came abruptly alert, his new thought obvious from his grinning mouth. "I've counted the days. The month is over, well, almost, isn't it?"

I nodded, smiling in spite of my resentment of his offhand dismissal of my wishes. With Henry I could admit my need for a man's embrace. He was gentle at first as he stroked my breasts, remembering I suppose that the month was by no means over. But as our desires rose, he caressed me more roughly until his passion refused to wait longer and he plunged into my eager body. Yet while I responded to him physically, my resentment still gnawed at me.

I had no chance to bring up the matter again as he slept instantly and left at dawn for Westminster, I think he said. Perhaps I'd have said nothing more anyway, insulting as it was that ambassadors should pay their respects to Becket rather than to me. How could I quarrel over a commoner being given honors that were due me? I wondered how long this curious attachment between Becket and Henry would last when it made Becket almost equal to the king. And forced me, the queen, to stand aside.

If anyone guessed my hurt feelings, he'd believe I was indignant at Henry's infidelities which were common gossip. As if I'd get wrought up over women he found in taverns or in his journeyings through the country. I shrugged them away. They meant nothing to Henry. At least the mothers didn't. I was annoyed when he returned with one of his by-blows and insisted the child be placed in our children's nursery. The boy, Geoffrey, was named after Henry's father whom I'd admired, but that was hardly enough for me to welcome the three-year-old.

I said contemptuously, "Do you really wish our sons to be brought up with a bastard? They can hardly profit by living with a child of the streets."

He shouted, "He is *my* son, madame, and I demand that everyone treat him as being his father's child."

I could see from his face darkening into purple that he was on the edge of a tantrum. And would probably have one every day until the boy was accepted. I said indifferently, "Very well. There'll probably be enough children of the nobility here to reduce any harm Geoffrey might do."

He wasn't too pleased at my answer, but he couldn't object too much since he'd got his way. My eyes narrowed as he left my room. I'd always been fiercely proud of my independence that was being chipped away by Becket's influence and Henry's rages. In one of his furies Henry could make me fully dependent on him. Well. I'd have some benefits from my position. An income of my own which no English queen had ever enjoyed. Practically all money raised in Aquitaine had to be used to keep up my estates and government there so I had to have an allowance which couldn't be cut off summarily even by the king.

I waited for the next meeting of the exchequer in the Painted Chamber of the palace. The ministers were sitting around a long table, every seat filled except for the king's massive chair that was placed under a colorful depiction of Christ and the apostles, the painting quite unlike those on the other three walls which showed mounted knights jousting, archers drawing impossibly long bows and an army charging into battle.

I sat down on the throne to make my demand courteously but firmly. I asked for what I called queen's gold. For every payment of taxes or debts made to the king, a part must be paid to me. The officials were so astonished at the curious request that they just glanced at each other and agreed. I thanked them and—I wouldn't chance the money not being delivered—said that whenever the exchequer met, I'd send my own officers to collect what was due me.

I was concerned at what Henry would say on

one of his fleeting visits home when he heard what I'd done, but on this I wouldn't back down if he raged for days. I'd threaten to return to my own provinces, which wouldn't please him since that might encourage my vassals, always hostile to him, to raid his borders.

There was no need for me to threaten. On his arrival I told Henry before he could see the exchequer officials and try to persuade them to change their minds. Henry gaped at the audacity of my move, a queen's allowance taken from his money and paid directly to her, he'd never heard of such a thing. Then with one of his swift mood changes, he threw back his head and roared with laughter. Who but I would ever dream up such a scheme?

A moment later he was serious, his brows drawn together. I wondered if he were speculating on what had led to my effort at independence. He wasn't. "By God's eyes, my love, you have a way of managing officials. I'm off to Normandy in a fortnight. I wish you to sit in with my councillors when you're at Westminster and if you can—" he eyed my waistline which was thickening again— "travel through the north. I want to know what happens there when I'm away. Or do you have to give up riding now?"

I scoffed, "When has pregnancy been a hindrance to me? I'm pleased you have enough confidence to have me share in the government." I bit back the sarcastic words that I knew why. He trusted no one as fully as he did his own family, not even Thomas Becket, though undoubtedly Becket would be ordered to watch my every action.

He was. I could feel his attention on me when I sat with the councillors the first week, but I carefully gave him no reason to be critical. After a clerk read a sheaf of documents, then laid the parchments on the table before us, I turned deferentially to Becket. "My lord chancellor, would you be good enough to explain the first request which has something to do with a sheriff distraining an abbey's lands? And the third—or was it the fourth?—concerning a dispute about the dowry a bride's father in Sussex owes her Norman husband?" I added with a smile, "That is, explain to me. The ministers, I know, understood every sentence."

Becket appeared surprised, but he picked up the documents and went over each word for me. His detailed explanation, I thought irritably, was aimed at the intelligence of a six-year-old. Still, he relaxed visibly at what he thought was my stupidity and at my acknowledgment of my need for his special abilities. I thanked him sweetly, and we went on with demands from the towns for special charters and from shipbuilders at the Cinque Ports who said they hadn't been paid for six months and would lay down their tools until they received their wages. But most of the complaints were on taxes.

I'd begun so well that I could put in, "As you may know, my lords, the king suggested I ride through the country and report to him on the affairs of his realm. So I could look into these grievances about taxes and send a report to you as well as to the king. You of course are far too busy to bother about these small matters, but I'm well able to take the time." My eyes slid toward Becket. I sighed with relief as he as well as the others nodded complacently, no doubt thinking me too inept to do any harm.

As I traveled north, delighted at my new responsibilities, I found there was discontent about more than taxes though they were mentioned most often. Journeying from town to castle to city, each morning I listened to the people who came to grumble about their ill fortune, and every afternoon I held a court of justice. Henry had introduced a new system so that a jury of twelve was given power to decide on a case instead of a single judge or lord. Most complainants went away satisfied when a sheriff was ordered to return taxes above what he was entitled to or a lord was told firmly of his tenants' rights so that the peasants had time to till their fields as well as his.

But one inarticulate man whose case had been dismissed by the jurors stood at the arched doorway, his knotted fingers clasped together. He looked frightened but evidently couldn't force himself to leave. I sent a steward to bring him to me and said, "You appear unhappy, but the jurors had no choice. You only mumbled that the king's officials don't treat you fairly, but you gave no instance of that."

"But they—they don't, Your H-Highness. They—they steal—" His heavy face lightened with relief as a small woman entered and bustled up to him. "Wife, you t-tell them."

She hadn't noticed me at first in her concern for her husband. Now as her eyes rose to mine, she curtseyed clumsily. She seemed too overawed to speak for a minute, but when she did words burst from her. They owed one goose for taxes, but the sheriff demanded two, and a day later the under-sheriff said they'd be put in jail since they hadn't paid, but he'd save them for the price of a goose and three ducks. They knew they'd go hungry, but what could they do if they'd escape jail?

I was angry at her story, but I couldn't take her unsupported statement. I sent for the two officials, and their guilty expressions at the sight of me and the couple were almost enough to condemn them even before they confessed and promised to make restitution. I said sternly, "Yes, you must repay what you stole, but I doubt if that's sufficient. We will let the jury decide if there should be a further sentence."

The jury took little time to reach a verdict, restitution and three months in jail. The couple watched the officials being removed by an armed guard, their faces not quite believing their good fortune.

Their feeling for me was reflected in the citizens. When I'd first left London to ride through forests and moors to the villages, the people were distrustful because I was foreign. But as stories drifted through the countryside that I was here to uphold their laws, not make new demands on them, I was cheered wherever I went. And I no longer looked at them as a strange people. They weren't my beloved Aquitanians, but they had a solidity and sense of fair play and were more hard-working than my southern subjects.

And they had compassion. I was wakened before

dawn one morning by a messenger from Westminster. I'd ridden long the day before and was still entangled in some vague dream so I answered drowsily when Alicia brought the rider in. But my eyes snapped open at his news. William, my first-born, was very ill. The words rang in my ears as I dressed and mounted and pounded out of the town, my escort strung out behind me. The only warmth that touched my chilled heart was that, the story of my son having gone through the countryside even faster than I, everyone I met promised to pray for his recovery.

Their prayers and mine were in vain. The following weeks were a blur. I sat up with little William night after night, but his fever continued to rise and his two-year-old body didn't have the strength to resist it. Sorrowfully we buried him at Reading Abbey. The shock of his death brought me early to bed with my third child by Henry, a girl I named Matilda after Henry's mother.

I loved the baby, but one child doesn't make up for the loss of another, and I moved in a stupor unable to shake off my grief. Alicia hovered over me, her plump face concerned. "Madame, you can't stay here in Westminster where every room reminds you of the prince. You must go away. No, not to your work in the north. That too would only be a reminder of the days before—before— You must be with your old friends. In Aquitaine." My heart lifted a little at the thought. I might find some comfort there. She went on, "The king is in Normandy. Surely he can leave his affairs for a while to be with you."

I nodded dully. I needed Henry beside me, yet

I'd been so stunned I'd scarcely thought of him since the burial. Alicia asked for no more consent than my nod and set to work so briskly that within a fortnight little Henry and Matilda and my staff were sailing across the Channel.

Henry met me in Barfleur on a sunny day with warm winds that mocked my grief. He started to say something about his province, stopped as he saw my expression and took me tenderly into his arms. "My love, my dear love, I too have suffered. I know what you're feeling."

I said muffled, my head against his chest, "You can't. You have so many distractions keeping the peace here. And you weren't with him when he d-died. Did my messenger tell you I'm—I'm going home? I mean to—to Aquitaine. Can you—"

I glanced up. He was grimacing and appeared ready to shake his head, said instead, "Anywhere if it will ease your pain to have us mourn together."

I thanked him gratefully, knowing how he detested my duchy with my lawless lords who were willing to bend the knee only to me. He added in an attempt to cheer me that our next baby would be another son. Instead of comforting me, his words brought on the tears I'd held back.

But my spirits lightened when my nobles greeted me happily and had troubadours and gaily ribald conversation at the banquets to entertain us. Or rather to entertain me. They ignored Henry as much as they could as if he were some unimportant vassal, and Henry raged. At least his storms were in private out of consideration for our recent loss.

And I could help him a little when my cousin Raoul de Faye rode into Poitiers. He'd been delayed by two new projects on the Garonne River to develop water power which the farmers greeted enthusiastically. Raoul kissed my hand and then my mouth but with a gravity which said he knew I wasn't in the mood now as I'd been in Paris for a lighthearted flirtation. His understanding made it easy to appeal to him, asking him to treat Henry with the respect due a duke and a king.

Henry was mollified enough to agree to spend Christmas in Bordeaux, but after Twelfth Night he insisted on returning to England. Since except for Raoul he'd put up with the veiled snubs of my people and their boasts about how much pleasanter life was here than in the cold north, I couldn't argue with his decision. I left more cheerfully than I'd arrived. Alicia had been right that I needed my old friends to regain my vivacity. Still, I was sorry to leave and promised myself I'd return often.

But soon I had little time to think of them or of myself. When we reached England word came that the Welsh were advancing on our city of Chester. Henry named me his deputy again, gathered up an army and hurled it across the country. He'd never paid much attention to Wales thinking the country insignificant, and daily I expected a report that he'd flung the Welshmen back across the borders. When I did receive news, I could scarcely believe it. Henry had been forced to retreat and negotiate with the Welsh leaders who fought as guerillas, not like chivalrous knights.

He came home crushed at his lack of success,

but only briefly. He said, "Let them have their wild mountains scarcely fit for animals. I shall make a progress through England, a civilized land. Come with me, love. Becket can see to the government."

I hesitated, finally said no. Not because of Becket. He and I made no pretense of loving each other, but he wasn't like Thierry Galeran who'd tried to set Louis against me. But I was eight months pregnant and riding was more difficult this time than in my other pregnancies. But the first week was dull with most of the court away and I decided impetuously to join Henry in Oxford. Alicia went along good-naturedly though she shook her head over the journey.

She was right for we'd hardly reached our lodgings in the Oxford fortress before I gave birth to a son, Richard. When he was put into my arms, I laughed with delight at his small body and wizened face, feeling closer to him than I had to any of our children when they were first born. I whispered to Alicia, "I didn't believe it possible, but this baby already is filling the emptiness in my heart that little William left. I'll give him the same title, future duke of Aquitaine." She nodded, smiling happily that I was recovering from the tragedy of William.

I hardly let the child out of my sight while I waited for my strength to come back so that I could go on with Henry. It was hard to leave Richard with his wet nurse, but I wouldn't risk his traveling. I knew too well Henry's mode of seeing the country. Not like mine where everyone knew my schedule. No one knew Henry's. If in the evening he announced he'd spend the next day in the village where we were lodged, he'd suddenly give orders at daybreak he wished to leave at once. The result was chaos as supplies were packed and his aroused household made ready to ride.

The next night he might tell his escort to be ready to leave at dawn. When he announced that I spent the morning in bed, knowing he'd sleep until noon. The servants, unfortunately for them, had to follow his commands, and horses and wagons and carts stood packed and waiting through the long hours. The chaos grew worse as we went on, and I looked back at the nights I had a bed to sleep in.

Henry would send a scout ahead to a castle to be prepared for his entourage. Then in the afternoon he'd turn off the road, and as it grew dark we'd find ourselves at some forest hut that hadn't been cleaned for months. Henry and I had the doubtful pleasure of a roof over our bed of rough blankets, but the court had to camp as best it could, and I could hear the clatter of swords and furious shouts as knights fought over a grassy spot or dry hollow for the night. Henry laughed, but none of the rest of us shared his humor.

However, I soon realized his unexpected stops and starts weren't due to perversity. I snapped one morning after an almost sleepless night, "We aren't at war, you could see to it we have a few comforts. Half the time the courtiers have beds of mud. And the food! You may not care what you eat, but have you heard the complaints? You're in such haste the bread's half-baked, and the fish and meat are often tainted and the wine's sour." I stopped for lack of breath.

Henry grinned. "I don't like to see you so ill used, my love, but a bit of hard living won't hurt my soft courtiers. They'll have to put up with it. I do have a reason. When lords or town officials expect me, everything's in order, and they can show me how devotedly they carry out their duties. What I want to see is how they work when they aren't expecting me. Remember Wakefield and Nottingham? Ha! By God's eyes those officials will have enough time in prison to think about their negligence and corruption. And the new officers will be fearful I might return at any time and see that their work is done properly."

I still felt cross as I pulled a wool robe and a heavy cloak around me to keep out the cold, but I agreed reluctantly his erratic ways had some merit. But I was grateful the next week was Christmas, a season that meant much to Henry, and we were near Lincoln. This time Henry sent ahead to warn of our approach, and we revelled in the ceremonies and feasting. Food and wine were properly prepared and graciously served, and tumblers and jugglers and musicians entertained us.

Too soon we were on our way again, and I was ill mornings. I hadn't expected to be pregnant again now since Henry spent few hours away from his continual roaming to sleep with me. Still, I was healthy, and except for those hours on awakening I felt well. But I was relieved when at last we rode south. Had I ever criticized Westminster? Everything about it looked elegant, especially the great silk-hung beds. But I had little time to rest because Henry was off to the Continent, and I was left to share the tasks of government with Becket.

And I had little time for my lying-in. But the birth was easy, another son, Geoffrey. I'd only a few days to cuddle and pet him—though Richard was still my favorite—as I had to return to issuing writs and attending courts of justice and signing documents endlessly. As usual Henry was delighted when I wrote him news of the baby. I thought drily he was probably already planning advantageous marriages for his small sons and daughter, then had to admit I too would soon be thinking of how our children could make alliances for us with other countries. But I could wait for that.

He couldn't. He was already deciding the future. While I was snatching an hour here and there to play with young Henry and Matilda—Richard and Geoffrey were still babies—Henry finished his business in Normandy and returned home with what he said was a great scheme. My former husband had remarried, but the fruit for poor Louis was only one more daughter, Marguerite.

Henry chuckled that we had sons while Louis might never have one. Then he added more soberly, "My idea—well, a Frenchwoman can't inherit the throne. But if our oldest son married—no, no, naturally not yet, he's too little—but if young Henry married a French princess—not the two older ones of course since they're his half sisters—but he could marry Marguerite and—and—"

He broke off, looking a little uneasy, evidently expecting me to be upset over any alliance with

Louis. But I was thinking of a dynasty just as he was. If Louis never had a son, wouldn't our Henry have a claim to the French crown through his wife? Henry sighed audibly with relief when I smiled and said, "That's a thought well worth considering. But the suggestion must be handled carefully. Louis must think our only purpose is a wish to bring peace to our countries and put a finish to these continual wars. You—" I shook my head. Henry was excellent in hard bargaining after a battle, but he'd stumble clumsily over delicate negotiations when one must conceal one's real goal. Perhaps I . . . I swallowed a laugh. Louis sit down with me over the marriage of our children? If he met with me at all, he'd say no before he heard me out. I frowned. "Who would you send?"

A ridiculous question. I knew the answer before he spoke. Thomas Becket. I wasn't pleased, the man already had far more prestige than he deserved. But who else could carry off this mission with his easy flair? And when the three of us met to make plans, I could see Henry was right. Henry would have sent him with a small suite, but Thomas and I were of the same mind. He must travel with a splendid escort that would leave the French gaping at England's wealth. Footmen to lead the procession, hounds and greyhounds, falcons, goshawks, great wagons with Thomas's wardrobe, pack horses with gold and silver plate, and in the rear two hundred knights, squires, sons of noblemen. We agreed laughingly the French would be overawed, thinking if a chancellor traveled so, how magnificent would be his king.

Henry's and my gaiety changed to uneasiness as the weeks passed, and we heard Becket was warmly welcomed but Louis would give no definite answer. I said irritably we'd find another princess for our son though I knew no other marriage would be so advantageous. I paced the floor restlessly, half hoping and half resigned to failure.

Then Becket returned, swaggering slightly. But that was justified. Our three-year-old Henry was betrothed to Louis's eleven-month-old daughter. And Marguerite's dowry was what my husband had his heart set on. The Vexin, that castled piece of land between our countries which Henry's father had surrendered to Louis when Louis recognized Henry as duke of Normandy. The French would hold the strip until the marriage, but after the wedding it would be ours again.

Louis had one condition. I grimaced wryly when Becket mentioned it hesitantly. The future bride naturally would be sent to grow up with her future husband, but I must have nothing to do with her bringing up. I, Eleanor, was unfit for such a duty. I swallowed a retort to the insult and told Henry to name one of his lords as guardian. That didn't change the terms of the betrothal.

Henry nodded absently, his eyes slitted in thought. "The Vexin." His hands were clenched. "We should have it now before the French use it to strike against our borders. Why should we have to wait until the marriage?"

Becket was taken aback. "I agreed to that, Your

Highness, or King Louis wouldn't have signed."

I half-smiled, saying nothing. I was sure Henry would find a way to get his clenched hands on his coveted land. He did. There was nothing in the contract saying when the wedding would take place. He did delay until Marguerite could stand and walk uncertainly. Then he had the two children married in a quiet chapel ceremony. As he said, child or adult, marriage was legal and binding.

Immediately he demanded the Vexin, and the French according to the treaty had to cede the land to us. Louis could do nothing about it, but he had to be furious, especially when Henry had the old fortress repaired and went on an orgy of castle building, not only in the Vexin but in Normandy and England. Henry gloatingly showed me sketches of his plans. He chose the wrong moment. I glanced at them indifferently. "They'll be cold and drafty like all your old castles. In Aquitaine my palaces have wide windows and private rooms and—" I stopped as my voice broke.

He stared. "You sound ready to cry. Why? My castles are strong, able to hold off an army. As for being drafty! My men aren't milksops, complaining about a bit of clean wind."

I dabbed at my eyes. "I don't care about your tiresome buildings. Do you know that—that this morning I had to say goodby to our little Henry? Your officers took him to b-be brought up in B-Becket's house."

He said defensively, "The boy can't live in a nursery forever, tied to his mother. Even noblemen's sons are sent away young to be trained in another lord's household. So certainly a royal child should learn to know his future subjects and be trained in the art of warfare and mathematics and foreign tongues."

I wailed, "But he's so small and what does Becket know of how he should be cared for? And I m-miss him."

Henry chuckled, pushed back the veil on my head to twist a strand of hair in his rough fingers. "Now that we can do something about, my dear. Another child will fill his place. Come!"

I stood up slowly. This was so like Henry. Soothe a mother's loss by greedily indulging himself. Still, I admitted I wasn't reluctant. He was away so much that my need for a man too often went unsatisfied. It was early afternoon, and I could see his face clearly as he lay beside me. He was weatherbeaten, and there were new wrinkles around his mouth and a slight sag below his chin. I wasn't sorry to see the signs, they made us closer in age. But could it be more than age that made his caresses fumbling, took him longer to be roused?

I felt a stirring of jealousy. Was there another woman who used his manhood, depriving me? Not some woman of the streets who was probably nameless to him and whom he turned to when he was away from home or forbidden my bed after a birth. But someone he cared for. Then he caught me to him, his eyes glowing, and I forgot my brief suspicion as his hands searched my body intimately. I sighed with pleasure, and he took me swiftly, impatiently.

Yet later when he left, the question came again. Did Henry care deeply for someone else? I thought fiercely, No. He was a lecher, but he loved only one woman, his wife. I would not let myself doubt him.

Chapter Seven

When our next child was born, a daughter, Henry insisted on naming her after me. For a moment I wondered if that were to placate me for some secret liaison, then firmly dismissed the thought. He meant it as a mark of his love for me, and I kissed him in gratitude. He beamed with pleasure at his growing family, and I smiled with him. Until he said abruptly, "The old Archbishop of Canterbury is dead. I shall appoint Becket to the see."

"But—but he isn't a priest, Henry. And everyone knows how lavishly he lives, not the way people expect from the most important bishop in the country."

Henry just grinned. "Thomas can be ordained easily enough, no problem. And think how convenient it'll be to have my chancellor and the archbishop the same man. You know how the church courts judge their own clerics if a crime has been committed instead of—as it should be—every citizen being accountable to our laws, not to the easy church discipline. He'll help me change that so I'll no longer be in conflict with the pope over this or that affair."

I made my voice sound weak, irritated though I was that Becket should be given more power than ever. "I can't argue with you now, but I'm sure you're wrong. Promise you'll wait a little before you decide."

He scowled. "I have thought it over, and I don't want to delay. I have to fill the position soon because—did I tell you—I intend to follow the example of some French kings and have our Henry crowned so there'll be no trouble over who succeeds me. And only Canterbury's archbishop can anoint a king. Becket will do anything I wish." The scowl changed to a pleased smile.

But he wasn't as pleased the next day. Becket was with him when he came to see me. "I offered this man the high post, and he refuses instead of being immensely grateful. Tell him, Eleanor, why it's his duty to become archbishop." Henry had already forgotten my objections as he often did when I disagreed with him.

As I groped for what to say, Becket turned to me, said earnestly, "You must be aware I'm not the man for the position, madame. An archbishop should be saintly, holy, and I am not." He waved at his expensive robes and smiled slightly at me, guessing I was as much against the appointment as he was. For the first time I felt some warmth toward him. At least he was honest.

I said with equal honesty, "Speak to the king. My husband listens more to you than to me." That truth wasn't as bitter to me today as it would have been yesterday.

He glanced at Henry. "If I accepted the post, I— You know yourself you try too hard to influence church matters. As chancellor I've always served you as best I could. But as archbishop, I'd have to serve God. You must not appoint me, Your Highness."

Henry looked surprised but said carelessly, "I'll think of what you say," and dismissed Becket. But Becket must have known as I did that Henry's tone meant he'd made up his mind and had no intention of changing it.

Within weeks Becket was ordained. A mistake, I thought, but I was too busy with children and my household and, when Henry was away, with administration to think beyond that. Though occasionally I heard stories that Becket was changing. His vestments were of silver and gold, but underneath he wore a hair shirt. And while others ate greedily at his overflowing table, he had only bread and fish and drank water rather than wine. I wondered cynically how long his Spartan living would last.

Henry laughed when I repeated the rumors to him. "He's showing off. Wants to impress me." He idly unrolled a message which was brought him with a package. We were in the office off the council room, and I looked up when he roared,

"Impossible! By God's eyes, the man must be mad."

He tossed the letter at me and tore open the package. I skimmed the brief letter. Thomas had written that he could not undertake the burdens of two such positions as chancellor and archbishop since they might often be in conflict. He was returning the Great Seal. The seal was in the packet, and Henry slammed it on the table between us. His hand was shaking, and he was speechless with anger.

When his voice came back, he raged for days at Thomas's base ingratitude, stopping only long enough to summon Thomas to see him at once. Becket arrived quietly. He was gaunt so the tales of his fasting had to be true, and he was firm in refusing to remain chancellor, undaunted by Henry's fury though he knew Henry didn't forgive anyone easily who went against his wishes.

If he didn't know, he soon discovered that. Henry called assembly after assembly to try to force the archbishop to take an oath that clerics would be judged by the law of the land if they were accused of a crime, not by the Church court. Becket wouldn't agree, and Henry stormed that after all the favors he'd heaped on Becket, what did he receive in thanks? Not so much as a word of appreciation. And he asked so little, only that Becket say the English law was above the papal law. In the clashes that followed, Henry threatened his old friend with imprisonment and worse, hinting at castration.

I was bored with the constant battles and dismayed at what they were doing to Henry. I'd always thought him a great king, but in this bickering he behaved more like a spoiled boy, brushing aside state affairs to carry on his quarrel with the man he'd raised up. His threats grew so savage that Becket fled for his life, disguised as a monk, to the Continent.

I was pleased at his escape, not only because I was weary of the endless wrangling. With Thomas gone, Henry turned to me, probably feeling I alone understood his violent frustration as neither his whores nor his courtiers could. He'd neglected me of late, but this time I had no suspicions of another woman. All his ardor had gone into his battles with Becket. I was sure of that when he came to my bed with his old passionate demands, and my body responded to his urgency. He slept swiftly after our embrace but woke me during the night to plunge into me again. I submitted laughingly.

Soon I discovered I was pregnant, a bright satisfaction since it proved that, though I was in my forties, I was young enough to be with child. Before I was brought to bed, we had news of another birth. Louis had sired a son, Philip Augustus. That meant the end of hope for our Henry to inherit France through his wife, but I had to smile at the grand name of the new prince which proclaimed Louis's happiness in at last having an heir.

As if that drove Henry on, I was scarcely recovered from delivering a daughter, Joanna, when I was pregnant again. I was pleased because now he'd almost forgotten Becket, I feared Henry didn't need me so much. I knew from whispered tales that he preferred younger women though his restlessness and continual affrays to keep his vassals loyal had aged him so that many said he looked older than I now.

He must have worried about his aging too because again and again he brought up the problem of young Henry's coronation. Only the archbishop of Canterbury could anoint a king, and Henry wanted to be certain our eldest son was recognized now as his heir. He stormed at Becket's flying to the Continent. The archbishop must return. Becket refused. At last I said tiredly —this pregnancy wasn't as easy as the others, and I often had to rest afternoons—"There are other archbishops in England. What if it is the tradition that Canterbury's should crown the king? You've never before hesitated at changing customs that are as old or older than this one."

He bit his lip hard, then grinned. "You're right. I'll speak to the archbishop of York. He's my friend, he'll perform the ceremony."

It took little persuading before York's archbishop agreed. Some of the lords were hesitant, but soon they were talked around, and the rites were carried out quietly. Young Henry was delighted, and I was relieved there'd be no fear of civil war when it was time for him to inherit. I was pleased too that now I was in my fifth month I was feeling myself again and could devote myself energetically to Henry's affairs when he was away and to Henry when he was home, a too rare occasion.

Far too rare. I almost wished I were sickly so my thoughts would be on my health. Instead I was continually probing at Henry's absences which seemed longer and more frequent this year. I soon gave up questioning him as he impatiently gave the same answers, muttering about trouble in Normandy and western England or appeals from courts of justice that kept him in some village or town for days. I explained I was only interested in his welfare, afraid he was trying to do too much. He shrugged that off. A king's duties couldn't be measured in hours. He must be ever alert to the needs of his subjects.

That was true. I'd had to rise too early from a lying-in many times to be his deputy. But I hoped this time he'd be with me when I gave birth. He shook his head. "Trouble in Anjou, my dear. But I'll travel with you to Oxford since you can't stay in Westminster as it's time for the yearly cleaning. The palace at Oxford has been repaired, and it's healthier there and you like being more out in the country."

I nodded. Richard had been born in Oxford, and I hoped I'd have for the new child the same feeling I had for Richard. Two days after we arrived, Henry said he had to leave for Anjou. I didn't try to hold him. He was right that a king's duty came before his comfort. The palace had been carefully restored, and I hummed one of my troubadour's airs as I looked over the rooms with a housewifely eye, then strolled in the gardens where the leaves were sere and late-flowering plants were nipped with frost on this early winter day.

My humming broke off at the sound of two guards behind a tall thicket, one saying something about sharing a mug of ale when they were relieved by the night sentries. The other grunted, "Uh huh, I want to drink to the downfall of that girl who thinks herself the new queen of England, the bitch."

Alicia darted forward, screaming at the men to hold their villainous tongues. They swung around and saw me where I stood paralyzed. They gaped in dismay. I tried to ask what they meant, but I couldn't get the words past my thick throat. Shoulders hunched they turned and hurriedly began to patrol another stretch of the gardens.

I touched my lips with my tongue, licked them again and swallowed convulsively. I was able to speak now, but only in a whisper. "Alicia—what did they . . . what girl?"

"Oh, that was just some silly soldiers' talk." But her face was white with anger. "Nothing, madame, really nothing. You mustn't let yourself be upset, not now when it's so near your time."

I gasped through clenched teeth, "Tell me."

Alicia glanced imploringly at the three other women with us, but they were as reluctant to speak as she. She said finally, "Rumors, madame, that's all, about some sly bi . . . some girl in Woodstock being treated as if she were queen." Her furious voice made it clear the story was more than idle talk. My frozen expression forced her to go on. "A—a knight's daughter." A girl of the gentry. So this wasn't one of Henry's tavern sluts whom I could dismiss indifferently. And she was being treated as if she were queen. Alicia added as if the words were forced out of her, "Rosamond Clifford. The—the king brought her to—to Woodstock where he's visiting her—" She clapped her hands to her mouth.

So Henry wasn't in Anjou. He'd known I'd soon be in childbed yet he was with her. I was in a state of shock and wondered almost coolly how often I'd thought him on state affairs or at war when he was really with his young love. For a moment I couldn't believe it. Then knowledge this was true exploded inside me. I moaned, moaned again as the first labor pains stabbed me. The women put their arms about me and helped me to the palace.

The birth was long and difficult, but I was scarcely aware of my wrenched body. The man who'd sired this child spent nights with me for the sake of the dynasty. Never again, not ever again. The hurt of his betrayal and his leaving me at this time made the agony of birth seem trivial. If the guards could speak so casually of this Rosamond, and Alicia was able to tell me where Henry was, all England must know the story. Were the people laughing at the neglected wife?

Mechanically I made the final effort to push out the baby. The child was quickly sponged and held out to me. Another son, John. I turned my head away, though not before I could see he wasn't bright-haired like my other children, but small and dark. Through the days of my recovery I tried to love him, but the sight of him brought back too clearly the bitter moment I'd learned of a young beauty—she must be young and beautiful—who'd captured my husband's heart.

My husband? No, I had none. I hesitated. I must not be impetuous, reject him because of a few words though I was convinced they were true. They fitted in too well with the stray suspicions I'd had. I sent Alicia with two other ladies and a guard to Woodstock to stay inconspicuously in a small manor house whose owner, an elderly widow, I'd met when I'd traveled through England.

They returned gray-faced. The king was flaunting his liaison at Woodstock palace, occasionally dropping broad hints she'd soon have the right to the honors he bestowed on her. Was that to keep his Rosamond content, or was he really considering divorce? It didn't matter. I'd forgiven him too often for his lesser infidelities. This I could not forgive. There'd be no easy divorce. I would go to Aquitaine and never come back to this foggy island where I'd been hurt past bearing.

We rode to London. Westminster was still being cleaned and aired, and I lodged at the Tower. Bermondsey was more comfortable, but I could not go there where every room would bring back memories of the days when Henry and I, young and in love, had stayed before his coronation. But I would not hurry my departure. I was as furiously bitter as the day I'd heard of Rosamond, but I was the queen. I would not fly home like a criminal. Nor would I go empty-handed. I had jewels and furniture collected and sent to Dover for shipping. Then I wrote Henry that I was returning to Aquitaine with the children, saying my provinces needed a ruler there. That he'd believe because when he visited my lands, the lords were in an uproar, fighting at the least excuse. But they were loyal to me.

I was sure he wasn't sorry for his unexpected freedom though he thought it wouldn't be long before I returned. He made only one demand, that the baby John be left to be brought up in England. I consented. John was the least favorite of my children, and perhaps Henry was right that one of the princes learn English ways. His freedom didn't last long. Word came that Louis was stirring up Normandy, and Henry had to leave his light o' love and rush to the Continent within a week after I'd left.

I was cheered wildly when I reached Poitiers, citizens and lords all saying I'd neglected them too long. Their outpouring of goodwill eased my bruised heart, and that night I could laugh again at the tumblers and musicians and singers who were summoned hurriedly for my entertainment. I laughed and shook my head over future plans for amusing me. Further entertainment must wait until the children were settled with their tutors and governesses, and I'd looked into the business of government. I knew I'd be a better administrator now with the experience I'd had in England when Henry left me to rule.

I should have known that my lighthearted cousin Raoul wouldn't take my questions on state affairs seriously so soon after my return. He arrived the next day, galloping in from the country when he heard I was there. We went into one of the private rooms of the palace that Henry dis-

Anne Powers

dained for his castles, and I asked to see the latest
decrees that had been passed. He grinned and
leaned forward to touch my cheek with his
fingers. "You're beautiful. Everyone else ages but
never you. What secret is yours?"

I hadn't meant to speak of my hurt, but at the
soft admiration in his voice I blurted, "I'm no
longer a fair young girl. Ask my husb—" I tried to
gulp back the word too late. He didn't look surprised. So. The story must be known here too
though I'd heard of it only months ago. Was Raoul
only trying to be kind? I stiffened defensively.

His eyes crinkled at my expression. "I wouldn't
ask Henry what he thought of my mare, certainly
not his judgment of a woman. No, you aren't some
ordinary pretty young girl. You have a woman's
mature beauty that is far more seductive." He
kissed my hand, pushed down the low neckline of
my gown to kiss my breasts. He looked up, said
mischievously, "This is quite all right now. You've
left Henry, haven't you? So don't draw away. You
do like me a little, don't you? And I—I need you."
His narrow sardonic face held a mute appeal.

Against my will my rigid body melted against
him. His thin body was muscular, and his arms
around me were almost painful in their intense
grip, but it was a pleasant pain. It reassured me he
wanted me not out of pity but as a lusty man
desires a loved one. As he had in Paris, but I had a
husband faithful to me whom I wouldn't betray,
not then. Later in Antioch it had been different, I
didn't look on Louis as a husband just as now
Henry of his own will had ceased to be my
husband.

Raoul muttered, "My own love, you will be mine." His low voice was husky and masterful and yet lightly wooing. My heart beat unevenly. His caresses were insistent, but not like those of a man who couldn't wait for his own pleasure. Raoul was gentle under his steel, and his seeking hands didn't try to rouse me quickly. He was more like one who enjoyed the slow preliminaries of love before passion would shake us both into a need for each other.

Breathlessly I slid my arms around him as tightly as he held me. He pushed up my skirt and undertunic, gazed with delight at my naked body before he thrust into me, murmuring loving words that changed into a cry of happiness. Everything was blotted out for me except the feel of his flesh, the weight of his demanding body that answered my clamoring senses.

We were more discreet after that, meeting when others wouldn't know we were together. Not easy to manage when we were in the palace, but soon I had to travel through my provinces to settle disputes among my vassals and have them renew their vows of fealty to me and to Richard as my heir. My journeys were peaceful, not like Henry's with his mercenaries to raze walls and take hostages, so our touring was gay and lighthearted.

And anyone could see it was necessary for my former deputy and myself to be together often. What they didn't see was Raoul's return to my pavilion later that night to fulfill the promises our exchanged glances earlier had made. We had hours then of delight, and of laughter that was stifled when we reached the heights of love that answered the cry of my passionate heart. Then we lay smiling at each other while he caressed me gently, no longer driven by desire.

When we returned to Poitiers, I was ready to enliven my court and make it into the center it should be with troubadours, musicians, scholars, fairs and tournaments, processions and pageants. My children were wide-eyed at the change this was from Westminster where there was seldom entertainment except for a great event, and even then Henry begrudged the time and expense. I had new songs written too about the knights of the Round Table, of Arthur and Guinevere and Lancelot. Their stories had been bandied about for so long they were almost lost in their disjointed forms, but now they were romantic ballads sung liltingly, and the people treasured them.

So many guests came that palace and knights' castles were crowded to the walls, yet no one complained. But my greatest joy was when two young ladies arrived with a royal escort. I saw them from a wide window in the hall and ran down to the yard hoping, hoping they were—it was a royal escort—Louis's and my daughters. They tossed back their veils and I cried out, "Marie! Alix!" knowing instantly who they were though it was so long since I'd seen them.

They almost fell from their horses in their eagerness to touch me, kiss me. We clung together laughing. I said, "But—but Louis, doesn't he mind?" They laughed again at that. They were young women now and had a right to see their own mother. Louis had agreed, reluctantly I imagined. They added they could stay a fortnight, and I hugged them again.

They became part of the court immediately, and taught chivalry and the Code of Love to the young men who gathered around them, each knight vying for a smile from the two girls. I was sadly aware the fortnight was slipping past too quickly. Richard also looked downcast as the day for leaving approached. But when that morning came, Marie said gaily, "We should go as Father said, but—"

I seized on that but. "You can stay on? I wish you could live with me forever, my darlings, but I'll treasure every minute you can be here." We smiled happily at each other.

There were less pleasant stories from Henry's lands. He'd met Thomas Becket on the French border and insisted they be reconciled, that Thomas must return to England and take up again his duties as Archbishop of Canterbury. There'd be no more hindrance from him, the king. An empty promise I was sure, like so many of his promises. This was soon borne out. Henry objected to every move Thomas made. Thomas ignored the royal strictures, and Henry shouted furiously why would no one rid him of this pestilent bishop?

He hadn't long to wait for the answer. Four of his knights crossed the Channel to Canterbury and attacked Becket in the cathedral where his blood was spattered on the floor and his head beaten in. A horrifying deed that shocked all Europe and instantly raised Thomas to sainthood. Henry of course, always intemperate in his emotions, went into a spasm of grief and declared he'd never meant Becket to be martyred.

That was probably true now, but not when he was in one of his uncontrollable rages as he'd been when he shouted against Becket. I shivered, grateful I was well away from him. His proclamation that he hadn't meant Becket to be murdered was believed nowhere since the four knights weren't punished, and to escape the angry snarling from every corner, he recruited any army to invade Ireland.

I turned with relief to my own court with its laughter and light conversation and music from viol and lute, though we were all depressed when Marie and Alix could put off their departure no longer. Still, they promised to visit again often. I gazed at my other children, saw how they were growing up. There was joy in that but a little sorrow too. Eleanor was married to the king of Castile. Young Henry was seventeen, Richard two years younger, Geoffrey fourteen. All of them were handsome, especially Henry, who was said to be the most attractive prince in Europe, though Richard was still my favorite.

They weren't each other's favorite. They were forever quarreling, Richard calling Henry handsome but weak and vain, and Henry retorting Richard thought of nothing but fighting. That charge wasn't true. Richard was a born warrior but also a poet and musician. The arguments came mostly from young Henry's restlessness, and they often turned from their bickering with each other to unite in a diatribe against their father.

Young Henry, just returned from a hunt, threw his gauntlets on the floor, sank into a chair and said furiously, "Richard is recognized here as the future duke, but Father thinks I'm good for nothing except whiling away the time on this or that sport. He gave me a title too, king of England. Ha! Who has the revenues? Father. He only doles coins out to me when even he realizes I might need a new cloak or to have my horse shod. And am I ever consulted on the least important edict? Never."

I had to agree he had a just complaint. I said, "I'm afraid he forgets his own father turned Normandy over to him when he was younger than you, Henry."

Geoffrey looked glum. "Then I'll never be given anything either."

Richard glanced from one to the other, his eyes gleaming. "If we stand together—I never object to a fight, I'll be with you—maybe we can force him to acknowledge we are adults and have our rights."

They went on noisily about the way their father clutched both authority and money. I too thought they should be given their proper places in the world, but I knew Henry. Never would he stand aside an inch to grant young Henry and Geoffrey space to grow as I stood aside for Richard, giving him a place in my council and his rightful revenues, proud when I saw how my vassals accepted him as my heir. I wished the other two boys could also command respect from their future subjects.

No use to appeal to Henry. Or would I have a chance? I had a hasty letter from him that we should celebrate Christmas as a family this year in Normandy. I hesitated, then agreed. It would be poor policy to have an open breach between us for the gossips of Europe to bandy about. Better to let the world think we lived apart because Aquitaine needed a ruler the lords would heed, and that Henry was too occupied in his own provinces to join me and the children. So I journeyed north.

Within days of our meeting I wondered if I should have followed my first instinct to refuse. I waited until an hour seemed calm—the servants of our households were continually quarreling—then walked into the hall where Henry was critically eying the candles and boughs brought in for the season's celebration. I said quietly, "I've been thinking about our Henry. You did have him crowned king, yet he has no authority in the smallest matter. He told one of your gamekeepers to bring in a hart for his friends, and your man just yawned and walked away though our son is the next ruler."

"Authority? That boy? I should say that child." Henry's voice shook.

I said coolly, "He's almost eighteen, quite old enough."

"Old enough in years," Henry sneered. "He'll never grow up. When he was in England, I tried to teach him something of government, of what it means to be a king. Do you know what he did every time?" He didn't wait for my answer. "He'd say yes to everything, and an hour later was off to some tournament to meet his own kind of good-for-nothings. And don't say that was a while ago." Color flamed in his face. "Just yesterday he was, as usual, asking for gold, to spend lavishly on his followers I suppose. I invited him to a council meeting to learn about the exchequer and to talk about his needs to my ministers. He laughed, said they were as tightfisted as I so why should he bother?"

I knew why young Henry hadn't attended. The invitation had been halfhearted, and if he'd ventured to say a word at the meeting, his father would have ridiculed him. But I said nothing though it was difficult not to lash out. Tomorrow was Christmas, and I wanted the holiday to be peaceful.

It wasn't. While the great roasts of beef and veal and peacocks with their great fantails replaced were served, Henry taunted our son about his self-indulgence and his spendthrift ways. Young Henry was generous, but since money was given him so grudgingly he could hardly be called a spendthrift. Our son stabbed at a piece of meat on his plate and laughed.

I shook my head at the boy, then was stunned as Henry turned on me and roared, "You, you are to blame for our son's lightmindedness, his irresponsible ways. Your court with its romantic nonsense has corrupted him. Instead of attending to administration and keeping order and seeing that laws are obeyed, what do your idle people do? They think of nothing except the next amusement —singing, dancing, jousting."

I swallowed my flare of anger. "My dear Henry, we attend to business first. But when that is done, why shouldn't we have a *civilized* court—" I hadn't swallowed all my anger—"where lords and ladies can talk of philosophy and poetry as well as war and the latest instruments of torture?"

Young Henry and Richard and Geoffrey loudly agreed with me. Henry's eyes narrowed to slits as he tried to answer but could only choke in his fury. He flung back his chair and strode from the room. The boys and I exchanged glances in a wordless resolve to leave for home, all of us aware Henry would soon be in one of his uncontrolled rages.

I hadn't feared his black Angevin tempers when I was younger and Henry cared enough for me that he'd never flaunted one of his prostitutes. But now that he treated his Rosamond as if she were rightfully in my place when he was in England, no one could be sure what he'd do. I was not going to risk having our sons or myself in his power. I ordered my servants to pack, and we were away before light broke the next day.

The cold was bitter and snow drifted across the roads, but we stopped only to eat or to sleep at the nearest abbey. By this time the boys were chatting about Christmas as if the day had been amusing, but I felt I couldn't draw a deep breath until we were in Poitiers. When I reached the palace, Raoul hurried to meet me, his dark face unusually solemn.

At my startled glance he said quickly, "Nothing to be concerned about—yet. But your scouts rode faster than your escort, and they reported you left the king just in time. Three hours later he commanded that you and the princes be put under restraint. What he will do next—who can say?"

I said crisply, "We must be prepared for an attack."

Raoul nodded. "Exactly what I thought, my love. When the scouts were finished, I ordered that the fortresses on our borders be strengthened and more soldiers are marching in openly so he'll know we're ready for an assault."

"Good!" I stared beyond him, narrow-eyed. "Even so we may not be strong enough alone. We need an ally." I grimaced, knowing young Henry and Richard would urge this move. "There's one who'll join us gladly. Louis is not a great leader, but his vassals hate Henry and his grasping for their land. They won't need any persuasion to be with us." The statement wasn't amusing, but I couldn't hold back a laugh. "I'm sure Louis will be ironically pleased to be asked to protect his first wife and her family. And here we have not only our own lords who also hate Henry, but our sons to lead our troops. I'll send a messenger to Louis at once."

"There's no one else to turn to." He smiled warmly. "When you've written King Louis, we'll have done all we can. Let us think of other matters then, my love."

That evening I gave myself to him gladly, a deep relief at having my devoted kinsman to aid me threading through my delight in his embrace. But we had only snatched hours of pleasure, both of us too concerned over reports that Henry's scouts were watching just across the border to allow us to give ourselves wholly in our love for each other.

A fortnight later when a messenger stood before us shaking with exhaustion from a long ride and fear over telling me his news, I thought instantly of invasion. His message was worse, I think. Young Henry, out hunting, had pursued a hart too far north, and his father's soldiers had swooped down on him and taken him prisoner. I could imagine the boy's helpless fury which matched mine, a fury that was intensified when we had a further report. The king wasn't risking leaving our son in a castle where he might persuade a kindly jailer into leaving a door unlocked. Instead he kept young Henry at his side, night and day, never letting the boy sleep alone.

I shivered at the thought of my son being a prisoner. It was unendurable. But I must not give way to my anger. That clouded one's thinking. I said to Raoul, "The last messenger said my son is in a castle near Gisors. I will send three of my men—with a bag of gold—to post horses along the road to France and then to get into the keep and bribe a sentry to let the boy out on a night when the king has been drinking too much and won't waken easily." I bit my lip. "I wish he could come home, but the road to France is shorter, and he'll be safer there."

I waited tensely for news. If our son was caught trying to escape, what would Henry do? But three weeks later my men returned with news the boy had got away, and I had word from Louis that young Henry was safe in Paris. I laughed happily, laughed again when Henry sent me threatening letters commanding me to return to him with all our children. When I didn't answer, he sent an archbishop who said if I didn't join my husband with the boys he would, regretfully, be forced to excommunicate me. I listened to him politely, but I didn't answer him either. My father, all my family, had always respected the Church, but we refused to be bullied by any churchman.

Still, the threats made me uneasy. If Henry did invade, could I be sure of protecting Richard and Geoffrey if they stayed in Aquitaine? No. I sighed and told them too to go to Louis's court. And I gave them money for weapons and horses for the time Louis would call up his own men to help them strike against Henry in Normandy. I was applauded by my own lords and, surprisingly, many of Henry's who preferred young Henry who wouldn't burden them with the heavy taxes Henry demanded. They wouldn't take up arms against their king, but neither would they support him.

When word came that my sons had invaded Henry's provinces to the north, I dispatched my troops to cross the southern border. We had to strike first before Henry could gather up his army and carry out his threats to capture me and our sons. For weeks we had reports that Henry hadn't stirred, and young Henry and Richard conquered one town and castle after another. I was sure Henry would be defeated soon. Then our son could take his rightful place in England, and Richard could return and live in peace in Aquitaine. I'd no longer have that fear nagging at me that Henry might attack and take over my provinces.

Abruptly he came to life. He said since he couldn't trust many of his nobles, he'd hired ten thousand mercenaries. With the tax money his lords had been forced to pour into his treasury. Quickly he threw back my sons' troops. And almost the same day we heard Louis broke off. His vassals had given the forty days' service they owed their liege each year and declared they were needed at home so they left in spite of their antagonism toward Henry. Without French help, young Henry and Richard hadn't enough men to face their father and had to return to Paris with Louis and wait for spring when Louis would call on his nobles again.

I was dazed at the sudden reversal. Raoul tried to comfort me, but there was little comfort even in his arms. For he too was worried, knowing as we both did that a vengeful Henry would march his riffraff of an army against my lands. Any pale hope there might be disorders in Normandy that would delay him was shattered within days.

Refugees streamed into my walled city of Poitiers with stories I could scarcely bear to hear about burnt vineyards and crops and prisoners sent to Henry's dungeons.

Raoul said decisively, "My love, you cannot stay here. Poitiers will soon be under siege. I do not want you to go, God knows, but you must. You are the person your husband is seeking."

He was right. I knew that, but I said, "How can I desert my country? I can't, not yet, not yet."

I had the same answer for the lords and servants who also begged me to escape before it was too late as I hoped grimly my vassals would somehow be able to stop Henry's advance. But refugees continued to pour in and I knew I must leave. Perhaps my absence would deter Henry from devastating my city. I said, "Tonight, I'll go tonight," thinking drearily I had only one place where I could seek protection—Paris.

But first I had to have an hour with Raoul. I agreed when he whispered, "My love, we don't know when we'll meet again or if we'll—" I put my fingers over his lips so he couldn't say the dreadful words on his tongue. This wouldn't, couldn't be the end for us.

When he came to my room, I stretched out eager arms, and he caught me to him violently as if he'd never let me go. Then he swept me up, almost threw me onto the bed. There were no gentle caresses, no soft murmurings of love. His voice was harsh, his hands demanding and urgent. I was blind and deaf to everything about me except the passion of his embrace, the heavy pounding of my heart when he took me savagely.

I wanted to stay here forever, feeling safe and protected and loved. But Raoul prodded me out of my lazy content. "My dear one, we must plan your escape. We don't know how close some of Henry's soldiers might be. If one of them saw a woman leaving the city secretly at night—"

I stirred, said smiling, "Then they won't see a woman. I'll dress as a knight and ride out with an escort of only four lords so I won't seem too important to anyone who might be watching."

He agreed heavily, knowing he was in command here and couldn't be at my side to guard me from possible dangers. All he could do was to be with me and my escort to the gate and try to smile cheerfully when we went out into the night.

We continued traveling only at night, breathing more freely as Poitiers was further and further behind us. We were nearing the French border. One more night's ride would see us across, we thought gratefully, as we drew up at dawn and started to dismount in the forest to make camp. At that moment the sound of hoofs came from the faint trail ahead of us. We looked at each other and slid back more firmly in our saddles. My knights had their swords out as we leaned forward warily, peering to see if the horses ahead of us were ridden by friends or by enemies.

The hoofbeats became louder, crashing down on broken branches. Then the riders came into view.

At sight of us they stopped short. There was no insignia on their tabards to tell us whose men they were, and equally they couldn't recognize me in my armor. We raised our hands in a brief salute while I pondered how best to pass them—there must have been a dozen. They didn't answer our gesture. Before we could spur our horses on, they charged. I was inept trying to defend myself, but my escort fought bravely to protect me. Bravely and uselessly. In a few minutes the clash was over, and we were their prisoners.

One of my knights said loudly we were willing to pay ransom. Their leader glanced at his men who shrugged or nodded. I breathed in relief until the leader demanded to know who his captives were, and our helmets were jerked off. My hair slid to my waist. Two of their men-at-arms knew me instantly. "The duchess! King Henry will give us a reward lots bigger than any ransom."

They were echoed by the others' curses of delight at catching me. My breathing was shallow as the men shouted with laughter and yelled ribald jokes about how they'd spend the king's reward. I wanted to cry out that I'd double, triple the money the king would offer, but the words stuck in my throat. My heart hammered unevenly. Whatever I promised, they'd never let me go. I must not let them see how frightened I was. With an effort I straightened my shoulders, sat more erectly in the saddle, and my lips stretched stiffly into a smile for my escort. I swallowed, managed to speak this time though my words stumbled together as I thanked them and added swiftly they were dismissed.

It was a moment before they understood my meaning. Then they realized I didn't want them to be prisoners too. Little attention was being given them by my captors. They swung their horses about quickly and plunged into the forest. The thud of retreating hoofs on the camp ground made the men surrounding me curse and shake their fists, but they didn't pursue my escort, not daring —as I'd hoped—to risk my escape too if they scattered to stop my men.

Two days later I stood before Henry. I was bedraggled and still in my knight's tunic, but my head was high. Even without the victory of having my escort gallop to freedom that had heartened me, never would I let him see I was afraid. I said with contempt, "So, like a true knight, you fight women now."

His malicious grin of triumph faded, and his ruddy face grew redder. He sneered, "You call yourself a woman in that gear? But the finest gowns in the world couldn't make you one. You should take lessons from my sweet—No matter. What I see before me is a traitor who deserves a traitor's death. Or do you repent now and would beg for mercy?"

"Mercy from you who're called the devil's pawn? And what treason is there in my trying to leave a city you were about to besiege?"

He gasped for breath, choked out, "Ask why I was attacking. Who would not attack the arch-rebel who led my sons to revolt against my rule? Without your corrupt advice, they wouldn't have raised one sword against me."

I laughed defiantly. "They needed no counseling from me. A two-year-old would understand how you've misused them. The boys are no longer children though you treat them so, giving them empty titles and nothing else, not even a father's love."

He sputtered he loved them dearly. It was I and my ridiculous court who had stolen his sons from him and transformed them into monsters. I think that was what he said. He was starting to gibber, and now I couldn't understand a word he gasped out. His tirade gave me time to hold on to my poise though it frightened me. I expected him to roll on the floor in one of his Angevin rages and roar out who knew what kind of command about me. But abruptly he controlled himself and his bellow to the guard at the door was in his usual voice. "Take this—the duchess to a room in the tower and see that she is guarded day and night."

The order was bad enough, but at least this would give him a few days to remember I'd been his faithful wife until he betrayed me with that wanton Rosamond. I smiled tightly at the guard when he came forward. I turned to follow him, giving him a cool look that dared him to put a hand on me. He gulped and led me through small, drafty rooms to the tower door and up the narrow steps to a chamber that was scarcely large enough for the cot and chair in it and a stand with a basin and a pitcher of water.

As I sat down a servingmaid came in and curtseyed, then spread out the gown she carried over her arm. I said "Thank you," eager to change from my uncomfortable masculine attire into a woman's clothes. And while I couldn't forget I was a prisoner, it was pleasant to have my hair brushed and untangled and to wash, though the basin looked inadequate after my hammered copper bath which was always carried in to be placed near the hearth on chilly days like this.

I would not think of complaints. I'd lost this gamble, but there would be others. With or without my encouragement my sons would take up their revolt again. And Raoul in Poitiers would wait watchfully to back them. Or a guard might be bribed to slip me past sentries. But when the doors were unbolted, it wasn't for my freedom. An officer entered with a formal document which he read from, slowly and distinctly in a tone which was drily official that revealed neither sympathy nor triumph.

I, Eleanor, queen of England and duchess of Aquitaine, was to sail to England where I was to be incarcerated during the king's pleasure. Did that mean forever?

I stared at the officer, paralyzed. I wanted to cry out, I wanted to weep, but the words were too terrible for me to find release so easily. What if my sons did rebel again? I'd be too far away for them to rescue me. And knowing Henry, the guards he'd place around me would not unlock a door for me.

There was one faint hope. The English loved me. Their outrage at having their queen imprisoned might force Henry to free me.

Chapter Eight

I clung to that hope in Barfleur where forty ships waited to take Henry and his prisoners to England. It was July, but a storm whipped the waves into foam and tugged at the anchored vessels. I moved back from the doorway of my hostelry into a small bare room. My hope was threaded through with sadness. I scarcely noticed the ever-watchful guards. It was the white-crested water I didn't want to look at as I remembered the day here twenty years ago and the raging winds on my first journey to England. A loving husband had been beside me then as we sailed through the rough seas to claim his English crown.

Except that I was not beside him, he was the same. Now like then he ignored the threatening skies and violent waves and had his prisoners herded into the ships that cast off one by one. But my companion was Elsie, a dour-faced serving-woman, not the king whose banner whipped arrogantly from the mast of the great vessel leading the fleet.

I would not think of him. I had pleasanter memories to recall. The days of the Crusade, tragic yet exciting. The massacre of our troops and the delight I'd found with my young uncle Raymond. I sighed over him, but I hadn't known him long, and first Henry and later my faithful Raoul had blurred my vision of him. Raoul. Oh God, I wondered, would I ever see that narrow sardonic face again, feeling him holding me passionately? I wrenched my thoughts from him too.

I'd remember the way that little by little I'd won over the English people, my rides through the green countryside to administer the government when Henry was away, and how I'd talked with lords and peasants, aware of their growing friendship. And I thought lovingly of my children, all of them handsome and strong and brave. Except possibly John. I knew little of him since Henry had kept the boy beside him, away from my so-called evil influence.

John's name made me shiver as the icy wind hadn't. It was the day of his birth that I'd learned of Rosamond and that Henry treated her as if she were his wife. Yet he couldn't understand, or pretended not to, why after I'd been pushed from my rightful place, I left him for my beautiful Aquitaine. Or why I encouraged the sons he'd neglected to fight for their rights.

Abruptly I was sick and all thought fled as I lay on the wooden bed fastened to the deck of my small cabin. The servingwoman brought a basin and wiped my face with a warm towel, but she gave no hint whether she was disgusted at the mess to be cleaned or sympathetic to my misery. I didn't care. The most charming companion couldn't cheer me at this moment. All I could do was stifle my groans. I didn't want Elsie to sneer at my weakness when she didn't seem to notice the rolling and jolting of the ship. I could only cling to the knowledge that soon, soon we'd be on land again where it would be warm and sunny and steady.

When we disembarked, wet and chilled, the shore was blessedly steady. But though it was summertime, the weather was cold and rainy. Still my spirits rose. We were riding north toward London, and when we reached the city I'd be cheered by the people. How then could Henry display me as his captive? He offended his English subjects by spending so much time in his continental provinces. He was too practical surely to risk offending them further by mistreating their queen.

I repeated the reassurances to myself as if repetition would make them come true. And why wouldn't they? Yet I was vaguely uneasy when Henry turned aside from the road and took lanes and forest trails to avoid an approaching town. I could think of only one reason for his actions, to be sure the citizens didn't see me. I wanted to throw myself from my horse, escape to the nearest village, but all I could do was rage at my helplessness.

Then I thought I must be wrong. We drew up outside Salisbury in late evening to camp and eat whatever food Henry's untrained cooks would provide. But for once the almost raw meat and thick ale looked appealing for we were so close that we must ride through the town in the morning, and then Henry would see how his subjects loved me. I hummed to myself as I walked toward my pavilion, not caring how closely my guards pressed around me.

One of the men threw the flap back for me. Immediately the escort captain stepped in front of the open space, preventing me from entering. Casually I gestured him aside, knowing that after tomorrow I'd no longer be treated as a prisoner. He didn't move, but stood nervously shuffling his feet and swallowing as if he found it hard to speak. Words came to him at last. "I—I'm sorry—that is, I mean you won't lodge here tonight, madame," I looked at him questioningly. "You—I have orders from His Highness that we are to bring you to—to Salisbury tower now that it's dark."

I shook my head, not understanding. Then, incredulously, understanding too well. To the tower, not to London where there'd be crowds to show outraged anger at the sight of their queen a captive. And when it was dark so that I wouldn't be seen by the citizens of even a small town. By the time news of my imprisonment seeped through the country, it would be too late for spontaneous demonstrations, and Henry could deal with scattered outcries.

I had only a few gowns with me, but I said haughtily, "See that my wardrobe is packed. I will not enter any home with nothing but what I have on. Nor unattended. Call Elsie to ride with me."

The captain appeared uncertain, but evidently he'd had no orders on anything except escorting me to the tower so he nodded agreement. The distance was short, and the mile covered too fast in the pale light of a full moon. I stared with dismay at the shadowed hulk of fortress and tower as we crossed the moat, a dismay that didn't lesson as I was led inside where a score of guards waited to receive me. The captain who'd brought me saluted clumsily and left hastily while I gazed around. My poorest vassal might have a home like this, straw on the floor, narrow slits of windows that the wind blew through but would let in little light, but they'd have decorated the hall, borrowed tapestries to hang on the walls if I were their guest.

There were only three women and a dozen menservants gaping at me. Ignoring them I turned to Elsie, said peremptorily, "Tell these people I wish the straw swept up and fresh rushes laid down. At once. And have one of the women take us to my rooms."

A frightened-looking girl stumbled forward, pushed by the other two, curtseyed awkwardly and led the way from the hall up the curving steps. I followed with Elsie, still dour, trailing after me. I should have said my room, not rooms, as the doors we passed on the way opened on emptiness. My room was slightly larger than the one in Normandy, but I could say little else in its favor except there was a bed with linen hangings, dusty of course but that could be corrected. Tomorrow.

I felt intolerably tired from the day's ride and the crushing disappointment of being sent here. I was afraid that in my exhaustion my jailers might glimpse my anguish, but I would not give them the satisfaction of gloating. I said to the girl to bring me water and a basin and that I wanted some refreshment served to Elsie and me in this room. I could see she was taken aback at a prisoner giving orders but didn't quite dare protest.

The next day, the next weeks went by with the pain in my heart that I must hide from hostile eyes. Each one was as dull and drab as the day before so that I had to force myself out of bed each morning wondering how to get through the long hours stretching ahead of me. Though the servants seemed to have little to do, they accepted any orders I gave sullenly. And Elsie remained as grim-faced as the first hour I'd seen her, speaking only when spoken to. But I made myself smile at all of them as if I were pleased with the solitude in this remote tower. I who'd been surrounded by the gayest court in Europe.

I discovered books and writing materials were forbidden, but at least I was allowed to exercise in the inner court, and every noon I walked briskly around the small flower and vegetable beds no matter what the weather. I'd always been healthy, and I was determined to be in condition against the day I knew I'd be free. That certainty was shadowed when word seeped back that my sons had revolted again but were defeated and had to come to terms with Henry.

He was generous with them, that is, generous for him. He gave three of young Henry's castles to John, but he forgave them, saying they were young and had been misled by—someone older and corrupt. I shrugged at Henry's malice as if it didn't touch me, though I'm sure he said more than the gossip I overheard while pretending not to be listening.

I was contemptuous of myself, straining to hear the whispers of servants as I went through my daily routine of rising, washing, dressing. I made each movement deliberate to spin out the empty time. That was difficult. There never used to be enough hours in the day for all I wanted to do, and now I had to force myself not to hurry through the small grooming tasks, and to walk down the circular stairs slowly to sit in the hall where the serving women spun or wove. And where I continued the despicable eavesdropping.

I had to know what I could of what was happening in the world, and there was no way else to learn. While the chatter seldom went beyond village gossip, it was here I'd heard of my sons' revolt. But not from my sons. Henry must have forbidden my seeing any messages that might have been sent me and also forbidden the servants to give me news they might be told. Another sign of his spite. What harm if every word spoken in the court or the streets were repeated to me? None, but Henry knew how much this reinforcing of my isolation would hurt me.

At the thought I straightened in my chair and rose quickly. I would not let his tactics subdue me. I reached for a mantle and went outdoors. I'd double the times I circled the inner yard though each day the narrow view hurt me more. The vines crawlng up the walls were brown, and the flower beds held only withered stalks now. It might be far longer than I'd hoped before my release, but I'd make sure I was ready when the moment came.

The slightest anticipation of freedom brought as always the image of Raoul. When, when would I see him again? I craved his nearness. If he were with me, his loving companionship would change the tower from a prison to a lighthearted home. The ever-present pain of loneliness deepened at memory of him. I must not think of him. When I finished my exercising, I'd look over my few gowns, have a seam mended or a hem turned or refashion a neckline. I was careful with the bliauds so that if someone from the bustling, fascinating world outside should visit me, I'd be properly clad.

As the days grew colder and there was the first sifting of snow, a messenger did arrive. An unimportant middle-aged man but a man free to move about the country, one who could tell me of London, and fortunately he was garrulous. I greeted him coolly, not showing how avid I was for the unimportant scraps of news he mentioned of London and the court as he gave me a sealed scroll. I opened it slowly, glanced at it with pretended indifference.

In spite of myself, my eyes widened as I read. Henry was offering me freedom of a sort. But what a sort! He'd arrange a divorce between us, and I could leave Salisbury. If I gave up my worldly possessions, and if I retired to Fontevrault on the Continent where I'd be named the abbess. The thought of the vast abbey and its welcoming sisters and monks whom I'd often given grants to was tempting set against the cold harshness of my tower. And the very word freedom was like cool water on parched lips. Raoul would be near. Though for an abbess out of reach.

But give up my Aquitanian possessions? Never. The answer came instantly. Only then did I wonder indifferently why Henry wanted not separation but a divorce. I doubted if it was to marry Rosamond. He wouldn't raise a knight's daughter that high, and she was already wife to him in all but name. I shrugged aside the questions, tossed the scroll into the low fire on the hearth and said, "That is my reply, sir. Tell the king I refuse his conditions."

I heard no more from Henry until a hot summer day. Our youngest daughter Joanna was to be married to King William of Sicily and—reluctantly I was sure and only because Joanna had begged him—he invited me to Winchester to see her before she left for her new home. I wondered if he'd use my visit to tempt me with the feeling of freedom so he could again press his conditions on me. A travesty of freedom in return for giving up my titles of duchess of Aquitaine and queen of England. I smiled contemptuously, then forgot him in my delight that I'd see Joanna.

When I rode to Westminster, every lane, every hedgerow, every field seemed to sparkle with green to my eager eyes. The sky was a deeper blue and the towns warm and inviting nestling among the vivid hills. And my lovely Joanna was lovelier than ever, slim and elegant. We fell into each other's arms, eyes half blinded with tears. I whispered a fervent thank-you to God for these few days away from my prison and another thank-you because Henry was away.

Had he absented himself, afraid some faint stirring of our old passion might soften him? But he'd left orders because I was aware I was always under scrutiny. I was so used to being watched I was indifferent to that and savored every hour with Joanna when sometimes we just gazed at each other and sometimes both talked at once, wanting to share each small happening of the day.

I was sorry only that none of my other children were at the palace. Henry wasn't chancing that my sons might be influenced into taking up the sword for me. But Joanna told me of all of them, how young Henry journeyed to Paris whenever he could elude Henry's vigilance and later always used the excuse his wife Marguerite was homesick and needed to see her family. More surprising was the news that Richard was betrothed to another of Louis's daughters, Alais, Marguerite's sister. As was the custom, she'd been brought to live in England. I longed to see her, see if she were worthy of my favorite son, but she was in London.

I pushed aside the disappointment, and Joanna and I had long conversations on her trousseau as she said I had far more sense of style than she had. Then she stared at me, her mouth open in astonishment, as she must have realized my own clothes weren't in the latest fashion, and that they'd been worn too often. She said nothing then nor when we sadly said good-bye. Though her usual cheerful humor returned when I assured her that somehow I'd be free again and would visit her in her new kingdom of Sicily.

I carried the memory of her glowing face back to Salisbury, and the picture lightened the gloomy tower. The atmosphere lightened again when great packages of cloaks and furs and robes arrived, sent by Joanna. So she had noticed how scanty and unfashionable my wardrobe was. I was carefully unfolding a bliaud of deep blue with a flared skirt and wide flowing sleeves, holding it up to enjoy the cut of the gown and its silky texture, when Elsie came into the room.

She didn't enter silently and grim as usual but with animation in her face and could hardly wait to speak. She said breathlessly, "I know, madame, we're not to tell you any news but this—I think you have a right to hear. That strumpet Rosamond Clifford that the king has been flaunting before us good citizens, she says she's sorry for her sins and is retiring to a nunnery at Godstow to do penance. She should repent, that adulteress."

I laughed. Partly at her acid disapproval of royal immorality, but more because I'd refused to go into a convent and now one of Henry's women was there. I wondered how he felt when he was deprived of his precious love and what he'd do now. I didn't wonder long.

To my amazement the untalkative Elsie had more to say though she seemed to have difficulty in finding the right words. "And—and it's said everywhere that the king has—has a new mistress."

I said indifferently, "So I'd expect. Who is she?" I was more intrigued at my actually conversing with Elsie than with learning the woman's name.

Elsie reddened. "He thinks it's a secret, that no one knows, but everyone does. Except you, I mean." She stopped abruptly. "I—I—perhaps I shouldn't—" Then her voice roughened vindictively. "That—that girl—they call her a princess, Princess Alais—a wanton though she's hardly out of her childhood—"

"Not Alais, my Richard's betrothed." I was sure I'd heard wrong.

"Oh yes, madame, that's the one, the whore. I don't know why he believes no one suspects his sin. Why, he fondles her in front of half the court, then finds some excuse to draw her into his bedroom. And—and every time her father insists she be married at once, the king says yes to the French ambassador but somehow there's never a wedding."

I flared. "And there never will be a wedding." I thought, enraged, that Richard would not, could not marry his father's leavings. I gazed at Elsie considering. Did this sudden breaking of her dour silence mean this ugly story destroyed her loyalty to Henry? That she saw me now as an ill-treated queen, not a traitor who deserved to be imprisoned? I'd nothing to lose by trying her out. I said softly, "Richard's head is usually in the clouds, planning this or that military tactic. He may not have heard the whispers, and no one would dare tell him to his face. I wish I could write him. No, that's impossible. Even if I had something to write with, the letter would be burned before it left the tower."

Elsie gulped, and gulped again. "No, no, madame. I—I can get you a quill and a scrap of parchment and see that it's put in the right hands without none of them soldiers suspecting a thing."

"You would? Oh Elsie!" I smiled at her radiantly and put my arms around her. "You'd be my friend forever."

At my embrace she smiled stiffly as if it had been a long time since her lips had drawn back for anything except a sneer. "You—you honor me, madame."

"It's you who're being honorable. I will write Richard about his betrothed and tell him to slip away to Aquitaine where Henry would have trouble reaching him. If anyone tries to stop him, he can say our vassals there are stirring up trouble, and only he can settle the differences. Even Henry realizes that though Richard isn't twenty yet, everyone says he's a great military leader." As I scratched out my message with a blunt quill, I wondered how that slut Alais could so much as glance at Henry when she must know their affair would endanger the possibility of having Richard.

My eyes shone as I handed Elsie the rolled letter. Between us, with any luck at all, we'd rescue my dearest son from a repugnant marriage that Henry, if he tired of Alais, might try to force the boy into. I was so full of that thought that I scarcely noticed at dinner that the meat was tough and greasy as usual and the fish tasted rancid. The chill drafts didn't disturb me for I had Joanna's furs around my shoulders and to spread over my bed.

But the cold empty days were longer than I'd ever known them as I waited to hear if my message had reached Richard. I walked endless hours in the courtyard, begged Elsie for something to quiet my restless hands. She understood for she too was restless and afraid. If my message to Richard were intercepted, there'd be questions as to who had aided me, and she probably wouldn't be able to hide her guilt. And I'd be under stricter confinement, perhaps not allowed outside even in the inner yard, and deprived of my one friend.

She found work for us, the kind that once I would have scorned, helping the women servants mend small garments sent by the parish priest for the poor of the neighborhood. That helped pass the anxious hours and gradually the three women forgot their stringent orders and gossiped casually about village affairs—the sheep stealer who was caught, the latest bride who had to get married, a small inheritance that helped pay a farmer's debts, traders who planned to journey to London. At the last word their eyes brightened. They'd never been so far away themselves, and were eager to hear the tales the men would return with. Perhaps more tidbits about the king and the princess—They stopped, dumb with embarrassment as they recalled I was with them.

I said easily, "That story? I—" I stopped too. I mustn't let them know it was familiar to me as they would immediately guess Elsie had told me. "I'm not surprised at any story about Henry. But perhaps this is a different princess than the one the rumors mentioned when I was in Aquitaine." There hadn't been such a rumor, but they wouldn't know that, and my words put them at their ease.

They exclaimed together that yes, yes, this was a different one, Princess Alais was probably still at home in Paris before I came to—to the tower. They stumbled over the last phrase that reminded them of who I was, their queen as well as a prisoner. I smiled, looking mildly interested, and they went back to their gossiping that relieved the monotonous task of mending. But whether they spoke further of Alais or some other subject, I didn't know. I could only think I was glad Elsie's remarks were confirmed, and that I hadn't been wrong in trying to warn Richard to hurry to Aquitaine. But when, when would I hear if he'd received my message?

I was on edge for another month before a roughly clad young man arrived at the tower and demanded to see his kinswoman Elsie. I was in the hall when he was allowed to enter, but he didn't look at me. I eyed him sharply as Elsie went up to speak privately to him. For all his unkempt clothes and uncombed hair, it was apparent to me that he wasn't the countryman he pretended to be. He'd forgotten to change his elaborate leather boots. And while he'd smeared his face, he must have automatically washed the dirt from his hands, which were far too well cared for to belong to anyone but a gentleman of the court.

I turned my head toward the smoky fire so no one would guess at the excitement rising within me. If this man were from Henry, he'd be dressed as an official with an armed escort behind him. So he must, must have been sent by Richard. He swung away at last, saying in a loud voice he was glad he could give Elsie news of her family and left. The loudness didn't conceal the fact that his voice was too smooth, and he'd forgotten his disguise again as he strode toward the drawbridge instead of shambling as he'd done when he arrived.

I stood up, said sharply, "I hope talking with your kinsman won't make you overlook your duties, Elsie. We'll go to my room to—" to what?— "to see if you can coil my hair in that new style I saw when I was in Winchester."

Upstairs Elsie closed the door quickly behind her. "Did you really think he was my cousin, madame? He was from—you'll never guess—he was from Prince Richard! He just pretended to be a farmer so he'd be allowed in. But he was from your son!"

I leaned forward eagerly. "Yes, yes, but what message did he bring?"

She beamed, "Didn't I tell you? Prince Richard is safe in Poitiers. The man said he was also told to tell you," Elsie appeared puzzled, "that some count, I think he said the name was Raoul de Faye, is in good health and thinks of you every day. Why would he say that when it's your son you were worried about?"

Through my relieved laughter I managed to say, "I have relatives, my dear, besides my children." I wanted to sing, to dance, to cry out to the world that Richard had escaped, that Raoul remembered me as I did him. In spite of my happiness, the news made my confinement harder to bear, I wanted so much to be with them, to see them. I swallowed a dry sob, lifted my head. I'd borne the unhappy years with dignity. I must not lose that now my heart was lighter. I thought of Henry's holding me here so long, and anger, as I'd hoped, stiffened me as delight could not. I said, "We should go down, Elsie. They were about to serve dinner," I grimaced at the thought of what the meal would be, "and I want to exercise while there's still some sunlight on this gray day."

I moved toward the door, stopped and swung back smiling in derision at myself. Had I criticized Richard's messenger for his carelessness in disguising himself? I pulled out the silver pins from my hair. "Elsie! The new style, quickly. I'd forgotten my excuse for bringing you up here."

We looked at each other and laughed. We'd both forgotten. Hurriedly she reached for a comb, twisted my long hair into a coil and shaped it around my head. From what I could see in the dull mirror, the style wasn't becoming but that didn't matter. Though when I sat down to eat some sort of thick soup with bread crusts floating on the lukewarm surface, the women said flatteringly the change made me look even more attractive.

I thanked them, thinking I'd accomplished something these last months. Before then they'd have sneered or pretended not to notice. The pleasanter atmosphere warmed me. We were becoming almost like a small family. Even the guards weren't as sullen as they had been and on occasions whispered flirtatious nonsense when I passed them. My imprisonment was almost bearable. If only the great drawbridge didn't always block my way to so much as a walk to the village.

At least it no longer blocked out what was happening beyond the high walls. There was more gossip of Henry and Alais and of Alais's father—I found it hard to remember Louis had once been my husband—who was infuriated at the stories and demanded vainly that Alais and Richard be married at once. I wondered if that would lead to war. No, Louis might storm, but he was futile in military affairs. Unless he had an ally.

He had one I found the next day. My eyes flew wide when one of the women said casually, shaking her head, "It ain't right. Do you know what the blacksmith in the village told me this morning? That that Prince Henry, him that was crowned king of England, is fighting his own father again in Normandy, riding beside the king of France. What is the world coming to when children rise up against their parents?"

The others agreed indifferently that the old days were better, but they were too far from any war to be interested in some distant disagreement. They preferred stories of romance and seduction in Salisbury or rumors of court life and instantly returned to their favorite subjects. I smiled as if I too were intrigued by the tale of a shepherd meeting some village hussy at midnight, but I heard only occasional words.

Henry must be on the Continent by now. If young Henry and Louis should defeat my husband, wouldn't they demand that I be freed? The possibility sang through my blood. But I mustn't let the thought make me too optimistic. How often was Henry defeated? Any slight hope I might not have been able to suppress was shattered by sad news. While young Henry was valiantly defending a castle from his father's army, he came down with a high fever. French physicians were called, but they said they could do nothing.

Night after night I walked the floor. Perhaps his illness was exaggerated? It must be. He was too young to die. But his youth didn't save him. The story flew across the country, even taking precedence in the household over gossip. Young Henry was dead. I wept when I heard, could not stop my tears. My eldest son—if only I could have been there to ease his last minutes. My hatred for Henry leaped high at the cruelty that denied our son whatever consolation I could have brought him.

My tears flowed for days until Elsie, patting me awkwardly on the shoulder, said the archdeacon of Wells was below and wished to see me. I wiped my eyes quickly and touched my reddened lids with rice powder, then went down to the hall where the archdeacon waited to tell me the tragic news. His voice was so kind and sympathetic when he spoke that I made a mistake. I nodded. "It was dreadful. I still cannot resign myself to—" I choked back a gasp at his surprised expression, horrified I'd let him see I'd known about young Henry before he told me.

When the archdeacon wrote Henry that he'd been with me, would he—perhaps not meaning to—let Henry know I had my own sources of information? If he did, Henry would change my household, send me servants who'd make certain I heard nothing of the outside world, as my present servants had during the first years of my imprisonment. I could not bear the thought of being so isolated again.

My mind touched and rejected one explanation after another, then I said in a broken voice, "You—you see I saw my son in a dream, lying dead. He was—was wearing two crowns, one the English crown, but the other was a circle of flashing light. While I can't yet resign myself to his death, surely the second crown means he's happily in heaven, don't you believe?"

He agreed gravely, saying only a mother would be vouchsafed such a miraculous dream. Then he eyed me closely and frowned. I wondered uneasily what I'd said that made him appear so disapproving, forgot it when he bowed and left, giving me time to think over my own words. While I hadn't dreamed of young Henry, I had a suddenly serene feeling that I was right and he was at heavenly peace, a peace he'd seldom known in his short life. And now—I was astonished the idea hadn't occurred to me before—now Richard was Henry's heir. Unless—would Henry pass over him for his favorite, John? He'd named John king of Ireland though little of that country had been conquered. Would he make that up to the boy by giving him England?

Surprise brushed aside the disquieting question when I sat down to dinner the next afternoon. My table was laid with fresh linen, there was a ewer of red wine next to a glass goblet and there was a tray with steaming roast of beef. I glanced around, my eyes wide. The women servants and most of the men were smiling. Elsie bent over me, her face beaming. "The archdeacon—he was angry when he saw how thin you are. He went to the kitchen and saw the meal being prepared for you. He said he'd take the re—responsibility," she stumbled over the unaccustomed word, "on himself, and that you was to be fed as your position demanded, not like some disgraced scullery maid, and wine too."

She poured out a glass, and I sipped it gratefully. The archdeacon's thoughtfulness lightened my heart a little though it was still weighted with young Henry's death. The courtesy made my imprisonment not quite so unbearable, knowing that even a stranger from outside could feel kindly toward me. Perhaps there were more like him who might persuade Henry that I'd been a captive too long.

The hope that stirred within me flamed higher a fortnight later. I had a letter from Henry written by his scribe that invited me to meet the king in Windsor for Christmas. Did the death of our son make him soften toward me? Or—my nature had grown suspicious from these years of disappointments—could he want something from me? No, I

would not think that. I laughed happily as I told
Elsie to pack my clothes, musing over the delight
of seeing at least some of my family again.

Chapter Nine

When I reached Windsor I didn't wait to change
but hurried into the great hall with its bright wall
tapestries glowing in the pale winter sunlight. I
saw Geoffrey first. He came forward quickly, a
dark young woman shyly holding his arm, and
said proudly, "You must meet my wife, Mother.
Constance, you know, the heiress to Brittany. Isn't
she lovely?"

I agreed laughing. "But married! You seem such
children to be man and wife though I'm sure
you're happy together." I was so happy myself to
see any of my family again that everyone appeared
happy.

I turned as John's voice sounded behind me.
"How delightful to have you with us for Christmas, Mother. You look beautiful as always." I
leaned forward to kiss him. He still wasn't tall like

his brothers, and his waist was thickening, but his smile was charming and I could forget my distress the day of his birth and that he was more his father's son than mine.

Beyond the door I could hear the clatter of Henry's booted feet, and a moment later he strode into the room, beaming at me. He said genially, "I'm pleased you look so well, my dear, it's so long since we've been together," as if he weren't the reason for our separation. I smiled and thanked him. There was some satisfaction in the thought that my enforced idleness and my daily exercising were kind to my appearance. I looked younger than Henry, who'd aged in his frantic warring to control his sons and vassals. Though that was little comfort when I didn't know how long it would be before I had to return to my drab life in Salisbury.

I could not ask when that would be, could only show my appreciation for today when we sat together after trestles were set up for dinner, and I saw how Henry had spent lavishly on wine, spices, beef and exotic sweetmeats to make this holiday special. It was Sunday so there wasn't the usual fasting the Church imposed on Christmas Eve.

Christmas day I woke to the sight of snow drifting across the fields and plastering the round tower with spirals of white. I stretched, was about to huddle under the blankets again. Then my eyes snapped open. I rose and ran to the fire burning on the hearth while the castle maids brought in a copper bath. I washed quickly. This wasn't another day in prison when I'd wonder how to fill the endless hours. It was Christmas, and in spite of the weather there would be mock tournaments and archery contests and later dancing in the great hall.

Even with a fur-lined mantle I shivered through the jousting and archery, but it was so delightful to be out where I could see beyond gray walls that I didn't leave my place beside Henry on the hastily built tiers until the last arrow was drawn. I missed Richard, who'd have won every tournament, but I was glad he was safely in Aquitaine until I learned why I'd been invited to Windsor.

Henry gave no indication of his purpose through the morning events in the fields or through the leisurely dinner with its roast capons and beef and pork and fish and fruits and candied sweets and red and white wines. Henry as usual gulped down his food and walked restlessly back and forth between courses, but Geoffrey and Constance and John and I talked animatedly of Brittany, Constance's home, and of the latest news from London while we enjoyed each of the elegantly prepared dishes, and later I watched the young people dancing to lute and tambourine.

Not until the instruments were laid aside and most of the guests had drifted away with Henry's permission did he tell me what he had in mind. We were sitting amicably in front of a roaring fire speaking idly of a new tax law when he interrupted himself to say pleasantly, "I'm sure you appreciate this taste of freedom, my dear wife, and would like it to go on forever." He paused, and my heart beat heavily as I waited. Did this mean he wanted to give up Alais and have me with him again? Or did he wish—

I couldn't stop myself from asking the question. "Do you intend to suggest a divorce again and have me retire to a convent?" My voice was hard.

"No, no. I want to say you can return to your old position at court as the queen if—" He paused again. Queen. Excitement flared within me, but the years of imprisonment made me cautious. I repeated, "If?"

"A small matter. If you'll just sign a document I've had drawn up."

I said carefully, "I hope it's one I *can* sign."

He frowned at the hint of defiance. "After ten years of prison, I'm sure you'll find it easy to agree. This is only to have a fairer distribution of territory among our sons. You know how John has always been called John Lackland. That is not right. He should have a proper inheritance. There is one way to manage that. I wish you to dispossess Richard and make John heir of Aquitaine."

I stiffened. Freedom. But take my duchy from Richard and give it to John? I bit my lip as if I were pondering the idea. "It's true the boy wasn't given provinces like his brothers since there were none left then to bestow on him. But since then you've made him King of Ireland. Isn't that a grand enough title? And—well, you know how troublesome my vassals can be. Could John handle them as Richard has?"

"Ha! You believe Richard can do anything. By God's eyes, he does nothing but make trouble."

I held on to my reasonable tone. "Richard has the help of Raoul de Faye," I said the name softly, "to bring my vassals to heel. Since the two work so well together, isn't it better Richard continue in his post there?"

Henry's face reddened. "No! John must have his chance. I'll send for the document now."

"Wait. If I signed my provinces over to John, what would Richard have in return?"

His voice roughened. "That isn't your affair. You seem to forget what you'll have in return, your freedom."

"I haven't forgotten, lord king. But you should forget your document. I wouldn't sign it if I'd been imprisoned for a hundred years."

His eyes rolled up, showing the whites. "And so you will be with our stupid stubbornness. You go back to Salisbury in the morning." He stomped out of the hall.

For a moment I hunched forward, thinking of the grim tower and dreary, lonely days. Then my shoulders straightened. I came of a proud family, not easily defeated. And I knew that even if I were tempted to sign away Aquitaine, I could never force my fingers to scrawl my name on Henry's document. If I did, what would happen to Richard when he was deprived of the duchy we both loved? He wasn't promised so much as a castle in exchange. And Henry might be planning to make his favorite John his sole heir. Unhappily I could do nothing about England or Henry's Continental provinces, but I could preserve the inheritance Richard had from me. If I were willing to pay the price. And I was.

I held my head high as I returned to the gray tower. I was a prisoner. But I was a victor too. I must remember that when I rose each morning wondering how to fill the long empty hours of the day stretching ahead of me while I yearned for beauty and gaiety and laughter and songs. Still I had my memories. I drew them out to relive them, making it a game to keep my mind alert. I went over the days of my own brilliant court. And of the crusade and Byzantium and my uncle Raymond whom I'd loved. And after the dull years with Louis, there were Henry's and my first years together when passion between us was high, and those times in his absence when I'd ruled for him and enjoyed the taste of power.

I didn't want to think beyond that. Rosamond in a convent didn't stir me now though she'd forced me to break with Henry and encourage our sons to arm against him. But the thought of Henry bedding Alais hurt deeply. The French were clamoring again that Richard marry her, and Henry as always said soon, soon, though I was sure he'd no intention of giving her up. At least with Richard in Aquitaine, my son couldn't be forced into an unsavory marriage.

Within months Richard was in an even stronger

position. News came that stunned all Christendom, so shocking that my most silent guard spoke of it openly. The holy City of Jerusalem had been captured by Saladin and his Saracens. Western Europe was appalled at losing the sacred shrine. The people would not let the disaster go unchallenged. When archbishops and bishops traveled across the countries begging young men to make up a new crusade, recruits volunteered by the hundreds.

Among the first to join was Richard, and then Louis's eldest son who was now king of France, Philip Augustus. I was proud of Richard's taking the Cross. And relieved because now there would be no more talk of weddings. I was saddened though at the thought of Richard's being so far from me. I wasn't able to see him in Aquitaine, but I felt more at ease knowing he was just across the Channel. Still, it would take months to raise the money that would be needed and to organize untrained men into an army ready to fight against the disciplined Saracens.

War. The word was on everyone's lips. But soon no one spoke of a holy war. The crusade was forgotten because Henry took advantage of the confusion in France where crowds gathered about the preachers and made a quick thrust to retake Gisors, which had been returned to the French after young Henry's death. I wondered, now that Richard was Henry's heir, if my son would stand beside his father.

Unbelievably I heard within days that Henry

would not acknowledge Richard was his heir though he must know that would push Richard into an alliance with the French. Yet for myself that gave me hope. If Gisors would hold out with Richard's and Philip Augustus's backing, Henry would be defeated and I—I might be released. So my heart was with Richard, but my hopes had been disappointed too often for me to be optimistic.

Again there was head shaking among the women about the degeneracy of a son taking up arms against his sire. I wished to defend Richard, but I said nothing. I wanted them to forget I was with them so they would speak freely for without their chatter I'd be completely isolated. But one day, a week after we'd heard of Richard joining the French king, I came upon them giggling delightedly over some fresh tidbit of gossip. I caught Richard's name and Philip's and something about a public confession. I glanced at them inquiringly as I automatically reached for a torn peasant's smock to be mended. Abruptly they gulped and were silent and went back to their work.

I wanted to jerk the garments out of their hands and demand they tell me what news pleased them so greatly, but I went on sewing, knowing they wouldn't answer, so it was best I pretend to be unaware of their secret gloating. My guess was that the two young men were involved with some girls or women of the French court. But why should they hesitate to tell me such a tale when they shared the stories of Henry and Alais with me? Surely Henry's sin was the greater, seducing his son's betrothed. But perhaps now they thought of Henry as I did—as my jailer, not my husband—and they knew my deep feeling for Richard. Still, the liaison of a young man and a girl was too common to us for anyone to be shocked. I'd ask Elsie when we were alone.

To my surprise Elsie was as tight-lipped as the women servants. She said virtuously she seldom listened to gossip since it was often ill-natured so she hadn't heard what all the whispering was about. I didn't believe her and told her so angrily. At that she looked woebegone, but it was hours before I could draw the tale from her. I sank into a chair as she spoke, staring at her horrified. There were rumors, just rumors, about Richard and Philip. What if they did usually share a bed in Paris and on the march? Didn't that show they were merely fond of each other's company?

I said, "Yes, yes, it must be," trying to make my voice sound ordinary. "But there was something about—about a confession, a—a public confession."

"Oh that? That was before he met the French king. It was nothing at all." But her expression gave away the fact it was important, and she didn't meet my eyes. I gazed at her steadily until she had to look back at me. Her face was crimson, and she stuttered when she answered. "I s-s-suppose s-someone else will tell you if I d-don't. I was j-just

—well, just—m-madame, must I tell you?" I nodded firmly. "It was only—it was after Prince Richard took the Cross, he walked up to the bishop and said he must c-confess before he was worthy to be a crusader. And—and he said that he had lain—had relations with young men. B-but he didn't say anything about the French king."

I thought dazedly, No, you said it was before they'd met. I'd known men at every court who had such inclinations and was indifferent to how they chose to live. But my own son! The knowledge was intolerable that Richard who was a great warrior, the winner in any tournament, should have this—this abnormality. Briefly I admired his courage in proclaiming it to the world. Then I remembered it strengthened the rumors of the attachment between him and Philip.

I knew nothing of Philip—their friendship could be innocent—but why didn't Richard avoid a situation that gave rise to gossip? And why hadn't he confessed in private? Oh Richard, my most loved son, what must be done? The answer came quickly. He must marry. Not Alais, but some young princess who was too sheltered to be told any scandals.

I noticed absently that Elsie had crept out of the room. It didn't matter that she hadn't waited to be dismissed. Nothing mattered except that Richard must marry, and soon. I started to think of possible brides, and stopped tight-lipped. What did it matter if I could list five or ten or twenty? I was helpless. If I wrote Henry, I knew he'd only grin, that is, if I could get writing materials. He'd retort that Richard was already betrothed; besides, what girl would accept our son who'd been corrupted by his mother and her frivolous Aquitanian court? As if he'd set a shining example of how royalty should live.

I tried to resign myself to this fact of Richard's nature, and little by little I found I was no longer shocked. Whatever he did, he was still my loved son. And he was at war, in danger. That thought brought me out of my absorption in his public confession, and I was again eager for any scrap of news from the Continent. The women reluctantly gave up their gossip when soldiers who'd served their forty days returned with some word of the conflict. At first Henry's every attack was successful. As I'd expected.

But then came a report that he was being forced to retreat to the north. The man added that perhaps that was because Richard had sent to Aquitaine for more troops, and they'd joined him swiftly, led by—what was the name?—my deputy. I thought breathlessly, Raoul had marched instantly into Normandy himself, knowing that if Henry were defeated, he and Richard could demand I be released.

Glowing at the thought, I didn't hear what the man said next. I asked him to repeat himself, and he said disinterestedly, "It was nothing about your family, madame. It was only that the Aqui-

tanians helped to force the king to retreat, but
their leader—that deputy—was killed in the first
assault.''

I said conversationally, "Raoul—Count de
Faye—he's—dead?" His remark had come too
quickly after the news Raoul was fighting for me. I
could not absorb it. I stood up from the hall bench,
said, "I must walk in the yard now," realizing only
that I must get away, be alone. Outside the
merciful numbness slid away. Raoul. I'd never see
him again, hear his tenderly wooing voice, feel his
arms about me. I thought dazedly, This stabbing
pain is what the troubadours mean when they sing
of a heart breaking. My passionate heart,
Raymond had said, that I would always follow.
Now I had only Richard to spend that passion on.
Richard and my memories of my dark sardonic
cousin, of our last hour together. I must not weep
though Raoul's name echoed through me like a
tolling bell. I must not let anyone guess my
feelings. After hiding my love for him through all
these years, surely I could also conceal my grief?

I did, I discovered when I found that Elsie
believed any sadness I showed, absent-minded
moments or misty eyes at night, were for Richard,
and she apologized abjectly for having told me of
his public confession. I assured her that she'd
been right to let me know since everyone else did,
but I didn't add that Richard's weakness now
seemed merely a peccadillo, easily forgiven.

Still, since others might have sharper eyes than

Elsie's, I again asked eager questions of the war. After all, I asked myself, what was my private sorrow compared to the greater conflict which caused so many other women to mourn as I did? And Richard was still in danger. For weeks we heard nothing, and I was in agony over my son. If Henry could call up more forces and swing back from his retreat and managed to cut down Richard and his allies, the king would not forgive Richard this time.

When finally news came, we gaped at each other, not quite believing. Henry hadn't gathered up more men. He was so ill he could not fight on and agreed he would negotiate. Henry negotiate? Yes, he would. By bits and pieces from traders or returning soldiers we heard the terms for peace offered to him. I thought if Henry hadn't been sick, he would be furious at the conditions. He was to do homage to Philip for his provinces on the Continent, give up all border castles, he must take no revenge on the barons who'd deserted him for Richard. And acknowledge Richard as his rightful heir. Henry agreed with all the terms, but I was certain he'd forget his promises once he was recovered.

Surprisingly the next messenger who arrived came from Richard. The man had been at Henry's fortress where the king had been carried on a litter. The man spoke slowly as if working up to something dramatic. In spite of Henry's illness, he demanded to know the names of his barons who'd fought against him. Reluctantly an aide unrolled the list, but Henry listened to only the first name. John .

He shrieked, "No, no, no, not John. I loved him more than all my sons. Take the list away. I care for no one, for nothing, now," and turned his head toward the wall. The messenger paused, went on dramatically, "Within the week the king died almost alone. Most of his servants and soldiers left him after his defeat. The few who stayed brought him to the abbey of Fontevrault for burial."

I thought vaguely, to the abbey where he'd wanted to send me. Yet I felt an unexpected compassion, and tears stung my eyes as I imagined how those last, almost solitary days must have wounded Henry who always had a vast entourage about him as he hurled himself against this or that obstacle, never at peace with himself or with others. For a moment I visualized the youthful restless Henry and his rough virile loving. He couldn't be dead.

The messenger shifted his feet, cleared his throat to attract my attention. "An escort will arrive tomorrow, madame, to take you to Westminster."

I was as stunned as though the news were bad. Tomorrow I'd put this prison behind me forever. My tears for Henry dried. Weep for his solitude? His had lasted a few days, mine had been for years. At his orders. Orders which had put a wall between Raoul and me forever.

I half-whispered, "Raoul," then I smiled. I'd

never forget him, but my love of life was too strong to let the future be darkened. I could almost feel his presence, feel that he was delighting as I was that, after so long, I was free.

Chapter Ten

In her joy at seeing me after all these years, Alicia forgot herself when I dismounted in the courtyard of Westminster Palace. Instead of curtseying, she hugged me so tightly I could scarcely breathe. I kissed her on both plump cheeks while tears misted our eyes and we smiled tremulously. The sight of her brought home more forcibly that I was really free. Our arms around each other, we strolled toward the palace under the hot summer sun .

Inside I gazed lovingly at the rooms. Had I really once criticized Becket's furnishings and had him bring in tables and chairs more ornate than those he'd ordered? The plainest stool looked beautiful to me, and I almost felt lost in the chambers that appeared vast to me now. I laughed delightedly. My ladies stared at me puzzled, except for Elsie whom I'd brought with me from Salisbury. She understood why the elegance and spaciousness caused laughter after years in a gloomy tower.

I must not forget that imprisonment, I thought, and so set right some of the evils Henry had left behind him. For I was more than free. I was a ruler again. Richard wrote he'd join me as soon as he'd settled his affairs on the Continent. In the meantime I was to be in command of his English kingdom. I was happy, not only at the power given me but planning how to use it for him.

My vassals accepted him in Aquitaine, but he'd spent so little time in England that I was told his subjects considered him a foreigner. I must change that, make sure the country would be loyal to him. I sent word to the lords to come to court to make their oaths of allegiance through me to him as their new king. They did so willingly, but that wasn't enough. The people too must accept him gladly. It was up to me to bring Richard and them closer. I would make a royal tour of England.

I was cheered at each town and castle where our procession drew up with pennants fluttering, but Richard's name was seldom mentioned. I hunched over the hearth in the palace at York one evening, the fire giving off the scent of pine logs and acorns, thinking I had to do more than let the people see Richard's mother. They must be made aware he was their king. Absently I thought how welcome leaping flames like these would have been in the tower. At that I suddenly straightened. Of course, hadn't I resolved to remember my years as a captive? I'd correct some of Henry's evils, but

I'd do so in Richard's name. Henry had been a great king, I admitted, in bringing some order to the country, but his forestry laws were barbaric.

In the morning when we met in the great hall for a breakfast of ale and bread and bacon, I spoke to a knight, Sir Basil, who'd been left in charge of the palace while his master was overseas. "I've been told the jails in the town and in the tower dungeons are overflowing." He nodded, surprised. "I wish to know what crimes the prisoners have been charged with."

His surprise deepened, but he said quickly, "I will have a list made, Your Highness. It should be ready by tomorrow or the next day."

I said crisply, "Today." I knew too well how each day can be insupportable to the imprisoned. Within hours I was given the list. My eyes slid down the names. Three were in for murder. Their names I crossed out, but the others were in jail for breaking Henry's forestry laws. I said, "I wish to see the rest of these out in the courtyard at once."

They were herded into the yard, gray shuffling men, pale from the months or years out of the sun and fresh air. I stepped up on a dais that had been hastily built for me, said in a clear, carrying voice, "Men of England, my son Richard who is your king has asked me to see that justice is done in this great country of ours. I have noted the offenses you have been charged with, trespassing on our late king's forest lands. For your crime you don't know if you will be mutilated or hanged for killing a royal deer or boar to feed your family." I paused. There was a deathly silence from the prisoners who probably were wondering if they were to be sentenced now for their misdeeds, and puzzled glances from the household staff and the soldiers guarding the prisoners.

I went on more quietly. Every word would have been heard if I'd whispered. "King Richard says that trespassing on royal lands is no longer a crime. From this moment you are all free men."

If possible the stunned silence deepened. Then there was a roar, "Richard! Long live King Richard!"

Smiling gratefully I thanked them in his name. They scarcely heard me as they rushed toward a gate I signaled to be opened, afraid no doubt that if they lingered their newfound freedom might be cancelled. I turned toward Sir Basil. "King Richard will have all the prisons in the country opened for those who're there only for breaking the forest laws of the late king."

The knight looked astonished and then highly pleased as he nodded vigorously. "Your son is a great king. Those laws were inhuman."

I wondered idly if he too had been guilty of poaching and by good luck had escaped King Henry's wardens. I wondered too what Richard would say about my freeing these men, but I wasn't overly concerned. He'd probably laugh that this was an inexpensive way to buy men's loyalty, a valuable talent in a regent.

Now as our cavalcade swung back toward London, Richard was acclaimed for his clemency, and his name was cheered as often as mine. But there was more to be done, government tasks that didn't have the instant appeal of releasing prisoners whose only crime was to try to feed their families.

I met with members of the exchequer, asking them to set up a new standard coinage that would be accepted throughout England. Travelers and merchants were harassed by having to deal with money changers when they went even from one shire to the next. The members agreed this should be done but shook their heads over the enormity of the task until I said, "Gentlemen, there is no one but yourselves who could undertake this work which my son feels must be done. He and all the people of England will thank you."

The next day I summoned merchants and traders to meet me in the Guildhall. I explained how the coinage would soon be uniform throughout the country. The next step was for them to set up a system so that weights and measures would also be uniform for cloth or liquids or grain. They appeared as taken aback as the members of the exchequer had been, but they recovered more quickly as they realized how much this system would lighten their work in dealing with farmers and weavers and sheepherders.

Another matter was brought to my attention. Henry had kept horses in abbeys throughout the country so there would always be fresh mounts when he dashed from shire to shire with never a thought for the work and expense this meant to the monks. I commanded—in Richard's name—that the abbeys no longer be burdened with this policy.

I was rewarded for my intense work. When Richard arrived in England, I was on the quay awaiting him as he was rowed ashore. I welcomed him joyously, then stepped back to admire this young giant in his scarlet tunic embroidered with gold, hardly aware of our escorts forming around us, noisily happy at our reunion. Their pleasure was only an echo of my delight in seeing my son for the first time in a decade and a half. Yet I'd have recognized him if he'd been in beggar's robes. Tall and straight and broad-shouldered with his red-gold hair whipping in the wind, he lifted me from my feet as he embraced me again. My eyes were misty. I think his were too, but his face was too much of a blur for me to be sure.

Those first minutes neither of us could speak, just clung to each other. Then we both started to talk, asking questions of how the other was, what had been happening, and both answering randomly for the past didn't matter. It was this moment now that was important. Reluctantly we drew apart at last, but we were never far from each other on the ride from Portsmouth to Westminster. There was an outpouring of more goodwill as we rode through the towns and hamlets. The trip was slow, so many people lined streets and lanes to welcome him and shout their gratitude to the new king for his justice.

Londoners cheered him as heartily as his subjects in the country, and I revelled in how well king and people responded to each other. But after those first few delightful days, I was too busy to do more than share an occasional hour with

Richard. I was preparing a festive coronation which I resolved would never be forgotten. There was no need for hurry because, for the first time in a hundred years, there was no rival for the throne.

When the day came I could see the occasion wouldn't be forgotten. The crowds were wildly enthusiastic as they watched us enter Westminster Abbey. The royal procession was led by archbishops and bishops, knights, barons and officials carrying Richard's spurs, scepter and sword. Scarlet robes trimmed with fur made a vividly colorful scene, and the most vivid was Richard walking under a silk canopy, hair shining and blue eyes sparkling. I was proud of him as he strode up the nave to the altar to take the oaths of justice to all and to keep the laws and customs of the kingdom before he knelt to be anointed and crowned. The choir of monks chanted the Te Deum so vigorously that the sound rebounded from the walls.

I glanced around. There was one absence. . . . I must not think of Raoul. I would spend myself on Richard, who was England and Aquitaine, I resolved as we crossed to the palace for the great coronation banquet. As we were seated pages and squires ran breathlessly to serve us from huge joints of beef, mounds of fish, eggs, mushrooms, pork, lamb, small loaves of bread and platters of comfits and candied fruits and gold decanters of wine. I'd planned the dinner, but I couldn't recall all the various dishes even when they were offered to me.

For the citizens outside, wine flowed in the fountains, and oxen and boar were roasted in the streets. The city was merry for a week, red and green and silver pennants hanging from windows and brilliant processions marching from Westminster to the Tower. But after the first few days I couldn't respond to the gaiety as any other time I would have. Now that Richard was crowned, his personal problem was too pressing. He must marry. At first I hinted, then came out bluntly with the announcement that it was his duty to carry on the dynasty. He waved away my demand goodnaturedly. "Yes, you are right, Mother. Naturally I'll wed sometime. But it'll have to be later, you know. After I return from the crusade."

I said aghast, "A crusade isn't possible, not now. The treasury's almost empty."

"That I know." He stood before me frowning.

"Then you'll postpone your plans?" My voice was eager. "Your country needs you here, Richard. The people love you. But for how long if you use them only to raise money for your adventure?"

He stared. "Delay! With the tomb of Christ in the hands of infidels? No Christian should rest until we have recovered Jerusalem. For that we need not only food and arms but ships and more ships. I will not make the mistake your Louis did and travel overland through unfriendly countries. But ships are expensive, and the men must be paid and fed—" His voice trailed off.

I hoped desperately he was seeing the obstacles

as insurmountable. Then he'd agree to stay in England and govern wisely and so win the continued love and loyalty of all his subjects. I was abruptly disappointed, and my heart sank when he spoke. "I have it, Mother! About the money, I mean. I'll sell everything I own. Not only castles and manors but public offices too. No matter what their rank, I'll remove my officials from their duties. If they wish to regain their posts, they'll have to buy back their positions."

I choked down a retort that he could not, must not upset the country so soon after his splendid coronation and the acclaim he'd received. But he was sitting, his eyes half-closed, and I knew he wouldn't hear if I did speak. Or heed if he did hear. Why, why couldn't he understand that a new king couldn't just let his subjects see him and then be off again, and with their money in his pocket? I admired his dedication to his promise to rescue the Holy City—hadn't I too in my youth been excited by the same high desire?—but he could put off his crusade a year, two years, until the country settled into his new government and his people saw him as a great king.

I tried to put my thoughts into persuasive words, but as I'd expected he was oblivious to my pleas. He strolled over to the open window that was screened by a clump of pines, said as if speaking to himself, "Everyone from under sheriff to chancellor will pay me to be reinstated. That will make a pleasant profit. And, let's see, I've given special privileges to monasteries. Those will be revoked and will have to be bought back. And the cities are always clamoring for special charters. If they offer me enough, they shall have them." He grinned complacently.

I sighed, knowing how the first wild cheering for him would now be followed by desperate moans that would roll across the land. How could he throw away the popularity I'd worked so hard to achieve for him?

I was more depressed three months later when he said gaily he was leaving for the Continent. Enough money had poured in to let him begin his work, and his stewards would send the rest on to him. He sobered a moment later when he saw me blink back my tears at the thought of his riding to the coast where a hundred ships were being loaded with silver and gold and arms, bacon, cheese, wine, flour, spiced meats and pepper. he kissed me and said confidently, "I won't be long away, Mother. I'll sail back the day the Holy City is once again ruled by Christians."

I didn't tell him that it wasn't only his leaving that made me despondent. What if he were killed in battle? With no direct heir, John would be in line for the throne. My youngest son, but I couldn't trust him as I should trust a son. In his stubbornness and arrogance, he'd make a shambles of England if no one restrained him. And who could if Richard were slain? In spite of his indifference, he must marry soon. But what princess?

She had to be a girl who'd be—understanding. One who wouldn't question why Richard at thirty-two had never shown any interest in marriage And very little interest in women except, I'd been told, for a brief affair with a slut some years ago. Again and again I went over in my mind a list of possible brides. One princess was too old for him, another far too young for childbearing and who'd be looked on as a child in the crusaders' camp so he wouldn't respect her.

I remembered suddenly there was one young woman he'd noticed enough tto speak of her to me. He'd been at a tournament in Navarre two years ago and met the king's daughter, Berengaria. He'd even written a poem to her which he showed me before his coronation, but he'd said nothing more of her since. He'd probably forgotten her in his frenzied preparations for sailing, but at least he'd regard her with more favor than some unknown princess.

When I went to bed that night, I tossed and turned as I wondered whom to send to Navarre. With the need for haste, the affair was delicate since the marriage must take place before Richard went into battle, and he'd set sail for Sicily. So she had to be willing to leave her home almost immediately to join Richard. A difficult suggestion to make to a princess. I went over and over the names of all the English lords and officials, but not one seemed right to handle the difficult negotiations. I sipped a mug of wine left at my bedside to help me sleep and finally dozed off. But for only a few minutes.

I sat up in bed, all drowsiness gone. There was no one I had enough faith in to send on the mission. So. I must go myself. I laughed, forgetting I was sixty-seven and too old for a difficult journey with who knew what obstacles waiting for me at the end. The need was too great to be concerned over possible problems. And I'd see my city of Bordeaux as I traveled through Aquitaine.

Brisk winds brought us swiftly across the Channel, and I revelled in being in my own duchy again. But there was little time to do more than bow to the welcoming shouts of my subjects along the roads or to greet my vassals. Not only time prevented me from enjoying leisurely banquets in the Ombriere Palace while listening to troubadours and lutists. The chair where Raoul had always sat was taken by another count, and when I was compelled to glance that way, my heart beat heavily and I answered at random when someone spoke to me. Fortunately the urgency of my journey dulled my sense of loss.

If Berengaria or her father refused Richard, I would have to search for another bride. The possibility haunted me as I pushed south into the Pyrenees. There was no one else who was the right age or whom Richard had noticed. I prayed desperately that my wooing would go well as we rode over the mountains into a country with pastures and apple orchards and forests of pine, beech, oak and chestnut. A pleasant land, most of it a flat valley surrounded by hills, but again there was no time to indulge in loitering.

I'd sent heralds ahead to ask King Alfonso to receive me. After all my anxieties on the road, I was delighted when we reached the great square in front of the royal palace to see crowds of courtiers in scarlet and green and blue tunics drawn up to greet me. And then from their midst a huge man walked forward, hands outstretched to help me from my saddle. His welcome and his regal air told me, before his name was announced, that this was the king himself.

When I refused his suggestion to rest, he led me into a small chamber where wines and fruit and cakes were laid out. He dismissed his attendants and turned to me. "I'm honored, Your Highness, at your visit. This must mean you have something important to discuss so I'm sure you prefer meeting with me alone. We are very informal here."

I smiled a thank-you and sipped the wine he poured for me. I liked his directness and answered with equal directness. "Yes, my mission is highly important, sire. You have a daughter, Princess Berengaria. Perhaps you remember my son Richard when he was here a few years ago?" He nodded, not interrupting. "Richard didn't forget her when he left your country, and now I come to ask if you will consent to the marriage of your daughter and my son." I held my breath, waiting his answer. He looked startled. Had I been too eager because I wished so intensely that Richard marry, and soon?

My breath went out in relief as Alfonso's surprise faded and he grinned. "My dear lady, how did you know I've worried about her future? But I'd never have dared hope that a great warrior like your son would consider an alliance with my small country. I will send for her."

I waited anxiously. What if she refused or had to be coaxed? Months could be lost then, and Richard would be far away in the Holy Land. I swung around at the sound of a light footstep and saw a slim girl with dark hair and brown eyes which were lovely, though her mouth was too small and her face too round. I pushed the petty criticisms out of my mind as Alfonso explained my visit. She gazed at me, then at the floor as if overawed by the proposal and whispered, "Your—Your Highness, do you mean I am asked to be queen of England? It is—it is so great an honor—" She couldn't finish.

I wished with a touch of impatience that she was less awed, then mentally shook my head at myself. How could I complain when I was being given exactly what I'd come for? And I knew Richard would be pleased with her for the very reasons I wasn't. Her lack of spirit—not even asking what Richard was like now, what she could expect as his wife—showed she wasn't a young woman who'd inflame Richard with a passion that would make him forget his disinterest in women.

I shrugged the thought aside. Nothing mattered except that Richard be married soon and sire an heir. Winter was almost on us, but I wouldn't let the weather interfere. We must go on to Sicily at once. The roads through southern France weren't difficult, but our escort wasn't happy at crossing the Alps. I refused to listen to my captain of the guards. Richard was supposedly spending the season in Siciliy, but I knew his impulsive nature. He might suddenly decide to sail east in spite of the stormy seas.

I'd written Richard earlier of my plan, and he'd answered in a hasty scrawl he was willing to put the matter in my hands. Now I sent scouts ahead to tell him I'd soon arrive with his bride. But where was he? I felt I held my breath until the messengers returned with word that Richard was still in Sicily and would have a ship waiting for us at Brindisi to take us to his camp in Palermo. I laughed with relief. So he really was agreeable to marriage. Now I had time to think of the joy of seeing my daughter Joanna again. Her elderly husband had died four months ago. Perhaps she'd return to England with me.

The thought of having her beside me, bright and laughing, reminiscing as only members of a family can, nostalgically remembering none but the happy hours of long ago, kept my spirits high in spite of rain and muddy roads as we crossed Lombardy. That and the pleasure of seeing Richard soon. I'd little else to distract me. Berengaria seldom spoke. For some reason she seemed almost as much in awe of me as she did of the prospect of being Richard's wife. So she didn't grumble. But my escort did. How could they care about the weather when we were on our way to see the king and an English Princess? I shrugged all of them aside and indulged myself in dreams of the near future.

They were all more cheerful when we reached Brindisi with its picturesque houses and Roman ruins and at the port found a ship waiting for us. The crossing to Sicily was choppy, but at least we were protected from the rain as we sailed down the coast, reaching Sicily three days later at midnight. No one was there to meet us at that hour, and the captain insisted we stay aboard until dawn. But I was too excited to waste more time and demanded we be put ashore at once. He mumbled a curse and gave in, though before returning to his vessel he found us transport for our baggage and two guides to take us to Palermo.

We reached the city when the first faint light was washing over the quiet homes, and even I could see the need to stop at a hostelry to rest and freshen ourselves before Richard met his bride who was pale and exhausted. She must be at her best, I thought, and said we could delay a few hours.

She looked fresher after a short sleep, and her complexion was lovely, the wild rose in her cheeks brought there no doubt at the prospect of seeing Richard again, and this time as his bride. She said shyly she'd never forgotten him and hoped he'd have at least a faint memory of her. I reassured her vigorously, reminding her of the poem he'd written about her. She smiled at that and kept smiling as we rode through the city to the palace where Joanna lived and Richard stayed as her guest.

But Richard wasn't there waiting for us though I'd sent a messenger ahead. I thought with annoyance he was probably talking with his captains about arquebuses and slings and supplies and hadn't noticed the time slipping past. But Joanna came rushing down from her rooms, hugging us both, then stood back to gaze at me lovingly, though she remembered to put an arm around Berengaria's shoulders, the gesture drawing the bride into her husband's family. Joanna laughed. "You never change, Mother. Oh, it's so delightful to see you, and not looking a day older than when we were together years ago."

I laughed too. "If there's any truth in that, it's due partly to your lovely gifts, my dear, or warm gowns and furs." I glanced at Berengaria wondering how I could possibly excuse my son's absence.

Joanna did it for me, saying airily, "Isn't Richard tiresome? When he left this morning, he said he wanted to search for you—the messenger didn't mention where you were—so eager was he to meet his future wife, Garia. You don't mind if I call you that, do you? Your name's much too long! But I was firm that you needed your rest, and he should go off to his camp." She grimaced. "I should have seen to it that he stayed here under my eyes. When he's with his beloved weapons, he can think of nothing else. But once he meets you, he'll be sorry for every minute that he's lost through his own carelessness."

Some of the color which had faded from Berengaria's cheeks returned at Joanna's lighthearted words. Then before any of us could speak, we heard someone striding across the anteroom and we turned quickly. Richard stood in the doorway. He saw me first, and a moment later I was swept into his arms. I whispered, "Richard, please, my darling, let me go and see who came with me."

He set me on my feet and looked over my head at Berengaria who was staring at him. I wished she had appeared less overwhelmed for it made an instant barrier between them. Richard stepped forward to kiss her hand and greet her formally. Joanna said gaily, "Isn't your bride lovely, Richard? I know we'll all be great friends—"

I interrupted. "But aren't you—? I hoped you'd come back to England with me, Joanna, now that your late husband's cousin is king of Sicily."

My longing to have one of my children near me after my years of isolation must have shown in my voice for Joanna smiled sweetly. "My hope too, Mother. I want to live in my own country again, but surely we'll wait for the wedding? When will it be, Richard? Tomorrow?"

We were all amused at her impetuosity though Richard shuffled his feet and didn't appear as eager as his sister. Berengaria spoke for the first time. "But—but we can't." She turned to me. "Lent's early this year, and no marriages are allowed until after Easter, madame."

"Oh no. I mean yes, you're right. But now what shall we do? Or will you put off your sailing until then, Richard?"

He shook his head. "Impossible." In spite of his agreeing he should marry, did his tone hold a trace of relief? "My captains and I have made plans to leave in three days. We've already delayed too long waiting for my bride. That is," he corrected himself politely, "not too long for you, Princess Berengaria. But every day the Saracens infest the city of Jerusalem is a blow to all

Christians."

I bit my lip at the dilemma. Berengaria couldn't go with Richard attended by only a few waiting women. That would scandalize our countries and cast a shadow over the marriage. Reluctantly I glanced at Joanna. She understood immediately and nodded. "These last years have been dull, and the Holy Land should be an adventure. I'll be Berengaria's companion and go to England later, Mother, after they're married."

I sighed, but there was no other way. Richard said incredulously, "Joanna! You mean you'd act as chaperone for us?" He frowned thoughtfully, then smiled at me. "Why don't we all sail east together, Mother?"

I wanted to say yes so badly that it was hard to hold the word back. To be with my son and daughter and my future daughter-in-law, to live again through the excitement of a crusade was almost too tempting for me to refuse. But I said, "I wish—but I can't. Since I left London every message from there that has reached me has been disturbing. John's traveling about England demanding deference as if he were already the king. And worse, he's been saying you'll never return from the crusade, Richard. Who knows what harm he'll do if left there alone?"

Richard shrugged. "I've heard the stories too, but I'm not going to break off now because my younger brother is stirring up a little trouble."

Joanna and I said in one breath, "A *little* trouble?" She added, "You're right, Mother, you can handle John better than anyone else. I'm sorry, it would have been—but you'll have to keep an eye on him."

Richard said, "Splendid! I'd rather you sailed with us, we'll miss you, but I'll have a document drawn up to give you full power in my absence as you had before I was crowned. But now," he took Berengaria's arm stiffly. "you must all come with me to see the camp and the harbor."

Soldiers we passed on the way to the encampment cheered Richard heartily. I gazed at him with pride, the perfect warrior, then remembered painfully the tales of his preference for bedding a man instead of a woman. I looked at Berengaria trying to match her short steps with Richard's strides. She would change him, I encouraged myself, and he'll father sons and daughters whom his subjects will love.

I forgot even Richard when we paused on a hillock near the camp to look out over the ships riding at anchor, from small fishing boats to great galleys. They brought back too vividly my own crusade. I no longer remembered the sickness and nausea, only the sense of high adventure in a holy cause. My eyes went over the vessels longingly. Then I brought myself back to the needs of the moment and said briskly, "Impressive, Richard. You can carry all the men and horses and weapons you'll need. How can you fail when your army will also have the best warrior in Europe?"

I cast a last glance at the fleet before we went down to the camp where the tents were in straight military formation and the noise unbelievable. Trumpets blasted, horses whinnied and servants were filling chests with cuirasses, hauberks, gauntlets, helmets, lances and battle-axes. Pack horses loaded with equipment were being led toward the quay, and huge wagons with wardrobe chests and provisions creaked past. I laughed and put my hands to my ears, telling myself I wasn't envious of Joanna and Berengaria's part in the venture ahead. But I knew I should start on my journey home the hour they sailed, or I'd want to scramble aboard the last ship leaving to share Richard's victories.

At least recrossing the Alps was in spring, and it was pleasant not to battle the winter snow and heavy winds as we had before. But I hadn't time to enjoy the scenery. I pushed on to London and sent for John who was, I heard, playing the king in Nottingham. He didn't hurry to Westminster, but he did come. He was arrogant and waved away the stories I'd been told, then leaned forward to kiss me and said, "Now you're here, Mother, there's no need for me to act as Richard's deputy and try to keep the peace. As you know, a country always is restless when its king is away."

I had to admit the truth of that, subjects needed a king to rule them. Perhaps I'd misjudged John's activities. But I was sure I'd been right not to sail east and leave John with too free a hand. But the next day I discovered I couldn't stay in England. An irritated message from Richard said that Philip Augustus had joined him but was returning early with the thin excuse that he was ill. Perhaps Philip was sick. I'd seen for myself that the Holy Land wasn't the healthiest place in the world, especially for westerners. But I suspected part of his reason was jealousy of Richard, who was acclaimed by the soldiers of every camp as the Lion Heart, I was told, while Philip was scarcely noticed.

I found some pleasure in the fact that there would be no more tales of Richard and Philip being too fond of each other, but this situation wasn't good either. Philip's jealousy might lead him to make forays against our borders. I sighed. I'd have to go to the Continent. To Rouen, I decided. From that city my officers could quickly bring word of what was happening in England, and I could watch the borders of Normandy and Anjou. A pity I couldn't hold the court in Aquitaine since that province was too far away, but I could invite some of my vassals and troubadours to give some of our elegance to the Norman castle in Rouen.

In spite of the tension of being constantly alert, the court was gay. I could never forget Raoul, but the memory of him now held pleasant thoughts as well as sadness, and I could exchange reminiscences of him with my lords who also felt his loss. I missed them too when they could no longer stay away from their estates. The Norman barons tried to please me, but they weren't lighthearted like my own people, their minds forever on war and despising frivolity.

Perhaps they were right I thought when I received reports from the Holy Land. Berengaria wrote little, not having overcome her stiffness with me though she was now Richard's wife. But Joanna sent off long letters. I smiled as I started to read the last one. She'd known nothing of marching and sieges, and her description of crossing the desert and plains to Acre, which was held by the Saracens, would have been a long grumbling complaint except that her natural good nature came through as she laughed at herself when there was scarcely enough water to wash her face, let alone bathe, after a day's hot and dusty ride. And when she had to stay cooped up in a small house while Richard's forces surrounded Acre.

So she couldn't tell me much of the siege or the attack when Richard felt the defenders too weak to resist. She could write only that he'd used assault towers and wheeled mangonels and battering rams, terms I was sure she put in to impress me with her military knowledge. She added as an afterthought that Richard naturally had taken the city. I smiled again at that though I was as certain as she had been that Richard would be successful.

But her next lines wiped away my smile. Richard had insulted Duke Leopold of Austria who'd joined him recently. The duke had dared to raise his flag beside Richard's on the captured castle though it was Richard who'd stormed the town. Richard had glared at the banner and flung it into the moat, and Leopold immediately left the crusade, swearing he'd be revenged. I shook my head. Didn't Richard have enough Saracen enemies without affronting a man who might have remained an ally if he'd been handled tactfully? First Philip Augustus had withdrawn his army, and now Leopold.

The thought of Philip made me wonder uneasily if Leopold would try to persuade him to move against our provinces. I dispatched officers to see that our fortresses and garrisons on the borders were continuing to keep their defenses strong, and I sent scouts into France to discover if Philip and Leopold were making an alliance against us.

I was walking on the ramparts of Rouen tower, admiring the fields and orchards surrounding the city, when the first scout returned, a young man whose usually cheerful face looked drawn. I said, "What—? Is Duke Leopold—"

"Not—not the duke, Your Highness." He went on reluctantly. "Emissaries are traveling between Paris and London."

I was puzzled. "To make sure the peace is kept? But why wouldn't Philip send to me since I'm Richard's deputy?"

"The emissaries aren't carrying peaceful messages, madame. King Philip Augustus sent money to Prince John to—to prepare a fleet and hire mercenaries in case—well, in case there'd be trouble in Normandy."

I gasped, "I don't understand. John and Philip, why should they be allies? And why do they think there might be trouble here?"

He explained unwillingly. "Prince John promised to give the French king castles and towns on the border if—if King Philip would recognize him as duke of Normandy. The mercenaries are to put down any disturbances here if the Norman lords refuse to accept our prince as their duke."

I stared at him in dismay. John yearning to be the duke of Normandy? I'd been looking in the wrong direction, at Leopold instead of at my son. His traitorous plot to become duke was only a first step. The next would be to treat with Philip and be recognized king of England. Absently I told the scout to refresh himself while I thought swiftly about what had to be done. My instinctive hope was that the messenger's report was garbled, that John was living quietly in England. But I could not risk waiting to have the story confirmed or denied. I must leave for England at once.

As often happened the winds were stormy and the Channel was rough and, as usual, I couldn't delay because of the weather. We had a miserable crossing, able to snatch only a few hours of sleep in the rocking ship and dining on bread and wine when we could force even that down. But when we landed at Portsmouth in the early morning, I didn't take time to rest or do more than swallow a crust and a slice of beef before riding on to London.

Officers sped ahead of my escort to call the barons to meet me at Westminster. They came clattering in from the countryside expecting, as I gathered from their loud questions that clashed against each other in the council chamber, that France had attacked on the Continent. I said quietly, "No, my lords. A scout told me a story which I hoped—desperately—was not true. But within an hour of my arrival here, a messenger came from the Cinque Ports to report— well, that the story was correct." Like the scout I had trouble going on, unwilling to confess that my son was ready to betray his brother, the king. I told them quickly.

They were outraged at John's grasping for power and demanded to see him. I agreed, said I'd already sent an officer to him at Dover. He should be here tomorrow. They said grimly they'd return to the chamber early and broke into small growling groups, muttering what they'd like to do to John, from stripping him of his title of prince to throwing him into a dungeon.

Their anger didn't ease overnight, and when John entered the room, they glowered at his smiling face and only grunted when he greeted them airily. I forced myself to speak calmly. "My son, I've told the barons about your planned alliance with King Philip. They are—they disapprove."

At the mild word the lords shouted furiously. Any agreement with Philip must be cancelled, and the mercenaries and the fleet in the Cinque Ports must be disbanded. I looked warily at John, afraid their hostility would arouse his. With mercenaries and a fleet at his back, he could signal for an uprising. Another civil war like in the days of King Stephen would tear the country apart. I prayed silently that John wouldn't answer their challenge with a threat of force.

I should have known. John was smiling. When he was confronted with powerful antagonists—his father, his brother, a justifiably enraged vassal—he backed down gracefully. He said now, "My lords, you must have been misinformed. You know the Pope sent out an edict that the lands of any crusader are inviolate. Would I risk excommunication and strike against my brother who is on a holy mission? As for what you call an agreement with Philip, that is only a natural kinship between princes of the blood to assure ourselves there'll be no outbreak on either his or our borders."

Some of the barons appeared mollified at the plausible statement, but several called out loudly, "What of the mercenaries and the fleet?"

John shrugged. "A safeguard to make sure Philip keeps his side of the plans for peace. But if you believe they disturb the country, I'll send orders at once for them to disband. In fact some of you—as proof of my good intentions—may wish to carry those orders for me."

"We will." Three of them spoke together, but all seemed satisfied with his capitulation. Yet I, his mother, was still uneasy. John made promises casually and as casually broke them.

I hurried from the chamber, not joining in the good will growing between prince and lords. I must write Richard, urging him to return at once if he wanted a kingdom to return to.

Chapter Eleven

I waited restlessly for his answer. He must come home though I knew how difficult it would be for him to put aside his dreams of freeing Jerusalem. Still he could return another year, and he should be satisfied with his Lion Heart victories at Acre and in the field against the Saracens, victories which were talked of through Europe. But would they be enough for him with the Moslems still holding the Holy City? The thoughts went round and round in my mind between council meetings and meetings with citizens who had grievances and discussions with the merchant guilds.

At last a messenger arrived with word from him. I seized the scroll, tore it open, then laughed delightedly. I realized his first sentences shouldn't be smiled at. Twice he'd almost reached

Jerusalem, so close that towers and minarets could be seen—so he was told. He himself would not gaze at the city since God hadn't seen fit to let him capture the Holy City. He'd had to retreat and sign a three-year truce with Saladin which at least left the coastal cities in the hands of Christians and allowed them to visit the holy shrines.

How could I help being overjoyed when the truce meant he'd soon be here? I longed to see him again for England's sake and for my own. To have him, strong and handsome and loving, beside me, what more could I ask for? He wrote that Joanna and Berengaria were sailing the next day. He'd follow in a week after the final negotiations and was sure he'd overtake them before they reached Italy. I thought happily, why, he'll be home by Christmas, all of them would. The only regret was that there was still no mention of an heir.

Every morning I woke thinking—today I'll have word of him. But weeks passed and there was only a letter from Joanna saying Richard hadn't arrived there yet, but she and Berengaria were safely in Italy. I was pleased they were halfway home but disappointed when she added they'd wait for the winter storms to be over before taking ship to England. Well, perhaps it was sensible to delay until spring.

There was also a short note from Berengaria which puzzled me. Not so much the actual words but the undertone. If I were hoping to meet a loving husband, I'd have sped to England, careless of stormy waters, in case he'd been forced to return overland. But Berengaria scarcely mentioned Richard and showed no eagerness for a reunion. I swallowed hard. Was that the reason for her carefully phrased scrawl that spoke more of the weather than of her royal husband? Had he outraged her by letting her see his preference for men?

But when Richard arrived, he'd mend that somehow. Only when would he come? More weeks passed without news. And then, even more disturbing, two of his crusading knights came to Westminster to see him. They were astounded that he wasn't here since they'd left the east a month after the king. Too late they tried to hide their dismay so I wouldn't be anxious, but how could I not be? I sent word that lookouts should be placed along the coast with scouts to let me know the minute his ship was sighted.

December came, cold and frosty with the Thames half-frozen, but there was still no sign of Richard. The Christmas I'd happily looked forward to was drab and dull, the court sharing my fear for Richard's safety. Though John wasn't gloomy, saying it was always Richard's way to keep others guessing. Richard had probably been blown about by winter storms, but he'd soon be home and wondering why anyone had been worried. I prayed fervently John was right, spending long hours in the chapel on my knees begging God to bring my son safely home. Soon. Tomorrow. Or let me know he was alive and well, wintering in some Mediterranean port.

A fortnight later a dozen clerics from the archbishop of Rouen arrived in London and asked for an audience with me. In spite of the cold, I was walking along the banks of the Thames in the daily exercise I'd begun at Salisbury, gazing around me with a pleasure no worries could quite dampen for now I was free to go where I wished, look at whatever pleased me. I wondered why the archbishop sent such a large delegation on what was probably some church matter, but I hurried inside to greet them and offer them wine.

I picked up my glass, put it down quickly when the oldest priest started to speak. They brought news of my son, King Richard. He stopped, cleared his throat. I said hoarsely, "What—what news? Where is he? Tell me, tell me."

He threw out his hands. "I regret we do not know that, Your Highness." He added instantly before I could speak, "But he is alive."

"Thank God, He's heard my prayers. Go on, go on."

His words were clipped, and he spoke as though reading from a document. "High winds drove the king's ship ashore in Greece."

"Is he—is he there? But you said you didn't know?"

"The king wanted to return to the sea, but no captain would agree so—he felt he shouldn't delay his return to England—he and four knights and a clerk and a page set off overland."

I said proudly, "He was the greatest crusader of them all, he'd be safe anywhere in the west. But then why—why haven't we heard from him?"

Several leaned forward but didn't speak as the oldest priest held up his hand. "He wasn't sure that he would be safe so he disguised himself. The knights were to travel as merchants, and he'd be their servant. Only, you know the king's appearance, madame, he couldn't hide his height or his bright hair or the way he walks as if he had a royal right to everything around him. In Greece that didn't matter, but after he crossed the Austrian border—" I gasped, waved to him to go on—"he was recognized in a small town, and an official galloped off immediately to inform Duke Leopold."

"No, no, not the duke who hates him. Sorry, go on."

He nodded his gray head. "Yes, we've all heard how the duke swore he'd be revenged for the king's insult in Acre. He rode to the town, just south of Vienna, and himself made the king a prisoner. Since then no one has seen King Richard though the knights who'd been with him searched the countryside until they were ordered to leave or they too would be put in custody." At the last words his voice held a note of relief that he'd got his story out.

Richard a prisoner. My heart cried out a denial that my restless son should be locked away though with no word from him I knew it must be true. And less than an hour ago I'd revelled in my freedom to go where I wished, see what I wanted to look at. It was unbearable that Richard couldn't. I jerked my thoughts away from that desolate picture and thanked the clerics gravely for traveling so far to tell me what they knew of my son.

But I hardly waited for them to bow themselves out before I sent for my ministers. They must immediately send men to every Austrian city, town, village, isolated fortress, to search for some clue. Surely someone there must have heard a rumor, a whisper of where Leopold had imprisoned a king.

Report after report came back, all saying nothing. The scouts were diligent in following every garbled tale they heard, but not one came to anything. I prayed feverishly every day, but my pleas went unanswered as the days dragged into months. Then one morning my hopes were raised briefly. Anselm, the clerk who'd been with Richard, asked to see me. He was still dusty from his journey when he entered the hall. I brushed away his apologies for his appearance. "Have you anything—any—any news?"

My heart beat painfully when he said, "Yes, Your Highness," but it slowed as he went on. "The king was imprisoned in the castle of Durrenstein. I hurried there, but by then he'd left." He added in explanation, "I wasn't important like King Richard's knights so I wasn't ordered out of the country. But I've done no more than they. All I found out was that two days before I reached Durrenstein, Duke Leopold was forced to hand over our king to the Holy Roman Emperor. Beyond that I know nothing."

My Richard still a prisoner. Then I said breathlessly, "The emperor has no reason to be revengeful. Perhaps—no, if he'd freed Richard, we'd know by now. But at least, at least I can send emissaries to him and beg for my son's release." I thought hopefully we might somehow bargain with the emperor who wouldn't dare slay a crusader.

I wrote a careful letter, and by afternoon three lords and their retinues were on the way to Dover.

I saw them off and then went slowly back to the great hall and sank into a chair, worn out by the conflicting emotions of hope and fear, a fear that was reinforced when John, chewing on a sweetmeat, came up to me. I started to say automatically, "Don't, you eat too many sweets—" and was stopped by his smiling expression. "Oh, I'm glad, you too think Richard will be all right."

"Quite all right so far as I'm concerned, Mother. Why, I'm as good as king now. Emperor Henry will never let Richard leave his prison alive."

"Oh no, you're wrong, don't even think such a dreadful thing." But I couldn't help dwelling on it though I didn't take John's childish posturings seriously. So long as he was under my eyes he wouldn't repeat his bold venture of recruiting mercenaries and fleet. I forgot he was in his late twenties, no longer a child.

I could think of nothing except how long would it take my emissaries to reach the emperor? And what would his answer be to my appeal? As the weeks went by, I felt I'd been waiting forever for some hopeful word of Richard. A message finally arrived when I was at a council meeting trying to keep my mind on endless government details. I reached for the parchment, both eager and reluctant to unroll it. My hands shook as I broke the seal and scanned the first words. Then I looked up, my eyes shining. "The emperor—this says he will accept a ransom for Richard."

A dry voice cut through my haze of happiness. "Excellent, madame, but what is the ransom demanded?"

"Oh, oh yes." I read on, leaned forward so that the table cut into my ribs. The slight pain was welcome to distract me from the greater pain of the words before me. I said stunned, "The emperor demands a—a hundred and fifty thousand marks of silver and—and two hundred members from noble families to be held hostage by him until the last coin is paid." We stared at each other in dismay.

The ministers broke into furious speech. "Infamous to treat a great crusader so!" "Outrageous!" The dry voice spoke again. "Our late King Henry left little in the treasury, and after that—"

We all nodded, no need for him to finish. After that Richard had sold his own property and all royal posts to pay for his crusade, and used every piece of silver in the treasury. Where was there enough money to pay even half of the incredible ransom? I drew myself up, said firmly, "My lords, the demand is unchristian, it's sinful when my son was fighting for all Christendom. But Richard is alive. We have no choice, we must pay."

Some muttered agreement, others appeared skeptical. If we couldn't raise the hundred and fifty thousand marks, what families would allow their children to be used as hostages? I rose. "We will meet again in a fortnight when we've had time to decide what measures we can take." I left quickly, fearful I'd break down in front of them, torn as I was between anguish that we might not be able to pay the ransom and joy at being told Richard was alive.

Or was he? My days I spent going over one suggestion after another on how to raise money. But many nights were sleepless when, overtired, I had treacherous suspicions he might have been killed and a ransom still demanded. That fear at least was gone when the day before our next council meeting I received a letter in Richard's own hand addressed to his "much loved mother". He was in Haguenau, being well-treated and happy in the knowledge he'd be home soon. He knew the ransom was outrageous, but he also knew his subjects. They'd do their duty. I kissed his scrawled signature. He said well-treated, but that was only to comfort me. Who realized better than I what torture imprisonment could be?

Richard's letter put fire into my ministers too. The king of England couldn't be allowed to die in a foreign country because of imperial greed. We must impose a new tax, and no one would be exempt from the least to the highest. Many of the devout paid willingly, but they were horrified that churches and abbeys also must give even when for lack of money they had to melt down the crosses on their altars. And the Cistercians, who possessed only their flocks, had to donate a year's crop of wool from their sheep. I liked that no better than our subjects did, but how else would the ransom be raised?

The barons, who had to give a fourth of their year's income, were only halfhearted in their protests since if we couldn't raise enough money, their sons and daughters could be held as hostages. It was agony to ask the lords for members of their families to sail with me—for I would trust no one else to face the emperor—but I promised that if the hundred and fifty thousand marks were in my hands, the hostages would return with me. And I could comfort them a little by explaining that the Pope had sent a bull, threatening the emperor with excommunication if Henry Hohenstaufen didn't release the crusading king.

Silver and gold began to pile up in the crypt of Saint Paul's Cathedral where I had it so securely guarded that even I had to give the password to be allowed in. The stewards counted each coin carefully, then poured the precious metal into chests which were locked and strapped with iron. Every evening I looked at their precise entries until at last I could rise from the table where the accounts were kept and say, "We have the ransom to the last farthing! Tomorrow we sail."

I scarcely noticed how the December winds lashed the Channel as our score of ships sailed east with the ransom money that was still under heavy guard. I'd soon see Richard, a year after I'd happily expected him back from the Holy Land. Travel across the Continent into Austria was little smoother or warmer than the sea crossing, but I scarcely noticed that either, aware of the discomfort only when my companions complained. How could they when the end of the journey meant Richard's freedom? Had he kept his health or would he be worn down after more than a year in prison?

At the border we were told that Richard had been moved to Speyer, and we hurried north to the imperial palace. We were led into the great hall between lines of heavily armed guards as if we were an invading army. Emperor Henry didn't rise courteously, only leaned forward, dark brows drawn together in a frown as though he too were facing an enemy. The watchfulness made me uneasy, but I smiled and bowed my head, then forgot him as I turned tensely toward the doorway at a clatter of steel outside. More guards entered. I gasped with joy at sight of the prisoner they surrounded who towered above them.

Richard was too pale. Then he saw me and color flooded his grinning face. Seemingly without effort he shouldered the men around him aside and strode toward me. He was too thin too, but his arms about me were strong and muscular. And he was his old exuberant self, laughing and tossing words of greeting to my escort and the hostages, looking as if he wanted to embrace our whole delegation. My heart sang when I turned gaily back to the emperor.

Henry Hohenstaufen's grim expression hadn't softened. Perhaps seeing how delighted we all were at sight of Richard he wished he'd asked for a higher ransom. The thought reminded me of the money, and I signalled my guards to bring in the iron-strapped chests. The two captains who held the keys unlocked the chests, flung the lids back and started to count out the silver and gold and copper coins. The emperor spoke irritably to an officer beside him. The officer stepped forward, said crisply through an interpreter that it was the emperor's will that his imperial stewards must check the money before he could begin to make arrangements for releasing his prisoner.

I said lightly, "You will not find a ha'penny missing so there should be no delay over freeing Richard and allowing our hostages to return with me."

His men went over and over the amount in each chest while the emperor ignored our restlessness at the interminable clank of metal. With my hand in Richard's I wasn't as annoyed as my suite was. Still, I wouldn't be really easy until we were well away from this castle. With reason I discovered a moment later. The emperor nodded morosely when informed the sum was correct, then said to my horror, "I must think further on this. I have had another offer for my royal prisoner. Twenty thousand more silver pieces if I continue to hold the king here. Or if I turn him over to—others."

I gasped, "Impossible! We have your signature on a document that you will release Richard on payment of this ransom." Then almost as an afterthought, "Others? Who would give so much as—" I stopped, knowing as I asked the question what the answer would be.

He scowled, said reluctantly, "King Philip of France and your son Prince John."

Even though I'd known the names, I shook my head violently. "Not Richard's brother, never. And surely not Philip who was a fellow crusader."

My words were drowned out by Richard's furious shout and the surging forward of the English lords, their angry voices rising and clashing. The storming went on for two days before the emperor agreed to honor his commitment. And he was persuaded to do that only because his own lords were as shocked as we were at his considering breaking his promise to us.

He said harshly, "Very well. Your son will be released today, but first he must do homage to me for all of his possessions."

Richard was incredulous. "I? Your vassal? I, king of England and duke of Aquitaine, Normandy, Anjou? But you cannot be serious."

The emperor's eyes narrowed. "I am quite serious. Give me your oath of fealty for all your lands, or I will accept the better offer for you from France."

I couldn't speak at first. I was watching Richard intently as he slowly realized the humiliation of this demand. His face looked as if he were about to fly into one of his father's Angevin rages, and God alone knew what he'd say or do if he lost control. I pressed against him, managed to say softly, "The oath's meaningless, the emperor's too far away to have any influence in your domains. So why not swear fealty and go free?"

He swallowed convulsively, and his hands clenched and unclenched. I waited, unable to breathe. Then the high color faded from his cheeks, and he laughed though there was no humor in the sound. He walked forward, knelt and placed his fingers between the emperor's, muttered the vow and rose swiftly. We wanted to swarm about him, cling to him, but even stronger was our desire to be away from these gray stone walls.

There were few complaints on our journey home about the weather or the icy roads to the

coast or the choppy Channel. We were all too
happy that Richard and the hostages were free.
His mood was bright too when we landed in
Portsmouth and rode through cheering villages
and crowded roads on our way to London where
banners or colorful strips of cloths decorated the
houses. Bells pealed a noisy welcome, and the
streets were so full of citizens trying to touch him
or his horse that we could only inch forward. No
one seemed to remember how they'd been
stripped of much of their wealth to ransom their
king but saw in Richard their beloved Lion Heart.

One person was missing. When I asked for John,
Elsie said "That one! He knows what's good for
him. When he heard our king was returning, he
made for Paris so fast a hawk couldn't have caught
up with him."

I thought, This isn't right. Whatever follies
Philip led him into, John's a Plantagenet. He must
be persuaded to come back to his family. Well,
that would have to wait for there was another
missing too. Berengaria. I sighed. What
persuasions could I use to urge her to join her
husband? That too must wait for a little. Now
Richard must show himself to his country.

He agreed laughing. A small way to prove his
gratitude to his subjects who'd save him years in
an imperial prison or an unknown fate at Philip's
hands. I accused only Philip. I was sure John
would never harm his brother. He must have been
misled somehow when he'd signed the document
to the emperor. I put aside the thought as we rode
north. It was spring, and the sun shone on budding
trees and plowed fields and herds of sheep grazing

on our way to Nottingham and Sherwood Forest and then up to Northampton.

It was the afternoon of our fourth day at the palace. Richard and I were walking in the garden, chatting desultorily about how peaceful England was after his years in the Holy Land and Austria. Almost at the word peace, three men burst past the sentries at the end of the path and flung themselves forward, shouting at Richard. He swung toward them haughtily, his expression so commanding that they stopped abruptly as the sentries ran up and seized them roughly.

Richard shook his head. "No need to hold them. They can't harm me, and they appear to have something to say. Well?" His crisp voice wasn't unkind. The men gaped at his mildness. Richard repeated, "Well? You must want to speak to me or you wouldn't have risked forcing your way in here."

A heavy man in a ragged smock swallowed noisily and said, "We—we was—would have gone to yer justice court but just heard youse leaving tomorrow. But we—it's our duty, see?—to tell you—"

He broke off, and the second man whose clothes were a little less ragged than the first said hoarsely, "Ain't fair what yer doing. Prince John—now he'd listen to us and he said it ain't fair. That is, if you came back. Which he said you wouldn't."

I bit my lip, regretting the unpleasant reminder of John. But Richard continued to be surprisingly patient. "If you'd tell me what isn't fair, I might find an answer."

The third man, gray-haired and gaunt, glanced
uneasily from one to the other of his companions,
apparently saw they weren't able to go on and put
in, "The prince—he said your sheriff was told he
could seize our holdings and give them to you, but
that we'd have them again soon as the prince was
really king now because you wouldn't never come
back. So what does it matter if you throw us into
prison? No worse than begging a crust of bread
and sleeping along the road in rain or snow. Least
we'd have a roof over us." He spat on a budding
rose in the flowerbed beside him.

Richard's mouth tightened in fury. "Vile lies!
And you believed them! For that you should be
thrown into—I was in Austria. How could I take
your land? It was my bro—" Family loyalty
stopped him before he finished the word. "There
was some mistake. I will see that it's taken care of.
Give your names to the sentries."

I touched his arm as he started to nod a
dismissal, whispered, "Let them have a few coins,
Richard, so that until they have their farms again
they can eat and sleep well."

He grinned. "I should have thought of that!" He
sent one of the guards to fetch his chamberlain
and have him bring money for these men who'd
been so ill-used. At his words the ragged and
stained men raised astonished faces, not believing
him until the chamberlain arrived and distributed
silver. Then they were kneeling before Richard,
incoherent in their gratitude.

There were no more startling scenes when we
circled back to Winchester. Everywhere was the
same outpouring of thanksgiving that the king was

safely home. I was as pleased as Richard at the loyal demonstrations, but my joy abruptly changed to cold fear when I noticed how often Richard retired to his room in the palace with Bertram, a young man who'd lately entered his service.

I'd been casually aware of their friendship on our tour but saw nothing significant in it until now. Richard must not, must not fall back into his old ways or how could I persuade Berengaria to come to us? I started to write lovingly to her that evening to say we were eager to see her again, that Richard needed a wife and England needed a queen. Then I remembered she was never at ease on the sea according to Joanna, and that might give her an excuse not to cross the Channel. So I added how happy we'd be if she'd join us in Normandy as Richard should show himself to his faithful Norman subjects.

They'd be heartened at sight of him, I thought as I sent off the letter, and I'd find a way to leave Bertram here, give him a new post and new duties. A scandal now would be disastrous. Richard, always ready for action, needed no persuasion to cross to the Continent. But he'd no intention of leaving Bertram in England. "He helps me in a hundred small ways, choosing the best robes to wear, making sure I don't forget a meeting of the ministers, reading documents they send me so I'll take care of the most important ones first and—well, he's always at my elbow to assist me when some new problem arises."

I said drily, "He sounds invaluable, but I believe you'll discover among your suite several others who can take his place." I hesitated, decided not to voice my suspicions unless I was forced to in order to overcome his obstinacy. "They may not do as well, I realize, but you won't want to stand in Bertram's way. I was planning to have you knight him, and we'd give him a fortress near here. The owner died a week ago without an heir so the land reverts to the crown. But Bertram—Sir Bertram—will be expected by his people to take up his duties at once. If he sails with us, we'll have to look for someone else."

Richard bit his lip angrily. "But I wish him to accompany me. I'm the king, madame. I make my own decisions."

"Certainly, my son. If you believe I'd honor Bertram too highly, why the matter's ended." My voice was cool, but inside I was shaking. Since I'd noticed his preference for Bertram, how many others also did? And should they travel to the Continent together, how swiftly John, or rather Philip, would seize on the story.

Richard said sharply, "You can't honor Bertram too highly, but—" His shoulders slumped, then he brightened. "He could stay on his new estate for a while until he learns all he needs to know and then can find someone to act as his deputy. After that he can take up his duties with me again. So we won't be separated long."

I thought grimly, Longer than you expect. Then more lightheartedly I recalled that he soon forgot companions who were absent and turned to someone new. But this time, I was determined, he'd turn to Berengaria. However, this wasn't the moment to mention her. I said briskly, "Since we plan to sail Friday, I must see if my women are packing my wardrobe chests properly." Not much of an excuse, but I wanted to leave before Richard might think again about Bertram. I didn't want to argue further, which might lead me into saying why I objected to Bertram's presence in his suite.

Besides, my mind was on John. Surely our being on the Continent would intimidate him, and he'd be anxious to be with us again. If I could talk Richard into forgiving his brother. The hope stayed with me as we sailed across the Channel to Barfleur and marched up through Normandy. To Richard's delight Norman lords and peasants were as wildly enthusiastic at our procession through the province as the English had been. So he was in a softened mood when I brought up John's name and asked if I might invite him to come to us. The Plantagenets should be together.

Richard hesitated, then shrugged, and I hurriedly sent a messenger to John in Paris to join us in Lisieux. He must have heard of Richard's popularity since his release from prison for when we reached the city John had taken up residence in a small manor there and wrote Richard, begging permission to meet with his king. Richard agreed coolly, and when John entered the council chamber where we waited him, Richard scowled at his younger brother.

I said hastily, "Welcome, John. I'm delighted to have the family united again." Then I shook my head at him. "You are too easily led into rash acts and listen to evil advisers."

"I know, I know, Mother." His voice broke, and he flung himself at Richard's feet, cried out with a half sob, "Forgive me, forgive me. I—I—I did not realize what I was doing, I didn't mean to hurt you. I—there's no excuse, but I implore your forgiveness."

Richard glanced at me before leaning forward to draw John to his feet. "Brother, we will forget the past. Come, let us dine together."

I knew he forced the difficult words out for my sake, and I loved Richard more than ever for his generosity. And he too must have been pleased the rift between brother was healed because as we ate, his stiffness wore off, and we had a merry meal. Richard recounted tales of his prison guards who rolled dice with him and were disgruntled that they usually lost. They had to make up for their lack of funds by asking for extra gyves and chains to secure their prisoner and then selling the articles. And John told stories of the French court, caricaturing king and nobles, unkindly but amusingly, until we were laughing helplessly.

The pleasant atmosphere continued as we traveled through the province, visiting vassals and conducting courts of justice and reviewing old laws that had fallen into disuse. Perhaps now was the time to speak of Berengaria since she hadn't answered my letter. I drew my horse up beside Richard's as we rode toward Anjou. The road was narrow here, and tree branches arched over our heads, deep green against the cloudless sky.

I said casually, "A beautiful country, isn't it? And everyone cheering the sight of you. But wouldn't your subjects be even more pleased if your wife were riding beside you? Send for her. She's living on her dower lands in Maine. Or did you know? She must be lonely now that Joanna plans to leave her to marry the Count of Toulouse."

His face set. "I shouldn't have to send for her. She knows there's always a place for her at my court." He shrugged. "Oh well, if you wish I'll write her."

I was afraid his message wouldn't be too pressing, but at least it would open up some communication between them. My faint hope was strained as whispers began again of Richard's liking for men companions. I was furious with him, even angrier with Berengaria when she didn't answer him either. A wife beside Richard would help silence the stories of him, and he must have an heir. John was too light-minded to rule England and our provinces on the Continent.

A month later the need for an heir became more acute. Richard was out hunting and returned with his face alternately pale and flushed. By the next morning he was too feverish to get out of bed, and by evening his fever was rising. I sat beside him through the night and every night for a week, shaken with fear for him and for the future. Richard could not, must not die.

As if my will reinforced his zest for life, he turned his head toward me at midnight. His face was thin, but he was smiling. Cautiously I put my hand on his. His fingers were cooler than they'd been an hour ago and tightened around mine. I breathed, "Thank God, thank God," and rose, saying I'd send for a physician.

Richard said faintly, "Not yet, Mother. First I wish to see my confessor." I nodded and hurried out, my heart light in spite of my exhaustion, not only because Richard was recovering. His asking for a priest must mean he repented of the way he'd been living and was resolved to change his life.

That bright hope was true I discovered hours later when he woke again. His voice was still weak but determined. "Mother, you are right, my wife should be with me. Write to Berengaria and beg her to come here, and I will sign the letter so she'll know it is my wish as well as yours."

I must have written persuasively of Richard's illness because the answer to my urging wasn't a letter but Berengaria herself. I hugged her joyfully. "Oh my dear! Now I know Richard will get well quickly."

She looked down at her fingers twined together. "I should have come before, but I—I didn't realize—I do care for him, madame, and I hope that he cares—" Her stumbling words broke off.

Afraid she was going to cry, I said briskly, "With you here, of course he'll soon be better. Don't blame yourself for the past, child. Often it takes something serious like his sickness to make a couple see what they mean to each other. Now let us go in to Richard so he can speak for himself."

She raised her eyes to mine, and for the first time she smiled at me as woman to woman, her shyness forgotten. I kissed her again and hurried her into Richard's room, hoping they'd meet before her natural timidity returned.

At our entrance he turned his head tiredly, then grinned and tried to sit up. Berengaria ran to his bed and pushed him back gently. "You mustn't strain yourself, Richard. I'm here to nurse you and make sure you take proper care of yourself." Her severe voice without a trace of her usual hesitancy with him, made him grin again, and he agreed meekly to follow her orders.

Their eyes shone as they gazed at each other. He held up his arms, and she knelt beside him, her face lifted for his kiss. I was delighted at their absorption in each other and backed quietly out of the door but not before I heard them murmuring endearments. I sighed with enormous relief. When Richard was well, they'd be husband and wife and England would have an heir. And the ugly rumors about Richard would no longer be whispered gleefully.

He improved swiftly under her devoted nursing, so devoted I had to insist she take a few hours to rest each day while I watched at Richard's bedside. At last he was able to walk around his room, call meetings with his ministers and finally able to continue his royal progress. He and Berengaria set off side by side, looking happy like a newly married couple. I was intensely grateful for Berengaria's selflessness, grateful too that now I wasn't needed to ride with Richard. The long days and nights of his illness had been exhausting on top of last year's fear for him and the plans and work to raise his ransom. I'd retire to Fontevrault for a rest.

I'd visited the Abbey often and liked the cool spacious grounds and the fact too, I admit, that the order was ruled by a woman though the place housed both a convent and monastery as well as a hospital. This was the same Abbey Henry had wanted me to retire to and be abbess of after I'd divorced him, and I'd refused. But now I felt the need to enjoy its peaceful quietness.

The room that the nuns said was waiting for me held little furniture though it was large and facing the south. Great flower and vegetable gardens spread out beneath my windows, and beyond them was a belt of green where orchards of cherry and apple grew. I could be alone and idly let my eyes rest on the lovely countryside, or I could walk in the gardens and meet nuns and friars who were almost too grateful for donations I'd made to this abbey and a dozen others. But we had pleasant times chatting of our own lives and of the restricted world around us.

Little news of the great world seeped through to disturb the serenity except for occasional rumors brought by tired travelers of sporadic fighting along the borders between Normandy and France, and infrequent letters from Berengaria of Richard's constant movements through his provinces. I read and reread her scrolls, delighted at the happiness that showed between the lines. But no word of an heir. That would come, I thought comfortably. The only unhappy note was caused by the fact she'd been raised in a small and peaceful country and now was horrifed at the brutality of war. At how casually Richard would order an enemy soldier or a rebellious vassal maimed or hanged. Well, she'd soon get used to the need for strong measures, I said to myself as I crossed to the hospital to see the patients I visited every morning.

Abruptly I was flung out of my serene life. A messenger galloped into the courtyard at noon and demanded hoarsely to see me. He was reeling from fatigue when he reached me at the bed of a young mother who'd just given birth to a daughter and could only gasp he had an urgent message for me. I took the document from his shaking hand, broke the seal and unrolled the parchment in one movement. The scrawled lines were from Berengaria and difficult to make out.

When I deciphered them, I clutched a table before me with one hand, my shoulders hunched. Then I straightened, said to the nun who'd brought the messenger to me, "Tell the captain of my guard to be ready with six of his men to ride in an hour. With me."

Her face was startled, but she left quickly. I looked back at the letter, my mind shrieking its disbelief in the words. Richard, besieging Chalus castle, had been struck by a poisoned arrow from a crossbow. If I wanted to see my son alive, I must go there at once.

I was numb when I went to my rooms and my ladies brought out a wool dress to replace the sheer gown I was wearing and adjusted the wimple over my hair and around my neck. They appeared puzzled at my haste, but I couldn't bear to repeat the horrifying words I'd read as if repetition would make them true. Chalus was over a hundred miles, and I was still numb as I traveled day and night with my escort, small so that it wouldn't slow my journey.

Dawn was just lightening the eastern sky when I stumbled into Richard's pavilion. The merciful numbness left me when I saw his flushed face above the blankets on the cot where he was sleeping. His left arm and shoulder were heavily bandaged. I whispered, "No, no, no!" while dry sobs shook me. I swallowed them as unexpectedly he opened his eyes and smiled. He tried to hold out his uninjured arm to me though I could see he was in agony at the slightest movement.

I sank to my knees beside him, forced myself to answer his smile though my heart knotted with pain. He said croakingly, "Mother, Mother, don't mourn for me. I've had a good life. I didn't free Jerusalem, but I'm at peace. You will look after Berengaria, and you must watch John, he knows little of the art of ruling. No, don't say you're too old," he was interrupted by a coughing fit, "you'll never be old. Knowing you will be working for my subjects, I can—can die without regrets."

There was a shadow at the entrance. I looked up, saw Berengaria come in softly. Her eyes widened at the sight of me, and she rushed forward to embrace me, then turned instantly toward the cot. She murmured something to Richard, lifted her head to exchange hopeless glances with me. A minute later a physician came in, followed by half-a-dozen attendants. He threw back the blankets and raised Richard's leg above a basin to bleed him. Berengaria and I said nothing, but we both knew he was beyond help from even the most skillful surgeon.

Richard slept then, woke fitfully during the day but could only whisper our names, and we could see he grew weaker every hour. Shadows were creeping into the pavilion when he opened his eyes for the last time to gaze lovingly at us, a smile on his pale mouth. Berengaria threw herself on him, weeping wildly.

I rose stiffly. I too wanted to weep, but his smile gave me courage to stifle my grief. I'd return to Fontevrault but only to bury my son and try to persuade Berengaria to stay there until her sorrow healed. I couldn't stay. There was work for me that no one else could do.

Chapter Twelve

My duty was to make sure we had peace, I thought as we rode sadly back to Fontevrault. A difficult goal when within hours of Richard's death quarreling broke out among courtiers and vassals on who was the rightful heir. I'd heard occasional stories earlier that some favored my grandson Arthur, the son of his late father, Geoffrey, Richard's next brother. But I'd paid little attention in my certainty that Richard would sire a son. Besides, Arthur was only twelve now, young to inherit so much territory and, worse, he'd spent most of his life at the court of France where he'd been taught to be arrogant and to despise the English.

Others shouted that John had a better right to his father's lands than a grandson could have. John was an adult, had lived most of his life in England, and Richard had expected if he hadn't a child that John would follow him. Like me, Richard had never thought of Arthur as the next king. That swayed me, and the fact that John would cause fewer problems than Arthur. In spite of John's earlier alliances with the French king, he'd be less apt than Arthur to be dominated by Philip if he had the title he'd always coveted.

He was intelligent. He was also unstable, with swift changes of mood which he soon flaunted to all. It was three days after we'd sorrowfully buried Richard in the Fontevrault vault when John arrived. He regretted he'd been delayed by contrary Channel winds, and to make up for his absence at the funeral, he piously attended every service for his brother from morning song to vespers.

Yet on the following Sunday when the bishop was delivering a sermon on the fate of good and bad kings, John stood up from his stool and told him loudly to end his preaching. The bishop went on, ignoring him, and John rose again to shout him down. The bishop was long-winded, but I was annoyed. Still, I said nothing, there'd be more important matters to disagree on later, I was sure, but the change from piety to insulting the clergy showed how quickly John's moods changed.

The small matter was forgotten before the day was out. Riders came in from the north with word that stunned us. Arthur, with Philip's backing, was already attacking our borders. I must move swiftly. First I sent for Richard's captain Mercadier who'd ridden to the abbey with us, and said crisply, "Gather up the army of my son

Richard," it was still hard to say his name, "and any men you can recruit, and I'll be ready to go north with you."

Then I crossed the hall to John who was lounging in a chair that had been Richard's. "You must go to Rouen at once and say I sent you to receive the ducal coronet. The Normans will have to accept you as their duke then, and you will demand the lords follow you to the French border. If there aren't enough men, hire mercenaries."

"I'm to have a coronet, eh? Good!" He smiled lazily but he rose quickly. I hoped, as I hurried away to prepare for the march with Mercadier, that he'd heard he was also to head his forces against Philip's army.

We were putting up tents on our way to Gisors when one of my scouts arrived from Rouen. The thudding of stakes into the ground and a blustery wind forced him to shout that John had been crowned duke. He paused, and his embarrassed face made it plain he had more to say but was hesitating. I jerked my head for him to come closer, said, "Go on!" He added reluctantly that during the ceremony, John and his friends had mocked the solemn rites, laughing when it was time to pray and making—well, odd gestures so that priests and barons were upset.

I was furious at the levity that would antagonize instead of drawing his new subjects to him. Perhaps I should have gone with John instead of marching with Mercadier, but it had seemed better to have two armies to converge on the French, and without me Mercadier wouldn't have enough authority to back up his orders. In any case, it was too late to change the unpleasant situation John had created, and I was never one to spend time uselessly regretting the past.

I went toward the campfire to eat bread and veal with Mercadier and his officers and discuss the latest news they had on the French army's march. Arthur was headed to a fortress south of Gisors. Since the scouts had no word of John's plans, if any, to raise his own army, we decided to go directly east tomorrow to strike against the enemy advance.

We were within a day's march of meeting the French when half-a-dozen messengers arrived, gaily shouting their reports to our forces before they even presented themselves to me. I could not fault them for that, the news was too happy not to spread. John had made another of his changes. He'd swiftly recruited troops and, with a shorter distance to cover than we had, swept in ahead of us to attack Arthur, sending my grandson flying to his protector in Paris.

Arthur was defeated. For the moment. Our march had been difficult through rugged country lanes, and I thought yearningly of Fontevrault's serenity. I couldn't rest, not yet. The next assault might be against my Aquitaine, and I had to make sure my vassals would be loyal to me. I idled away one day, then I sent Mercadier to join John, and I rode south to tour my province.

I was cheered everywhere as we rode south. My subjects crowded around me trying to touch me, to hear my voice. I smiled and waved at all the small farmers and peasants, but I must also be welcomed by their lords. I circled the country, riding hundreds of miles, stopping if only for an hour at fortress or castle to meet my vassals and discuss any problems, their crops, questions of boundary lines, and I invited them to visit me when I reached Bordeaux.

They were at the palace waiting for me, and I gave liberally from my own inheritance for those in need and had a document drawn up with new privileges for nobles and clergy and cities. Feast followed feast, and there were hunts and tournaments almost daily so I had little time to think of Raoul. How he should be here with me, how much shorter the thousand miles I'd traveled would have been if we could have shared the journey. Or if Richard . . . I thrust their names aside and took part in the merrymaking that ended when my vassals gathered around me to renew their vows of fealty before domestic demands forced them to return to their homes.

I had another thing to do in my search for peace which was as vital as ever even though I was assured of my own lords' support. It was difficult to bring myself to act, but I must. I wrote Philip Augustus that if he'd meet me in Tours, I'd acknowledge myself his vassal and do homage for Aquitaine and Poitou. He received me graciously, and there was no mockery on his young-old face when I knelt to put my hands in his. He quickly bade me rise so the gesture was scarcely more than a token. But he appeared satisfied, and now I could breathe more easily. With my submission, neither he nor Arthur could find an excuse to attack my provinces.

But we must have peace for the Plantagenet lands too. Since I'd humbled myself to Philip, John could also swear fealty to the French king for his continental provinces. I knew he'd be hard to persuade and resigned myself to more traveling. I'd have to see him personally before he'd agree, he'd toss a letter aside. But as I prepared for the journey, I found I had to rely on writing him.

A messenger came from my daughter Joanna, now countess of Toulouse. She'd somehow managed to escape from a castle under siege in spite of being almost nine months pregnant, and now was in a farmhouse ten miles from Toulouse where the farmers didn't dare risk sheltering her much longer, and she had no place to go. I told my escort captain we'd travel south, not north, as I eyed the shakily drawn map Joanna had given her messenger. With that and with him to guide us, we had no trouble locating her.

But I was plunged into grief which I had to conceal at first sight of her, could only murmur, "My dear, my dear, you will be all right now."

Seeing her was like my first glance at Richard on his cot and knowing it was too late for anyone to cure her. But I tried to keep up her spirit and mine with lighthearted chatter as I rode beside her litter on our way to Fontevrault where the nuns would care for her tenderly. The hospital staff was pleased to see us, glad to be able to repay the bounties I'd given the abbey but sad too when they carefully carried Joanna from her litter to a bed. They knew as I did that all their devoted assistance could do nothing for her. Within a week she died giving birth to a dead child.

Now I could put aside my determinedly cheerful air and weep for her wildly, my sweet adventurous daughter. Of all my children only John and my namesake Eleanor who'd married the king of Castile were still living. But after Joanna was buried, I knew I must not give way to my sorrow. I wrote John to meet me in Rouen.

At my arrival in the city he kissed me, but his first words were, "No, Mother, you're asking too much. Me do homage to Philip? Why should I?" He adjusted the gold-embroidered band at his wrist as if that were more important than my plea.

"For peace. Philip will listen less to Arthur's demands if you acknowledge him your overlord. And you know very well that it's traditional for Normandy and Anjou to be vassal to the French king." I stirred tiredly on the wooden chair he'd led me to. I didn't want to go on and thought crossly I shouldn't make weariness an excuse for letting the subject drop. I added, "You alone can pledge your provinces' loyalty to Philip. And if he's reluctant to accept your oath, your charm will break down his resistance." That was true. John could be charming when he wished.

"If he's reluctant? Oh, you mean because I tossed aside our alliance and returned to Richard after his release from prison. Hmm. As you say, it is traditional for the duchies to be vassals to the French. Well, I'll talk to him."

I said eagerly, "Then you can go back to England, a country you've always preferred and one which has been neglected of late. And your borders here will be safe." In my relief some of my exhaustion left me, and I made ready to travel again to Tours where Philip had stayed after my meeting with him. I felt I should be there when the two met.

Philip was friendly as before, but as John was ready to take the oath he said, "There's only one small matter. I'll gladly recognize your right to the duchies, but our expenses have been high—" he didn't give one of the reasons for that, that he'd provisioned Arthur's army to attack us—"so recognition depends on a payment from you of thirty thousand silver marks."

I gasped at the vast amount, and I could see John was equally horrified and furious too. Would he stalk away, refusing even to bargain? Another war would cost at least the thirty thousand marks and who knew how many lives? I said quickly, "It would take a long time to raise that sum. Perhaps twenty-five thousand marks would satisfy you?"

Philip looked thoughtful. "Y-yes. But you haven't asked what the money is for. It's time my son Louis was married. I've consulted with my ministers, and we've decided the bride should be a princess of Castile. Unfortunately her father can't afford an adequate bequest so I planned to use these marks for her dower."

I closed my mouth tightly so I wouldn't gape at his words. Then a smile forced itself to my lips. One of my granddaughters the future queen of France? I glanced at John whose eyes were narrowed over the same thought, his niece the queen of France. He shrugged, said airily, "Very well, since it's the tradition to bend the knee to France, but only for the duchies, not for England."

When the oath was given, Philip rose to embrace John, said over his shoulder, "To make you even more content, madame, I beg you to be my emissary to the princess. None of the daughters has yet been approached, and you would know which one would most please my son. He'll leave the choice in your hands."

I was overwhelmed at what must be considered an honor, but I was too old for such an arduous journey. I started to say that, stopped. The hope of seeing my daughter again after so many years was too strong. And I was pleased—I'm afraid I've always been vain, liking power—that I had the authority to select France's next queen.

Only one incident marred my traveling to Spain. My escort—small as usual so that we could move quickly—was attacked in Lusignan territory, and we were herded into the lord's castle. I stormed at the indignity, but the lord only smiled and said I could be on my way this very hour if I would sign over a strip of land bordering on Lusignan. I didn't hesitate. The territory was uncultivated and of no value to anyone except Lusignan since an enemy could conceal himself there. So it was better to lose the small property than to be delayed.

The rest of the journey was uneventful though the ride on twisting roads through the Pyrenees was maddeningly slow and rugged. But thought of seeing my daughter kept up my spirits. The image of her, small and untidy after romps with her brothers, was lovingly in my mind. So when I saw her, I was startled. I hugged her tightly, but it was minutes before I could believe this elegant woman in her thirties, the mother of eleven children, was the girl child who'd been sent off to Castile so long ago.

I'd hurried to the Castilian court to select a bride, but my urgency slipped away in my delight at being with Eleanor and my grandchildren. She'd taken after me in more than name. The court was gay like mine in Aquitaine with troubadours and poets and bright conversation. I revelled in it though I told myself I mustn't indulge myself too long.

I excused my tarrying week after week with the thought I must know my granddaughters better before I made so important a choice as to select the future queen of France. The oldest was already betrothed so it was natural I should speak for the second girl, Urraca. But each time my lips opened to say so, I found myself looking at the third princess, twelve-year-old Blanche. A sweet vivacious child, but she had something more though I scarcely admitted even to myself what it was. We'd been instantly drawn to each other because, well, because she was so much like me at that age, a little arrogant perhaps, but with a resilience and strength which had carried me through the peaks and low points of my life.

My daughter was surprised when I spoke at last, then smiled. "You're the best matchmaker in Europe, I'm sure, Mother. So if you believe Blanche is the right bride for Prince Louis, I know my husband will consent as I do."

Blanche herself sparkled at the adventure of traveling to a strange country and being its queen. She bombarded me with questions about the Dauphin, but I'd never met the young man. Still, I could assure her I'd heard a little about him, and it had all been good, that he was companionable, hard-working, pleasant. She was satisfied with that and threw herself into preparations, or rather goaded her parents to hurry so that a fortnight later we were riding through the Pyrenees with wagon after wagon of luggage lumbering behind us.

My daughter and her children accompanied us the first miles. When she had to turn back, Blanche was misty-eyed as she said goodbye to her family. But within a day the journey and anticipation of the future shook off her sadness, and she was gay company. We stopped briefly in Bordeaux in the Ombriere Palace, and I recalled the time when an earlier Louis had come to fetch me as his bride. Remembering, I thought only of the good times with him, how he'd been considerate and gentle, and assured Blanche that her Louis would treat her well.

The short rest there made me realize how weary I was now, but I couldn't give in to fatigue until I'd seen the child married. The wedding had to be in Normandy just across the border from France because France lay under an interdict and no religious ceremonies could be held. I'd forgotten the Pope's edict which was the result of Philip's taking too many mistresses. Philip, being excommunicated, couldn't attend the wedding, but he was liberal in providing entertainment of songs and tournaments and jugglers and banquets.

His absence was scarcely noticed. All eyes were on the radiant young bride and the bridegroom. I saw with approval that Prince Louis was lean and hard-muscled with an air of command, but an air he put aside when speaking with Blanche who, it was obvious, impressed him with her grace and vitality and lovely youthful face. I sighed happily when I noticed she too was impressed with her spouse and turned eagerly to him whenever he came near her.

The day after they exchanged their promises in the cathedral, I said a loving good-bye to her and turned thankfully to peaceful Fontevrault. I'd done everything I could to safeguard my provinces and the Plantagenet territories. The one thing left to do wasn't in my hands. I wanted John to marry, he was thirty-five, but he was indifferent. I was relieved it wasn't for Richard's reason even though I disapproved of the women he enjoyed.

I wrote him often and finally my letters or his ministers persuaded him to agree he needed an heir, and that he was willing to be betrothed to a Portugese princess. Disinterestedly he dispatched officials to negotiate terms. I was grateful he didn't ask me to be head of the group the way I'd been in Castile so I could rest in the serene abbey, feeling all was going forward as I'd hoped.

I should have known that John's marriage plans wouldn't go smoothly. Perhaps I did because I wasn't shocked when I heard what he'd done though I was deeply disappointed. He met a twelve-year-old girl, Isabella of Angouleme, and immediately broke off the Portuguese agreement, declaring Isabella was the only bride in the world he'd accept. She too was betrothed to another, but with the English throne to offer, John easily persuaded her father to break her contract and within weeks John and Isabella were married.

I was unhappy at losing an alliance with Portugal and possibly stirring up French enemies, friends of Isabella's discarded bridegroom, who might decide to be enraged at the broken engagement. Still, when John and Isabella came to see me at the abbey and he proudly presented his child bride, I knew it was pointless to be angry at something that was too late to undo, and I gave them my blessing, putting aside my uneasiness over what antagonism they might have stirred up with their ill-considered marriage.

I told myself I worried too much, perhaps because of late I was often ill with small complaints, but it was a state I wasn't accustomed to. Still I had my scribes send messages to Normans and Aquitanian lords to be alert for any sign of hostility from Isabella's former fiance and his friends. I breathed more easily when I was assured they were living quietly, apparently with no intention of revenge.

I was resting in bed when another message reached me, shocking me out of my drowsiness. Philip was raising an army, using the marriage as an excuse. First he had young Arthur do him homage for all John's Continental provinces. And then sent the boy to attack my city of Poitiers. I cried out, "No, that's impossible. What had I to do with John's marriage?" When I recovered from the stunning report, I ordered my ladies to dress me at once and sent word to my captain to have his men saddled and ready to leave in an hour.

My presence in Poitiers would strengthen the defenders of the city. But I was eighty, and reluctantly I had to admit I didn't have all my old resilience. Instead of riding through the night, I broke the journey to stay at Mirebeau with its walled keep and walled town. It appeared impregnable at first glance, but any experienced observer would note the defenses hadn't been kept up properly, and the walls appeared ready to totter into the moat. Still, what did that matter? We'd be here only for the night, and it was Poitiers that would be under assault.

We were talking optimistically and laughing in the great hall before we retired to sleep when a guard rushed in. The expression on his face silenced us before he said a word. He spoke at last. Prince Arthur had had me followed and now turned his army aside to take me captive so that John would agree to anything for my release.

As he finished, my captains hurried out, shouting for their men to shore up the walls. As I could not help there, I sent a message instantly to John of what his enemies were doing. I hoped he'd receive it in time. And act on the news immediately. I knew we couldn't hold out long against an assault, but my men were loyal and would fight valorously over every inch the enemy would try to take.

For three days they defended the town walls, but they were pushed back into the keep foot by foot. I was sickened at the bloodshed and said, "We will retreat into the fortress. It's better built, and there is a portcullis between the besiegers and us." I might have said only a portcullis for it wasn't a strong barrier. But I would not let even the sight of maimed and broken bodies change my cheerfully determined tone, and the soldiers responded as though I'd promised them victory.

I went up to the barricaded roof of the keep where I could look down at the town's streets. Arthur's forces were bedding down for the night under the starry sky or passing around mugs of wine, singing loudly and out of tune and choking with laughter at how they'd take the old eagle prisoner in the morning. I wondered dully if we could hold out against another attack, yet I couldn't put out a flicker of hope.

I stayed on the roof through the night. If my hope were misplaced and tomorrow would see me a prisoner, I wanted to savor every hour of freedom. At dawn I rubbed my reddened eyes sleepily, rubbed them again to be sure I was seeing what I thought I was. Could it be—yes, it was an army surging through one of the town's gates, an army holding John's standard high. Even Richard could not have come so swiftly.

Someone must have reported to John that the enemy had grown careless, believing success was already in their hands. My heart sang as his soldiers fell on Arthur's sleeping or half-roused forces. By the time the sun had risen above the horizon, our enemies were either slain or captured or had fled. Arthur, I thought. I could not have my son killing my grandson.

I stumbled down the circular steps of the keep to meet John, who dismounted tiredly though he was grinning happily. I held him close, wildly grateful for his rescue, not only of me, and for his destroying the army which would have struck against Poitiers. I tried to mention Arthur, but cheering shouting soldiers pressed against us, and it was a long time before my voice could be heard. "John, what of Arthur? Is he killed or have you taken him?"

His grin widened. "I have him, Mother, you needn't worry about that brat's taking up arms again."

"I know, and we can't thank you enough for what you've accomplished. But he is your nephew. You can't have him executed."

He shrugged. "I should think you'd want him out of your way as much as I do. But since you wish his life spared, why not? But I won't just turn him free to lead another army against us." He swung away to answer an enthusiastic shout from a number of my guards.

A prisoner. I felt a quick leap of sympathy though I realized there was nothing else John could do. But when I inquired for the boy and was shown to the house where he was held, I was appalled to see his legs were chained to the bench he was sitting on. And a guard said indifferently that Arthur was to be sent to a dungeon in Falaise. I held out my hands to my grandson and leaned forward to kiss his rounded cheek. I remembered he'd hoped to take me captive, but I couldn't believe he'd have treated me with such indignity. I said reassuringly, "The king can't know how you're being treated. I will speak to John. This isn't right."

He didn't return my kiss. His lips set thinly, and his dark eyes stared at me arrogantly. "King? *I* am the king of England and the duke of Normandy and Anjou and Brittany. He has usurped my rights. That does not make him a king. He'll soon find that out."

I reminded myself Arthur was only a boy, too young to weigh his words or to understand my offer of friendship. Yet I admired his spirit of defiance. I said gently, "Many legalists have said John has the best claim. In any case, since you're a prisoner of war—"

He interrupted before I could finish. "I won't be for long. My good friend the king of France will free me, madame, and restore my rights. Until then I do not wish to speak to one of the enemy. You may leave."

I was half amused and half shocked at his peremptory tone. But I went. Useless for me to speak to him when he was in this mood. And I didn't like his reference to Philip's aiding him which could be interpreted as a threat. It convinced me again that John as king would cause fewer problems than this boy. Yet I ached for my grandson, a prisoner at his age.

I hurried to meet John, who was overseeing the rebuilding of Mirebeau which had been plundered and houses demolished by Arthur's forces. I caught the sleeve of his tunic and begged him to promise Arthur's chains would be struck off when the boy reached Falaise. John shrugged. "If you wish, Mother. In fact, if Arthur will swear loyalty to me, I will put him only under house arrest instead of a dungeon."

I was pleased at that, and now there was nothing more for me to do, I could return to Fontevrault. Berengaria was the first to greet me at the abbey. She appeared to be recovered from the first pain of Richard's death and said she was going back to her dower lands where she was needed. After her the nuns and monks welcomed me lovingly, and I felt protected by the peace and serenity of the place I now thought of as home.

As usual I couldn't let the days drift idly past and again visited the hospital every day to talk to the patients, persuade some to take their prescribed medicine and cheer those who were despondent over their illnesses. I could give myself wholeheartedly to the small tasks for the English lords had willingly accepted John as their king, and the provinces on the Continent were quiet now that Philip didn't have Arthur beside him as an excuse to lead an army against us.

Arthur. I wished I could forget the boy, but no matter how violent and ill-mannered he was, how could I brush aside the son of my son? I wrote John to remind him of his promise to put the boy under house arrest if Arthur would give the oath of loyalty. John answered he hadn't forgotten but, from the tone of his letter, he seemed to be sorry he'd promised. And he was furious in his next message. He said he'd seen Arthur. And Arthur had sworn he'd never give up his claim to John's possessions which were his rightful inheritance. And if the territories weren't restored, he'd never let his uncle have a moment's peace. John added there was only one answer to that. He was sending his nephew to a new and stronger tower in Rouen.

I put down the letter sadly. I thought John was overly harsh, yet I acknowledged he couldn't risk another war because of a boy's obstinacy. I could only suggest that Arthur be treated well even though he must be securely guarded and tried not to dwell on my grandson. That was difficult at first. Soon it was impossible.

There were rumors that began as whispers but quickly swelled to accusing questions. "Prince Arthur hasn't been seen in Rouen for weeks. Where is he? Where? Is he alive?" Later it was said he hadn't been seen for months. What had King John to answer to that? Fontevrault was away from the world, but not far enough to isolate us from the ugly stories when John just waved away the tales. I wrote him again and again, and he replied that naturally Arthur was quite all right, I shouldn't worry about him.

How could I not be uneasy? And if the boy was still alive, why wasn't he brought out for people to see? John didn't answer that question. And the accusations became a roar. John was a murderer. He'd killed Arthur. I would not, could not, believe an uncle would slay a nephew. Was it possible that Arthur was dead but from natural causes? And

John didn't display his body because we all knew no one would believe such a report, not if a hundred physicians took oath it was true.

I put aside my restless questioning and simply asked nuns and monks to pray for both my son and grandson. I hoped Arthur's fate wouldn't hang over John, who might one day be a great king. I could believe that possible after his swift rescue of me at Mirebeau. But I need no longer concern myself with the world's doings. I'd done what I could, and France and England were at peace.

I'd lived vitally. Now I was willing to let the affairs of countries slide from my hands into those of the younger generation. My mind slipped back over the impossibly exciting events of my life. A long life, I thought, yet today I felt as young as when I was a fifteen-year-old bride riding to Paris to be with my husband. Riding on the crusade. Where I'd again met my young uncle Raymond. And later there was the demanding, insistent Henry. And when love failed between us, there was Raoul. And my beloved son Richard. I'd soon see them all again. I laughed happily. If I were to relive those years, there was little I'd change for I would always follow my passionate heart.

BE SWEPT AWAY
ON A TIDE OF PASSION
BY LEISURE'S THRILLING
HISTORICAL ROMANCES!

FOR THE FINEST
IN CONTEMPORARY
WOMEN'S FICTION,
FOLLOW LEISURE'S LEAD

Make the Most of Your Leisure Time
with
LEISURE BOOKS

Please send me the following titles:

Quantity	Book Number	Price
_____	_____	_____
_____	_____	_____
_____	_____	_____
_____	_____	_____
_____	_____	_____

If out of stock on any of the above titles, please send me the alternate title(s) listed below:

_____	_____	_____
_____	_____	_____
_____	_____	_____
_____	_____	_____

Postage & Handling _____

Total Enclosed $_____

☐ Please send me a free catalog.

NAME_____
(please print)

ADDRESS _____

CITY _____ STATE _____ ZIP_____

Please include $1.00 shipping and handling for the first book ordered and 25¢ for each book thereafter in the same order. All orders are shipped within approximately 4 weeks via postal service book rate. PAYMENT MUST ACCOMPANY ALL ORDERS.*

*Canadian orders must be paid in US dollars payable through a New York banking facility.

Mail coupon to: **Dorchester Publishing Co., Inc.**
6 East 39 Street, Suite 900
New York, NY 10016
Att: ORDER DEPT.